INTO THE
DARK

For Florence and Ed

INTO THE DARK

DARK

POLESTARS 9

Patrice Sarath

NEWCON
PRESS

NewCon Press
England

First edition, published in the UK November 2024
by NewCon Press
41 Wheatsheaf Road, Alconbury Weston, Cambs, PE28 4LF, UK

NCP341 (hardback)
NCP342 (softback)

10 9 8 7 6 5 4 3 2 1

Cover Art by Enrique Meseguer; cover design by Ian Whates
Editing by Ian Whates
Typesetting by Ian Whates

Table of Contents

Acknowledgements

No writer goes it alone. I've had a number of teachers and peers who have helped me sharpen my skills and tell the stories the best way possible. They are: best writing buddy Martin Owton, Cryptopolis (Matthew Bey, Nicky Drayden, Dave Chang, Steve Wilson, Melissa Mead Tyler, Jessica Sollace, Patrick Sullivan), Jessica Reisman, the Four Kids in a Trenchcoat (Laura Mitten and Kris Romero), the HepCats, the Free Divers, and the Slug Tribe.

Then there are the filmmakers: Austin Community College professors Christian Raymond, Caleb Johnson, John Moore, Nathan Locklear, fellow filmmakers Angela Reavis, Liberty-Joy Maldonado, Drew Schwemer, Omar Marroquin, and Joy-Serene Adams.

My agent Jennie Goloboy, who knows how to get to the heart of a story.

My family: Ben, Kim, and Aidan. You guys.

My brothers and sisters: Carol, Ed, Maria, David, Jay, and Steven – better story tellers than me, if you want to know the truth.

And finally: my readers. Thank you.

Foreword
by Martin Owton

Patrice Sarath has been my friend and critique partner for close to thirty years. In that time I've watched her grow as a writer, we've visited each other's homes, attended conventions and shared the joys and frustrations of the writing process. She has read every bit of fiction I've written and I've read all of hers. It has been a pleasure.

I first encountered Patrice in the mid-1990s in a critique group that grew out of the old Speculations website. "It seems like we write similar stories" she said. "Do you want to swap critiques?" I was a fairly new writer at the time and she gave good critiques so I readily agreed. Since then she has written many fine short stories as well as six novels (two duologies and two standalone). This collection is the pick of them and one of the joys of reading it for me is seeing the final version of stories, most of which I only saw as an early draft.

Patrice writes short fiction across a range of genres so this collection ranges from science fiction through secondary world fantasy to contemporary/urban fantasy that shades dark enough to be horror, so everyone should find something to their liking. This though does not cover her entire range; her most successful novel "The Unexpected Miss Bennet" is a Jane Austen sequel about Mary Bennet.

Among the science fiction stories "Murder on the Hohmann" and "Spider" feature some characters in common, "Pilot's Forge" and "Joe Fledge's Jump" are set in the same world hinting perhaps at a SF novel that I have not yet seen. "Bad Dog" offers us an alien invasion from an unusual viewpoint. "The Night of Their Conversion" is a bleak tale, dark enough to make it borderline horror.

The fantasy stories "Red Ned Mederos and the Sea Girl of Port Saint Frey" and "Theo Ballinchard and the Oranges of Possibility" are origin stories from Patrice's Tales of Port Saint Frey duology. The novels are adventure fantasy in a Regency setting – Georgette Heyer with magic – and are well worth checking out. "The Star Seed Witches Meet at Midnight" shows us a group of contemporary witches in small town America trying to help a sweet old lady with her dirtbag son only to find the old lady is far from sweet. "The Lunch Thief" documents weird happenings in a contemporary corporate office. "A Prayer for Captain La Hire" is an historical fantasy set in 15th century France and reflects Patrice's long-held interest in Joan of Arc. "Into the Dark" is another bleak contemporary tale of inevitable loss and was Patrice's breakthrough story, getting published in Realms of Fantasy. "Ice" is a strange contemporary fantasy that will make more sense if you are familiar with the plot of "Giselle".

Having already referred to a dark streak in Patrice's work it should be no surprise that there are some horror tales in the collection. "Hell: A Rescue Mission" is a contemporary tale exploring the limits of friendship. "Pigs and Feaches", a tale of an apocalyptic viral pandemic, is in my opinion, the darkest piece in the collection. "Blood on the Snow" offers a twist on the East European werewolf legend. In "Caro Comes Home" the central character is an alien shapeshifter that falls in love with its human victim.

What distinguishes all these stories is Patrice's ability to create complex and believable characters. This gives credibility to the fantastical elements of the stories, and is a rare gift.

I commend this collection to you.

– Martin Owton
London
June 2023

Murder on the *Hohmann*

My homage to Agatha Christie, Arthur Conan Doyle, M.R. James, and Raymond Chandler.

In 2065, after ten years as a shuttle pilot for the Bifrost asteroid mining complex, I took it upon myself to settle my affairs off-planet, return to Earth, and resign myself to look upon the stars from afar. This was a common migration, as miners and crew often found themselves with the same vague yearning for a planet many of us had not seen in decades. We none of us acknowledged that we *were* embarked on a migration, but all gave different reasons on official documents for our decision to pack it in. Yet humans are as instinctual as any animal; no doubt if you ask the wildebeests, you'd get a different answer from each one too.

My voyage from the Bifrost mining complex to Earth took eight months, my ship the venerable *United Nations Hohmann*, an ancient, chemical-propelled workhorse whose frame was laid in the early 21st century. The *Hohmann* carried supplies on the Earth-Mars-Bifrost run. It was a small, cramped ship, the bridge barely larger than the cockpit of my shuttle, and it had been retrofitted with two modules attached like train cars, and a big turning centrifuge of a caboose for crew and passengers to experience *up* and *down,* put on muscle, and salvage bone.

The first inkling that my voyage might not be as smooth as hoped came when I stowed my duffle under my assigned sleep pouch and found myself next to the two asteroid miners, Carter and Rose. We carefully did not acknowledge one another, but my heart sank. What other surprises were there going to be?

I was soon to find out, and my misgivings grew when I met everyone at dinner our first night out.

Besides myself and the brothers, the *Hohmann* carried three other passengers: Elton Haley, a talkative fellow with blond, receding hair and a portly figure, who never answered a straight question about what he was doing on the Earth-Mars-Bifrost run; Agnes St. Germaine, a first-generation Mars colonist; and Mrs. Paavo, a veteran of the Mars conflict of 2047.

I disliked Haley from the start. "Ah, Meredith Hawkes, the shuttle pilot. I've heard about *you*," was the first thing he said to me.

"All good, I hope," I replied lightly, and set down my cup. Yes, set down, for the *Hohmann*'s skipper, Captain Ngotu, was old-fashioned and requested passengers dine with him at a common table in the centrifuge chamber. Thankfully, the captain relaxed the rule that we dress for dinner, so we were all in some variation of ultra-lightweight T-shirt and trousers. Mr. Haley's had a legend advertising a barbecue restaurant.

"Yes, now what was it? There was something that rang a bell. No matter it will come to me. I have eight months after all. Ah, the brother miners! Which are you two – Dopey and Grumpy?"

At his jocular tone, Carter and Rose looked over sourly from their end of the table, and then back down at their dinners, forks clenched in their fists. Haley had better watch out, I thought. The brothers might be height-deficient, but they were more like trolls than dwarfs, and just as thuggish.

"What about you, Mr. Haley? Why are you leaving Mars?" I said, going on the offensive.

"Oh, I'm not from Mars," he said cheerfully.

I raised my eyebrows in surprise. A tourist from Earth? The *Hohmann* was a slow, chemical-fuelled supply ship, and lacked all but the most basic amenities for space travellers. The only reason I booked a ticket was because there were no passenger ships on the schedule, and I found it expedient to leave as soon as possible. I had resigned myself to an eight-month journey that on a newer ship would have taken four. As for the Martians, why had they chosen to book passage on a ship that was going an extra four months out of their way?

Mr. Haley turned to Miss St. Germaine. "Now Miss St. Germaine, are you remembering to keep up with your bone supplements? I see you aren't eating again, as usual. Our Bifrost friends will think you don't care about your health."

Miss St. Germaine murmured something and, at his jocular tone, made an effort to move her dinner around her plate. Like all first and second-generation Martians, she looked as if she were twelve years old, with a delicate bone structure and petite form. Her diffident manner emphasised her childlike appearance. Her ancestry was similar to mine – African and American – but her skin had the artificial pallor of genetic enhancement. She would need as much Vitamin D as her body could manufacture, even with the implants all spacefarers had that released a steady supply of vitamins and hormones. Her curly hair was wrapped in a colourful scarf, a startling print against the industrial background of the ship, and at odds with her shy personality. Unaccountably, I felt nostalgia. I had shaved my head for the last ten years out of expediency and simplicity. On Earth, I could grow out my hair.

Mr. Haley leaned toward me as if in confidence, lowering his voice but without any effort to hide his words. "Miss St. Germaine and I have become great friends. She's off on a wonderful adventure, back to the ancestral planet. Trading Red for Blue, eh Miss St. Germaine?" He winked at her.

The other woman, Mrs. Paavo, was an elderly white woman who had a no-nonsense manner and the erect bearing of a general. Her eyes were piercing blue, and I soon learned she had the habit of snorting indelicately whenever someone said anything she found absurd.

She snorted now at Haley's impertinence with Miss St. Germaine. "I must say, Mr. Haley, I have no patience for personal remarks and undue familiarity," she said.

"No doubt, no doubt, Mrs. Paavo," he said, with the same smirk. "But we have only each other for amusement, and I am resolved that we will become great friends before this voyage is over."

Ignoring the disgruntled looks of his fellow passengers, he raised his glass high. "Here's to the *Hohmann* and Captain Ngotu. May our journey be uneventful and fruitful. Captain, what an honour it must be to skipper the *Hohmann*. Did you know she was one of the first to establish supply lines between Mars and the Bifrost stations? Amazing how these old birds just keep going. She's fifty years old at least."

"She'll last another one hundred and fifty," Ngotu said, with simple pride. "These ships don't take off or land. They'll last forever."

"Sentimentality is all and well good, Captain, but quite frankly, I'm appalled that the only ship available is this ancient wreck," Mrs. Paavo said. From the way Miss Saint Germaine rolled her eyes, I gathered it was an old complaint which she had heard frequently in the preceding months. "And the price for tickets is extortion, plain and simple, considering that we've added four months onto our journey." She glared at our Captain as if she expected a refund right at the table.

"The government sets the ticket price, Mrs. Paavo," he said with admirable diplomacy. "As for the length of our journey, the *Hohmann* is a supply ship, not a passenger liner. We keep to our schedule and our route, and take on passengers only when there's room."

"Now, now, Mrs. Paavo," Mr. Haley said. "Poor planning on your part does not constitute an emergency on the Captain's. You could have booked the express if the local were too slow."

Mrs. Paavo's old eyes narrowed. I wondered how much capacity for violence existed in that birdlike frame – certainly the spirit was willing.

"There were no tickets to be had." Miss St. Germaine spoke up. "It was an inconvenience for all of us."

"Well, there you go," Haley said. He gave Miss St. Germaine a smile. "You see, Mrs. Paavo? Rather than blaming the good Captain, you should be thanking him. The *Hohmann* was the only ship available."

There was little any of us could say to that.

We grew used to the routine on the ship. Captain Ngotu ran a tight ship; everyone knew their position, and we all worked hard not to breach the artificial cordiality that was the mainstay of a long space voyage. All of us, that is, except for Elton Haley.

The man was an insensitive boor. Besides flirting with me, he adopted a fatherly approach with Miss St. Germaine and an overly solicitous one with Mrs. Paavo. With the former he joshed her unceasingly regarding the virile Earth men she needed to beware of, pushed her to pair off with one or both of the brothers or various crewmembers, and advised her of many pitfalls of life on Earth. With the latter, he could not lay eyes upon her without asking about her health and if she had grandchildren or great-grandchildren to care for her, and enquiring at every interval if she was taking her bone medications.

With Carter and Rose, he was simply patronising, assuming they were simple, ignorant miners. I did not bother to disabuse him of that notion.

I tried to stay out of Mr. Haley's way except at meal times. However, the voyage was long and the ship small, and so it was that when I was enjoying a bit of peace and quiet on the observation deck, he found me. The hatch opened and to my vast annoyance, Haley pulled himself inside. I had my feet hooked around a foothold, and pointedly turned away from him. He did not take the hint.

"Ah, Captain Hawkes," he said, holding on next to me. "I was hoping to find you here. Do you know, I remember why your name sounded familiar."

I supposed I could just go to my bunk, but all the passengers had were narrow sleep cubicles, and we hung there like bound-up spider victims. And blast it, the observation deck was the only place I could be alone, and I was there first.

"The feeds were full of the story," he announced, making himself comfortable. "The asteroid mining disaster that killed five. *You* were the shuttle pilot on that job, and according to the breathless reporters, if it weren't for your exemplary skills, the death toll would have been far higher."

I said nothing, willing him to close his mouth and knowing that he would not. Yes, the accident and investigation were public knowledge and part of the corporation's filings, but what ordinary person would look them up?

Haley just wouldn't stop. "You know, I just wasn't clear on one thing, Captain. Why were you hauling that particular asteroid in the first place?"

I pushed off, heart hammering as if I were in the centrifuge. As I irised out of the hatch, I heard him laughing behind me.

I didn't calm down until I was in the centrifuge, pedalling furiously on an exercise machine, and thought about how I wanted to murder the man.

After that, I avoided the observation deck except for the Mars approach. Normally, the view is a cause for great celebration – sighting Mars is a sign that the next manoeuver is on deck, when the Hohmann slingshots around the planet to gather speed for its final approach to Earth and then turns around and begins deceleration. As a result of the tension on the ship – no one looking at Haley as he beamed and prattled – the oohs and aaahs were lukewarm rather than enthusiastic. I noticed Miss St. Germaine looking more pensive than usual and thought how homesick she must be. She gave off such an air of childlike frailty that my ordinarily hard and cynical heart grew quite maternal toward her. We often ended up side-by-side on the weight machines, and she unbent toward me, her diffidence charming. She asked shy questions about what it was like to be a shuttle pilot, and I couldn't resist exaggerating my exploits.

"Oh my," she breathed, wide-eyed. "It sounds exciting. May I ask why you're leaving it all behind?"

Mindful of Haley's nosiness, I decided I had said too much. "Oh," I said, "It was time to retire, see the old homestead, feel one-g again. That sort of thing. And what about you, Miss St. Germaine?"

She stopped her frantic pumping, resting her arms on the handlebars of the weights. "My parents came to Mars twenty-five years ago," she said. "So did I, as an embryo put in a deep freeze and protected from radiation during the entire voyage out. They waited ten years to have me, and by then they were... old. When it became clear I had little aptitude for the life of a colonist, my parents decided to send me to Earth. So they could start over, with a new child. Another chance for their genetic legacy, despite the cost."

"I – Miss St. Germaine –" I faltered to a stop. I knew that things were hard on Mars, but to so coldly discard one's child – was it possible?

Her voice was hard now, though her eyes were wet with tears. "It's quite all right. I've reconciled myself to it. Do you know what Mr. Haley said?"

"I can imagine," I said dryly.

"He told me that I should be grateful my parents didn't leave me out on the Meridiani Planum to die as some Martians do. That they had probably bankrupted themselves to send me home."

"Mr. Haley is not to be listened to," I said. "He likes to get under people's skin."

"I know," she said, and now there was a catch in her voice. "I just wish he didn't hit so near the mark."

The Mars manoeuver was a success and we were on our last leg of the voyage. Dinner was especially celebratory, enhanced by Mr. Haley's absence from the table. No one cared to ask where he was. We were lively and talkative, and at the end of the dinner, Captain Ngotu came around and poured us each a tiny serving of coffee in real cups.

"We are six months away from Home," he announced, to a scattering of applause. "We are on the downhill side of our journey, and so tonight is a special celebration." He tucked his head into his collar and spoke briefly into the mic attached to his uniform. The lights dimmed, creating a candlelight effect with small electric tea lights on the tables. Everyone oohed. Captain Ngotu raised his small white coffee cup in a toast and we followed suit.

"To Home," he said and we chorused, "To Home." Even Miss St. Germaine echoed his toast, her eyes bright.

We lingered over dinner. Carter and Rose produced a flask of homemade vodka, and we all indulged. At last when I was forced to go to the head, I was quite tipsy when I bumped into Mr. Haley drifting in the passageway between compartments.

"Excu –" I started, unable to hide my irritation. The last thing I needed was him poking his nose into my business. I could have skin like a heat shield and he would still know how to get under it.

Then I realised that Mr. Haley would be getting under no one else's skin any more. He drifted sideways in relation to the corridor, not oriented vertically as we all did, and an expanding spray of round drops of blood scattered around him. His eyes stared blankly at the bulkhead.

I pushed myself forward and slapped at the emergency call button on the wall. The shriek of the siren blared. I grabbed onto Mr. Haley and anchored myself against the grab bars. I could hear hatches opening and voices raised in concern. With Mr. Haley captured against my side, and droplets of blood coalescing around me, I felt for a pulse in his neck. Nothing.

The ship's doctor pushed herself through the corridor from sickbay, expertly gathering momentum by thrusting herself off of each grab bar. With quick efficiency she readied a shot and jabbed him into his heart. He jerked, but sank back again. "Help me get him to my clinic," she said, and she and I and Mrs. Paavo pushed the man through the corridor after her. All the while she was barking comments into her mic, recording blood droplets, rate of coagulation, body temperature. I couldn't help but wonder if she could save him, and if so, if he could identify his attacker.

I don't deny I was in shock. It was one thing to idly contemplate the murder of a nemesis. It was entirely another to face it in reality. We all hated Haley, but which of us had taken matters into their own hands?

Word spread that Haley was dead. After a period holed up exchanging transmissions with both Earth and Mars, Captain Ngotu gathered us all in the lounge and briefed us with terse sentences. The comms officer had notified criminal investigators on both planets; and the authorities would be questioning all of us via radio and again when we made planetfall. The *Hohmann* herself didn't land – we would be shuttled to Earth to the Salto di Quirra base in Sardinia.

"Please be useful and open with the authorities," he told us sternly. "Tell them everything you know." He glanced at me when he said that and I stared impassively back.

"As for that, Captain, perhaps you could be useful and open with us," Mrs. Paavo said, steel in her voice and demeanour as always. She had seen more death than any of us, and her manner was of one who was irked by the inexperience of everyone around her. "Have you found a murder weapon? Do you know how Mr. Haley died? Have you accounted for the whereabouts of everyone on board this ship, and most importantly, are you taking measures to prevent another murder?"

"Mrs. Paavo, calm, please," Captain Ngotu begged. "It has only been a few hours. We can't discuss everything we've found out, surely you understand that?"

"It's hardly unreasonable to ask what you are doing to ensure the safety of your remaining passengers," Mrs. Paavo said. Her jaw jutted forward. "We are six months out and we are traveling with a murderer."

"Yes, madam," Captain Ngotu snapped. He took a deep breath, clearly reaching for calm. "And just like everyone else aboard my ship, you're a suspect."

Mrs. Paavo reared back in outrage. "What utter nonsense," she said. "Utter nonsense."

"Is it?" The Captain looked around at all of us. "Mr. Haley irritated everyone on this ship. We all had good reason to – well, there's no good reason for murder, but good reason to dislike him. And until I get further orders from Earth, I don't intend to release any information about the murder that could compromise the investigation."

Mrs. Paavo made some well-chosen remarks about the Captain's professionalism, but he ignored her, taking another calming breath before floating off to the bridge and further communications from Earth.

In death as in life, Mr. Haley was the topic of all of our whispered conversations, in the passageways, the centrifuge, the observation deck. Even in our sleep pouches with the lights dimmed to meet an ancient circadian rhythm, the whispers went on and on. More than ever I wished the voyage to be over and cursed myself for booking passage on an antique ship. Why hadn't I just waited for a ship with an ion drive?

We were all unsettled, even the crew. The first officer and the navigator, who had been conducting a brisk affair in the medical bay, now avoided their usual trysting place, since the body was stored there. The enterprising brothers Carter and Rose, who had a significant sideline in narcotics, now did a brisk business in sedatives, since no one was sleeping very well. Captain Ngotu, whose wrist implant dispensed blood pressure medication, took to tapping it almost compulsively. Tempers were snappish and easily triggered. Mrs. Paavo's stern good sense was driving me insane. She was relentless in her constant conversation on what Captain Ngotu should do and what his many failings were. Miss Saint-Germaine's childlike facade had cracked and she had become waspish. Not long after the murder I saw her in close conversation with Carter and Rose on the observation deck. They all three glared at me, and I took the hint and irised right back out the hatch. But with me Carter and Rose were as taciturn as ever, and I could tell by their constant sideways glances that they suspected me.

I wanted to shake them by their scruffy necks. Yes, Mr. Haley had brought up the botched tow and the subsequent inquiry. But I wasn't the one designing and dealing drugs. Nor was I the one who habitually carried what was referred to as a miner's mercy – a tiny shiv that could be used to jimmy the air mix on a miner's suit. Tether broken? Said your last good-byes? Rather than suffocate in the deep, alter the mix and go gentle into that good night.

It was the perfect device to exsanguinate Mr. Haley. The only problem was, both Carter and Rose were at dinner too.

And what had they and Miss St. Germaine been talking about, in such close conference on the observation deck?

We were all throwing accusing glances. I decided to take a leaf out of Haley's own book and look up my fellow passengers. The news on the *Hohmann* was canned; the archives got updated only when the ship docked. Those archives were surprisingly thorough, although they were silent on one name: Haley himself.

"May I join you?" I said to Miss St. Germaine in the centrifuge, where she worked diligently on the machine. She glanced at me and shrugged. I slid next to her. As I set the weights, I said, "We have to talk."

She gave a dry little laugh that was nothing like her childish manner. "Do I have a choice?"

"How do you know the brothers?"

"Never met them before this journey."

"Really," I said, my voice as dry as hers.

"Really," she agreed.

She was lying, but that was not surprising after what I had learned. Miss St. Germaine made me look positively wholesome. Maybe her parents should have abandoned her on the Meridiani Planum after all.

The days crept along excruciatingly. I was tempted to stay in my sleep sack but there was no privacy there and I couldn't allow myself to waste away. I couldn't bear to be around the others, however, so once again I went up to the observation deck, and contemplated the growing Sun. Mrs. Paavo found me there, and in her bracing, astringent manner, told me to get over myself.

"You're being a fool," she said. "For God's sake, Captain. You're the last person who should become moody over this."

"Hardly," I said. "Aren't you worried that I'm the murderer?"

"No," she snapped, and pulled herself in next to me. We watched the stars for a while. Finally, she said, "What did Haley have on you?"

"I caused an accident that killed five people." I kept it to that. What Haley knew, it died with him.

She gave me a sidelong glance. "So much for the heroic Captain Hawkes," she said, her voice dry.

"I never claimed to be, Mrs. Paavo, unlike you. I had to cross-reference – you took your husband's name for this trip, but you are better known as the Butcher of Dome Two. How did Haley find out?"

"As I was a celebrity, as it were, on Mars barely twenty years ago, it wasn't difficult. I served my time, Captain. I paid my debt to society. It was time to go Home."

The Dome Two disaster was back in 2047, during the Mars conflict. An outbreak of flu started in the primitive hab. Mrs. Paavo had ordered a quarantine, with no medicines or food to be spared. I could see her, twenty years younger with her same no-nonsense manner, explaining that compassion for the doomed hab would jeopardise the entire colony. They could not spare their meagre resources.

A merciless despot, two drug dealing thieves, and a conniving Martian black marketeer – the investigators would have more suspects than they knew what to do with. And in ironies of ironies, I would no doubt be considered their prime suspect.

There was no celebration this time when Earth loomed into view. She was surrounded by the blinking lights of the complex of half-way stations surrounding the planet, distinguished among the field of stars because stars don't blink. She grew in the viewscreen hourly, and we all crammed onto the observation deck.

"I'm glad we're all here," Mrs. Paavo announced, looking around at everyone. "There's something we need to discuss."

"You aren't the captain," Miss St. Germaine said. "I'm not discussing anything with you." Ever since the murder she had lost her waiflike appearance. All the hours spent at the weight machines had paid off. She was hard now, and her eyes glared.

"You'll discuss and you'll like it," Mrs. Paavo snapped. "We're all under suspicion of murder and I'm not taking the fall. I'm due to be on Earth in two weeks' time and that's where I intend to be."

"Are you sure they'll have you?" Miss. St. Germaine said sweetly. "The Butcher of Dome Two is hardly going to get a hero's welcome."

"I've paid my debt to society," Mrs. Paavo said, repeating the excuse she gave to me. "The same can't be said for the rest of you."

"Ah, after causing the death of hundreds of innocents, Mrs. Paavo doesn't think she should be a suspect for murder," I said.

"Don't start, Captain Hawkes," she snapped at me. "I can do research too. You did more than just cause an accident on Bifrost – you were part of the gang that was diverting asteroids to the black market."

All eyes turned to me. "I was never convicted," I pointed out. "Charges dismissed."

"Oh stuff it, Hawkes," Rose said, glancing at his brother for support. "You ratted everyone out, and you got a plea bargain."

"Pardon me," I said. "But while I was lying in the medbay handcuffed to a bed, you were throwing me under the bus. Of course I sang."

"Oh, how surprising, the miners were involved too," Mrs. Paavo sneered. "I thought you two were just the local drug dealers."

"Sure, they were in on it," I said. I was tired of playing the lone villain. "Carter and Rose were responsible for finding the Mars buyer, and setting the tow. They're quite the jack-of-all-trades, our miners."

"That's enough," Carter said. He pointed at Miss St. Germaine. "Ask her what she's doing here, and you'll find out we're not the ones who killed Haley."

"Don't be absurd," she snapped. "I didn't kill him."

"Even though he was the reason for your exile from Mars?" Mrs. Paavo smirked. "You aren't the innocent daughter you like to portray, Miss St. Germaine. Your sole reason for leaving Mars is that you were the sorrow of your parents and the bane of Dome Four. Quite a black market in diverted goods you were operating."

Diverted goods… black market… I flashed back to her huddled conversations with the brothers. Our mysterious asteroid buyer was based on Mars. "You!" I cried. I was flabbergasted. She curled her lip at me.

"Oh, I'm sorry, did I let you down?" she said, and I flushed. I admit it – she had played me like a violin. "Too bad you couldn't pilot a ship *or* keep your mouth shut."

"Very interesting," Mrs. Paavo said. "I paid *my* debt to society."

"Stop saying that, you self-righteous madwoman." I had had enough. If anyone was a candidate for the airlock…

The lock irised open, and Captain Ngotu pulled himself in. "Good. You're all here." He grabbed a handhold and moved sideways. In floated Mr. Haley, alive and well and with the same irritating smirk, and holding up an InterSol badge.

To say we were astonished would not do justice to the moment. I had seen him – held him in my arms. There was blood – with a sinking realisation I understood that I had been duped.

"The good news is, none of you are murder suspects," Mr. Haley announced. "The bad news is, you are all under arrest for the various infractions that you committed while off Earth."

It turned out that the authorities on Earth, Bifrost, and Mars had coordinated efforts to apprehend and build a case against a ring of asteroid thieves and black marketeers. There were no tickets to be found on a larger, faster ship, because InterSol made sure the only berths available were on the slow, ancient *Hohmann*. Our confessions to one another were the last bit of evidence Haley needed to bring us to justice.

Miss St. Germaine was the mastermind of the asteroid theft; the brothers were her lieutenants. I was the hired pilot, lured by the money and the chance to go Home in style.

Mrs. Paavo was collateral; but it turned out that the irritating old bag still faced civil and criminal charges on Earth. She had not entirely paid her debt to society after all.

It was a subdued group that walked off the *Hohmann* onto Midway Station into the embrace of the authorities. I looked back once at the observation screen that offered a panorama of the vastness of space. I was conscious of a deep pang of longing. Maybe if you asked the wildebeest, in the maw of an opportunistic crocodile, she would say she regretted migrating too.

Bad Dog

There's no such thing as a bad dog. Not really. Not ever. This one is for you, Franklin.

Before he does the Bad Thing, the world Dog knows is a good world. Runs in the park, leaping into the air after the flat thing, food to fill his belly, and a bed to sleep on at the foot of the people. It is a good cave, with good fire.

After the Bad Thing, the people take him to the cage place. Dog huddles at the back of his concrete box, desperate to shut down the incessant barking and scents of fear, madness, chemicals, death. He loses track of time.

A new thing comes. Dog hears a roaring in the sky that is so loud it drives him deep inside himself, and then it gets mor quiet than ever before. The cage people don't come, and the cage place stays dim, unlit.

Dog hears a skittering sound. This is not a rat, come after the rations of kibble. This is a different sound. This skittering has too many legs. Dog huddles in the back of his cage. Another dog barks, then yelps and yelps, then is silent. The skittering thing passes Dog's cage, pauses, and then goes on.

Dog waits one more long day, unable even to mark his cage, desperate for food and water, and the next morning, he noses the cage door, and it opens.

Dog knows he is to blame for this too.

The good smells of his old world, and the smells of the prison (urine, faeces, fear, chemicals), are replaced with a new world of smell: fire and chemical spills that overwhelm the sensitive glands in his nose. Cars are abandoned everywhere. Highways and overpasses crumble. Dog picks his way through still-burning rubble. There are people but they are the wrong people. After the Bad Thing and the cage place, Dog doesn't trust people any more. He isn't sure he would be welcome in his old place, so he doesn't try to go back there.

When the people call to him, urging, beseeching, "Hey Buddy! Hey, dog! Come on, we're not going to hurt you!" He sidles away, galloping fast when they throw something at him, skirting trouble. His belly is hollow and he needs food, but he can't trust people.

There are new chemical smells along the river, and there is a fire all along the top of the water. Even Dog can tell that is wrong. Thirsty, he laps a little at the water in a small cove along the shore, but the taste burns his tongue. This is bad water. There's a dead turtle and a pile of dead fish wedged against the roots and mud, but Dog can tell they won't be good to eat. He doesn't even want to roll in them.

He finds an old wrapper with the scent of burger on it, and he eats that. Even if he vomits it up, the smell is strong enough to make him pretend that he is eating something.

At night, he finds a den in a pile of rubble and curls up nose-to-tail there.

He dreams of the Bad Thing. He growls both in the dream and in his sleep. It is just a warning growl. Go away, he tells the eyes. Go back. He doesn't like faces in his face. People don't get so low into his face, so these eyes are not people. The people are barking and no one is listening to his growl. The eyes get closer, and the not-person reaches out and touches Dog, even though Dog has clearly warned it away. Dog barks another warning, and in his sleep he yips and struggles.

The hand slaps at Dog, stinging his nose, and Dog loses control, snaps, his teeth biting flesh, catching the soft face just below the eyes. Coppery blood fills his mouth, startling him, and he jumps back. There is silence, a drawn intake of breath, and then screaming.

He wakes, his sensitive ears and sensitive nose pricked up and alert. It's dark, heavy cloud cover, no stars. In the before days, dogs watched the stars with the people. Dog hasn't seen stars in a long time and while he doesn't miss them, he knows something is missing.

He smells a person. All the person smells are there without the strong smells of soap and food and clean clothes that usually cover them. The person scrambles over the rubble, coming toward Dog's den.

Dog tenses. The person moves around, and then stops. Dog imagines the person curling up nose-to-tail. He hears whimpering, and then sniffling. Dog knows exasperation. This person is being too loud. If he is not a predator, he needs to be quiet before he draws predators down upon them.

Maybe the person knows that because the whimpering stops, the rustling stops, and Dog dozes, half-alert for danger.

The grey light comes. There is silence except for wind. It drones over the rubble of Dog's den in the crumbled concrete. Dog uncurls, fully awake, and sniffs the air. The person is still there, whimpering again.

Prey. His mouth fills with saliva. Sometimes the cousins are strong in Dog. Both aspects of Dog struggle inside him, the wolf and the cave, the pack and the pact. He gives a low woof, but Dog doesn't know which call he is answering.

Dog rises to his feet, yawns and stretches, and saunters out of his den. The person is only about fifteen feet away, tucked in his own den under a triangle of concrete, and he looks up when Dog approaches.

The person is small. His eyes are low, right in Dog's eyes, and the same fearful aggression rises inside Dog. He growls, despairing. If the small person comes near him he will bite, and more bad things will happen. He will go back into the cold cave with the bars, and the world will become even more strange and fearful than before. Dog backs away and trots off, stumbling in footsore weariness and with weakness from hunger.

He looks back once. The small person is following him.

Dog follows the food smells, picked out by his nose from the scents of burning fuel, twisted metal, and dead bodies. He follows the scent to a smashed car, its persons hanging half out of the seats. The bodies are dead and Dog will have to scavenge sometime, but for now the pact is stronger than the pack, and he noses around to the passenger side, half climbing in. There's a sack of groceries. The milk jug has burst, spewing rotten milk everywhere, and there are two plastic-wrapped steaks that have also turned. Dog paws at the steak, biting away at the plastic and tearing into the meat, bolting it down in huge chunks. Dog hears the small person come up to the car, and he gives a growl. This is his find.

The small person ignores his clear warning and climbs up into the car next to Dog. He doesn't look at Dog, just goes straight for a box of cereal, prying at it with scratched and dirty fingers. Since he doesn't go after Dog's find, Dog relaxes. Side by side the small person eats and Dog eats, and when Dog finishes the steak and noses around for something else, the small person holds out a small hand with a few bits of cereal in it.

Dog stops. The pact of the cave and fire is strong in him now, responding to the offering the small person makes. Dog forces himself to look at the small person, crouching despite himself, because he is afraid of what he might do.

Dog knows this person is a young person. His clothes are torn and dirty, and he smells of faeces and urine, and he has dry cereal on his breath. He is skinny and scratched. Holding his breath, Dog accepts the offered gift with delicate tongue. The small person plunges his hand back into the box and pulls out a few more bits. Dog takes the cereal and gives the boy's hand a tentative lick.

In this way the boy feeds Dog, alternating between giving Dog and himself handfuls of cereal.

The hurtling jets make them jump apart. Dog growls and the boy shrieks, throwing the box down and scrambling to hide in the footwell of the passenger seats. He cries and cries, and Dog doesn't know which way to turn. The Bad Thing has come again, and Dog doesn't know what he did wrong this time. He gives into his fear and he bolts.

There is a great explosion, yellow flame and white light, and black and grey smoke, and Dog is rolled over by the energy of the blast. He rolls and hits his head, yelping in pain. He is left unconscious in the middle of the broken road.

When Dog comes to, yelping and whining, he gets to his feet. His ear stings, and his hind leg drags. Gentle hands pat him and he snaps at the hands. He doesn't want hands. He wants a den to hide in until the pain stops. He wants to go away. But the small hands keep tugging at him, and dimly he recognises the smell of the boy. The boy's face is wet and he shows his teeth, and he tugs hard at Dog. Dog can't hear anything because of the blast but he knows the boy is barking at him.

Dog gives in and stumbles after the boy.

This den isn't bad. It's barely big enough for the two of them but that's good. Dog crawls inside, his bad leg throbbing, and snaps at the boy when he crawls in after him. The boy pats him again and curls up next to Dog, away from his bad leg. The boy opens his hand and tries to give Dog another bit of cereal, but Dog just turns away dully. He doesn't want food right now; he wants time and a dark place. Dog lays his head on the boy's belly, taking comfort from the warmth. The boy strokes Dog's ruff with one hand, and sucks his thumb. Dog and the boy doze.

Dog doesn't know how long the whisper of too many legs has been going on. He wakes to hear each reaching step, a long pause between every sound. His nose is blind. The thing does not smell, so Dog can't see it. He can only hear the slow, skittering footfall of too many legs.

The small person hears it now too. He lifts his head, his thumb in his mouth. Wet comes down his face and drips on Dog's back, but he doesn't make a noise.

Step. Pause. Reach. Step.

Something long pokes into the den, unfolding angularly, and taps almost at Dog's feet. Dog feels a growl come up in his throat, but he remembers the bark and the yelp and the silence. He remains still.

After a long moment the leg retracts and they hear the awful sound of its slow scraping retreat across the rubble.

Dog and the small person stay still for a long time.

It's night again, raining. The rain sizzles when it hits the concrete rubble. The rubble shifts around them as machinery moves over the broken roadway. The slab of concrete, the roof of their den, trembles and shifts. In the face of this new danger, Dog freezes. Somehow the boy understands. He lifts his head, and there is something, some resolve, that Dog recognises.

"Up, Dog," the boy commands, and the words pull at Dog's muscles as if with a string. Dog knows *Up. Sit. Leave it. Come.*

He follows the boy out of the den, struggling to move his injured leg. He yelps but quietly, forlornly.

The boy stops once to look behind them and Dog follows the direction of his gaze. He sees lights on a big machine, breathing fire and smoke, its giant tracks coming down over the pile of rubble. The boy scrambles and runs, and Dog follows, the machine chasing them.

Dog has seen big machines before but he has never seen a machine like this one. He sees another and another, and the machines point their long whiplike arms at Dog and the small person.

The roar of jets overhead, screaming in formation, make the machines jerk their whiplike arms around and point them at the sky. They throw themselves upward to rope in the jets, but the jets peel away. Dog and the small person scramble off the broken roadway into the shallow woods along the highway. Dog is relieved to be in the woods. There are good smells, like bugs and small animals, and there are old markings that make Dog feel almost normal. He wants to lift his leg to mark a tree, but his bad leg won't support his weight and he can't lift it. So he piddles on the ground, and throws the scent as best he can. It feels good to have something he knows to do.

"Bad, bad," the boy says, his sobbing like Dog's yelps. Dog knows the boy can't help his yelping. "Bad machine. Go away. "

There is a small dead furry animal. Dog bites into it, tearing away fur and crunching the desiccated bones. There is some meat and delicious marrow, and he eats. The boy crouches and watches him. Dog growls at the boy. The meat is his. The cousins have reared their heads inside him.

A distant explosion lights up the night sky, and for an instant the light is emblazoned on Dog's eyes. A whiplike arm rises upward from the highway, and catches a jet, flinging it out of the sky. They both watch with uncomprehending eyes.

Dog smells a new person before he sees him, and before the boy sees him.

"Hey," the person says. Dog knows *Hey. Hey* is like a bark. *Look at me. Pay attention.* The boy turns around and freezes.

The man is a dark shape in the night, but that doesn't stop Dog from seeing him as clearly as if it is full daylight. The man smells like the boy, urine, faeces, sweat, and dirt, and overlaid with that, fear. And something more – Dog smells craft, desperation, sourness.

"You got food?" the man says. The little boy stares at him. The man laughs, a dreadful bark. "Yeah, you don't got food. You got a dog, though. Come here, buddy."

The man picks up a stick, drops it, looks around, and picks up a rock. He hefts it. He is so intent on Dog he cannot see what is behind him.

Dog feels the growl start inside him. It's soundless at first. He quivers with it, and his hackles stand up on his thin neck and shoulders. His head goes low and his eyes bore into the space behind the man where the thing is coming. The boy hears it; the man doesn't. All the man's attention is focused on Dog.

"Good dog," the man says." Nice dog." His scent is vivid with fear. "Nice doggy. Jeez, bet you're rabid. Bet you are. I'm not going to hurt –" He breaks off and charges at Dog, swinging the rock.

Dog charges too, past the man at the thing. Its many legs reach for him and he is rolled over and burned where they touch. His yelp and the man's scream mingle in his ears.

Dog is flung clear of the thing, and he goes down hard, his bad leg burning. He scrambles to his feet to see the thing embrace the man with its too many legs, and the man's scream is cut off.

On the other side of the man is the small person.

His pack.

Dog barks.

Still grappling the man, the thing turns toward him, and Dog gathers his strength. He creeps in low and, driven by instinct, grabs a long articulated leg, and tears it off. Dark liquid flows and Dog jumps back, rips at another leg. The thing can't untangle from the man. It is hooked into him with its legs and teeth all down the centre of its body. Dog rips again and again, until the thing falls over, surrounded by ripped-away legs.

Dog comes to his senses slowly. He is blind in one eye. His ear has been torn off. His hind leg throbs and he has broken ribs. He raises his head, but that's as far as he can go.

The dead man and the dead thing are sprawled out in the small clearing, long articulated legs everywhere, blood and dark fluid mingled on the weeds and in the dirt.

He smells the boy. The boy is fully overcome with hunger and thirst, and he can't cry any more. He lies in the dirt, his desiccated thumb near his mouth, and his eyes stare up at the sky. Only the faint rise and fall of his thin chest under his t-shirt indicate that he still lives.

The sound of an engine creeps over him, as if something is growling at a register no one can hear, only feel.

This is not one of the bad machines. Dog has ridden in one of these vehicles, with knobby tires and wide seats. The vehicle drives along the road and then rumbles off into the clearing. Men and women get out. Dog can smell them. Under their clothes and dirt and sweat, behind the metallic and chemical scents of their gear and weapons, they are clean and healthy. He can smell fear, and tiredness but no sickness, no despair.

They see the bloody clearing and the bodies and break into a run.

"A kid! There's a kid!" The woman drops to her knees, hands off her weapon to another soldier, and gathers the boy in her arms. They cluster round, and try to give the boy water, talking in loud voices, all bustle and movement. A radio crackles.

The others survey the carnage, the dead man, the thing, the legs, and Dog.

"Jesus Christ," says a soldier. He kneels and puts his hand on Dog's shoulder. His hand is hard but kind.

"Come on, move move *move*, we're out in the open. There are more coming up from the south."

"Got the boy?"

"I got him," the soldier says, and she does, holding him as carefully as if she could carry him in her mouth. The boy has bags and lines attached to him, and even Dog can see that he is pinking up, that his skin is rehydrating, that he is coming back. He will not die.

"Sir, should we bring the dog?"

Everyone turns to look at Dog. He knows they are weighing a decision.

Weighing him.

The pact is clear: He has been a Bad Dog.

It is the boy who makes the decision. He reaches out his hand to Dog. His voice is muffled.

"Come," the boy says.

Dog knows *Up. Sit. Leave it. Come.* He gathers himself, pushing against the pain, and hobbles after the boy.

The Star Seed Witches Meet at Midnight

This story is a love letter to one of my favourite all-night diners in Austin. A lot of righteous revenge can be cooked up in a place like that.

The Open 24 Hours sign was a beacon of red neon in the rainy predawn darkness. Evelyn pulled into the lumpy parking lot in her old Volvo wagon next to Carol's Honda. The Star Seed Café windows were fogged up but she could see their table and three shadowy figures around it. Evelyn felt a pang. Was it just two years ago when they had been at full strength? Now there were just four left, and soon, they would dwindle even more.

They looked up at her when she came in, her frizzy grey hair a halo in the humidity.

"Well, look what the cat dragged in," Margie said. She pulled out a chair from a nearby table. Evelyn sat, shrugging out of her raincoat. Water droplets flew. The ladies grimaced. Carol handed her a napkin, and she mopped at her face and hair, the thin paper soaked in seconds.

Ginger said, "Don't drip on us, Ev. It's cold in here. The A/C must be at sixty-five."

Margie laughed. "That's Ev for you, always making a mess." She patted Evelyn's hand. "Just teasing, Ev."

"Are you?" Evelyn said, sharp. The other ladies looked between them. Ginger's fingers twitched and Carol looked worried. The dislike between Margie and Evelyn was well known, and normally the witches fed off it, but sometimes the spark could get out of control, and nobody wanted a fight tonight.

Margie grunted, took a sip of coffee. "Why're you all so jumpy? It's not like you've got work to do. Goddamn, I'm so tired I'm ready to take on the Dark One Himself."

They all made the sign, even Evelyn. She knew what Margie meant. Margie's shiftless son, his dirtbag wife, and three grandkids all lived with her, and she was the only one working, as a home health aide no less. She wiped grownup butts and she wiped cute baby butts, and she might have been younger than they were, but she was old and mean, a meanness brought on by exhaustion and devastation. Evelyn tried to feel sympathy, but Margie annoyed her sometimes.

"You want us to do something about that, Margie?" Carol said.

She meant about the son and daughter-in-law. It wasn't a matter of cursing, or calling up the devil. It was a matter of inclination. Push them where they were already headed. Just a boost. That's all. But there was the matter of the kids.

They might be witches, but babies were babies.

Margie smiled, a tired smile that gave her momentary dimples. "Nah. I got that covered." Before anyone could ask what she meant by that, Margie added, "Besides, I have another thing that we can do something about."

The waiter came by with Ev's standing order, migas, sausage, and French toast, and poured her coffee. While she ate, Margie filled them in.

One of her clients was a sweet lady in her eighties, bed- and wheelchair-bound due to a stroke. "She's still in there," Margie said, "but there's no connection. Nothing in or out."

Her son was in his fifties, and he was doing his best to fleece his mother of everything. "He comes in when I'm there, and he just takes stuff. Just walks off with it. He's taken furniture, the silver, the china, brazen as you please, and right in front of her, and she can't do anything about it. I've seen her expression. He gives her a kiss and says real loud, 'Thanks, Ma.' "

"Jesus Christ," Carol said. They all nodded.

"Yeah, he's a real piece of work. Thing is, he's a moron, because he thinks he's cleaning her out, but there's a bigger score in the house." She looked around and then leaned in, and they moved in around her, Evelyn trying not to chew too loud.

"I think her husband was stacking silver and it's still there somewhere."

She smiled at their reactions. Evelyn thought about what a silver cache could do. It was the difference between living off social security and getting ahead.

"After our divorce I found out Harold stacked silver," Ginger said. "Ended up being all of ten grand when he was through, and he took it with him when I kicked him out." She sucked up her last dregs of coffee. "Shame about the gas line explosion."

Even Carol smirked. All they did was work with inclinations, with moving things the way they wanted to go. Ol' Harold's new place was connected to an old Texas Gas line, and who were they to stop the gas from expanding the fifty-year old line?

"So have you looked?" Ginger asked, with her toothless cackle.

"No," Margie said. "I'm not gonna paw through Miss Jessica Bertram's possessions the way her son does." Her dimples appeared again, contrasting with her wolfish grin. "I'll read her aura the way the Dark One intended." They all made the sign. "Miss Jessica's hiding something, and I'm getting a strong image of precious metals along with a wish for revenge."

They all perked up. Revenge – the strongest inclination of them all. Margie was right. They could work with this.

That afternoon, Evelyn dropped off Margie at the Bertram house when her shift started. The Bertram house was a bit shabby – it needed paint, and the landscaping was straggly and overgrown. The driveway was cracked, and the garage door was crooked. Once, though, this mid-century bungalow had sheltered a family where Miss Jessica had kept this house and raised her children, including the son who was treating her like an ATM.

Evelyn waited for Margie to go inside, and a few more long minutes for when the morning shift aide, a tired woman in pink scrubs, came out. She was on the phone and didn't even look at Ev's car as she headed to the bus stop.

More long minutes, and then the curtain shook. At the signal, Evelyn got out of the car and hurried up the steps.

Margie let her in. The house was dim and cool, the place clean and uncluttered. There was little furniture – the son again – but for marble-topped end tables that would have bracketed a couch, centred in front of a missing television. There were photos on the mantel; a wedding, the family in front of the house when it was new, a frightened child on Santa's lap. In the middle of the room was Miss Jessica in a wheelchair.

Evelyn knew better than to deify an old lady, even an old helpless-looking one slumped to her right side. She was an old lady herself, and she was far from sweet. Maybe the Bertram son had good reason to hate and mistreat his mother. Maybe Miss Jessica was a right old bitch.

But also she was irritated by middle-aged men who thought the world owed them something. Lord, save me from men with a chip on their shoulder, she thought, making the sign.

"Miss Jessica, this is my friend Evie," Margie said. She didn't use the loud childlike voice people often adopted when talking to the elderly. "Evie, this is Jessica Bertram."

"A pleasure to meet you," Evie said. There was no reaction from Jessica Bertram. "I've heard a lot about you from Margie." She cast around for something to sit on, and ended up on one knee by the wheelchair. She could tell that getting up was going to be a pain. "She asked me to come visit with you today, because she thinks that maybe together we can help you."

Was that a flicker of something around Miz Bertram's eyes? Ev reached out and took the woman's hand, limp and unresponsive. She caressed it, and with her gaze locked on Miz Bertram's, she said, "Margie told me about your son."

That was a reaction. The woman moaned, and a bit of drool dripped from the corner of her mouth. Margie dabbed gently.

"So you see," Ev went on, "We think he's upset you. But if he hasn't – if you're okay with things – we can just go on the way we are, and Margie will keep taking care of you, and when he comes back for the rest of your stuff, well, it's his inheritance anyway, right?"

There was no other reaction, but Miz Bertram's eyes lost their unfocused expression. She sharpened. Oh yes, she's in there, Ev thought, and she wants out. It was time. Ev nodded at Margie, Margie nodded back, and with one hand clasped on Miz Bertram's, and her other clasped with Margie's hand, she and Margie began to chant.

On the third go round, something snapped, and Ev felt her head jerk, as she was joined by another consciousness, speaking in midstream.

"No, I wasn't a good mother," Ev said, speaking Miz Bertram's words. "I know that. I made mistakes, especially with Jimmy. But it breaks my heart. I didn't think he was this angry. I didn't think he could be this mean." Ev's voice broke. "I just don't think I deserve this torture."

Miz Bertram in Ev's body got up, Evelyn feeling every bit of it as she rose from a kneeling position to her feet. She could feel the old woman's pleasure at being able to move again and a deeper disinclination to let go. Evelyn fought the urge to resist Jessica Bertram, at least just yet. Sometimes the rider didn't want to dismount and had to be thrown, but now was not the time. They needed to find out where the silver was. And she wasn't worried yet. It would take a while for Miz Bertram to know her own strength.

"Miss Jessica, let me help you," Margie said, taking Evelyn's body by the arm and helping to balance her. "That's right, sugar, you're doing fine. Now, let me know when you feel it's too much."

"Can I go outside?" Miz Bertram said, Ev's voice wistful.

"If you aren't too tired," Margie said.

Jessica Bertram walking around her house, touching things, picking up photos and setting them down, caressing a loved bowl on the kitchen counter. Milk glass, still a collectible in some quarters – Jimmy Bertram obviously didn't know it was worth anything, or just hadn't had a chance to come for it.

"Do you want me to put that away for safekeeping?" Margie asked, and Jessica made Evelyn smile.

"Not yet. Not yet," she said, and kept walking. Over the next half hour Jessica opened up the cedar chest, checked the closets, visited old photo albums, and finally sat at the kitchen table near the window looking out on the backyard. There were two mature oaks out there, a falling down toolshed, and an old greenhouse, the plastic smeared and stained by weather. The way she sat on the old paint-stained chair, it was clear that she had sat here many a time, having her Maxwell House, leafing through the *Reader's Digest* or a ladies' magazine.

She turned Ev's body so she could see out the window, but also keep an eye on the front of the house.

"When the children went to school, it was my time," she remembered. She ran a finger over the scarred wooden table. "Sometimes I sat here for hours, just daydreaming. I'd sit so long, they'd come home after school and I'd have to jump up and pretend I'd been busy all day. That's the only thing keeping me sane in there." She nodded her chin at her unmoving, slumped body. "I've had lots of practice. Sometimes I dreamed that I waved good-bye to the kids, and then got up and packed a suitcase and took off in the car." She smiled. "That was a good one. I dreamed that one a lot."

"Did the kids know?" Margie asked.

"I don't think the kids knew anything. Children are so self-centred. My husband used to make fun of me – he always said it was just in fun – and after a while they all started to do it." Now she sounded spiteful and self-satisfied. "So I stopped talking to them. I'd stare right through them. Ellen could be whining about something, and I would just look at her as if she was a cockroach. Jimmy begged me once to talk, just to please talk, and it gave me great pleasure to walk away."

"I haven't seen Ellen," Margie observed.

"No, no, Ellen and I have been estranged for many decades now. She had her chance, but she took her father's side in everything, and she has to lie in the bed that she made."

She looked straight at Margie. Evelyn, deep inside, could see Margie's jaded expression at what they were hearing. Apple, tree, Evelyn thought. And that clearly leaked through to Jessica, because Miz Bertram said with great resentment,

"So you think Jimmy's spitefulness is because of me? I told you, I made mistakes, but he chose to steal from me. I didn't teach him to be the kind of son who robs his mother. I didn't teach my children to be snotty and disrespectful and hateful. I showed them nothing but love for many years, and when I grew tired of being the family joke, they didn't like it, did they." The deep bitterness burned Evelyn's throat. She lifted a hand with great difficulty, and Margie recognised the sign.

"Miss Jessica, we're going to put you back now, but we'll let you out for another chat soon," she said.

"Oh will you, eh? And what if I decide I don't want to go ba –?"

Evelyn snapped to, almost bouncing her head against the window. "Ow," she said, rubbing her neck. She looked over at Miz Bertram, and then at Margie. They gathered at the kitchen sink where Jessica Bertram couldn't see or hear them. They talked low.

"I don't know," Margie said. "I think I like him better now."

"What do we do now?" Evelyn said. "I don't want her back inside me." She shuddered.

"Did you get anything about the silver?"

"Nothing. Just Chatty Cathy talking about her stellar parenting skills."

The sound of the front door opening made them turn.

"Hey Ma!" Jimmy Bertram called. Margie and Evelyn gave each other deep looks and went into the living room to see the son kissing his mom on the cheek. He looked like his mother around the eyes and mouth. He was about Margie's age, tall and bulky, gone to seed. His belly overflowed his jeans.

"Hi Margie!" Jimmy said. "Who's your friend?"

"Hello, Mr. Bertram," Margie said. "This is Evelyn. She's learning the ropes and will be taking on a shift with your mother."

"Well, Evelyn, don't let my mother's mild-mannered exterior fool you. She's a live wire, right Ma?" he said, patting his mother's shoulder with extravagant affection. The last pat jarred his mother's unresponsive body. It was almost a smack.

"It must be hard for you, to see your mom in this way," Evelyn said. "But we take good care of all of our patients. They're like family."

He laughed, a little too hard, like the pat. "That's too bad. No, just joking," he added, before they could even react. "Just joking. That's the way we do it in the Bertram family. Everyone's a joker. Especially Mom. She was a real kidder, back in the day."

Evelyn couldn't resist. "You're a good son, to come by every day. Margie told me."

Jimmy turned to look at her, really look at her. The avuncular act fell away. There was a hardness around his mouth that was more than just a resemblance to his mother's facial structure, but an echo of her spitefulness and meanness. That anger and pent-up spite was the mother's true legacy. That was the Bertram way all right.

"Oh, I get it," he said. "Yeah. I see what's going on. Well, all it takes is one phone call, ladies, and you two are out on your ass, so if you want to keep your shitty job, you'll keep your opinions to yourselves."

He went down the hall toward the bedrooms, and they could hear him rummaging around. They all three looked at each other, although it was hard to tell where Miss Jessica might be looking at any given moment. They were all still like that when he came out with a clock radio and a bedside lamp. He gave them all a glare but said nothing as he slammed the door behind him, getting the radio cord stuck in the door, and having to open up the door again so he could get out.

A day later, Margie and Evelyn and Jessica inside Evelyn sat around the kitchen table, drinking coffee and eating Nutter Butters. Evelyn wasn't a fan, but Jessica had missed them. She raved over them, and the chance to drink coffee again. She asked for Maxwell House, but Evelyn put her foot down and they were drinking Starbucks.

"Why didn't you just get a divorce?" Margie asked, as Jessica dunked her cookie in her latte. "I mean, I can understand it was the Fifties, but –"

"Sixties, by then. And no one got a divorce. Also, they were my children." She made Evelyn shudder. "Can you imagine, if he remarried and they loved someone else?"

Evelyn was permeated with Jessica's sickening spite. It had grown like a cancer, so that the feeling of being put upon had blotted out anything approaching love. She had loved the chance to reject her children over and over again, become addicted to it. Revelled in it, every rejection, every gotcha.

And that's how we got here, she thought.

Miss Jessica snorted. "Your friend is awfully judgmental," she said to Margie. With great deliberation she took another Nutter Butter, and stuffed it in her mouth, and then another, and another. Evelyn tried not to gag.

Margie rolled her eyes and took the package away.

"We're trying to help," she reminded her. "We'll cut the connection if you don't behave."

Jessica made a face, as if she had eaten a turd instead of a cookie. "Well, I don't know what you think you can do, although I suppose you might kill him." A wave of self-righteous satisfaction swept through her, so strong that again Evelyn felt the strange allure too. Jessica imagined herself as a mother who would have the spotlight for her grief. Confined to a wheelchair, her only son visiting her, and now gone...

"We don't kill," Margie said. "We push. Whatever happens, they do it to themselves. Is Jimmy inclined to anything?"

But Jessica didn't want to talk about it, just thinking over and again about how she could mourn a dead son. The sympathy, the righteousness, finally the recognition she deserved.

When it was time to disconnect, she fought. Evelyn severed the link with a decisive snap, taking pleasure in shutting the old woman up in mid plaint. After she left the house, Evelyn drank a bottle of water and spit and spit until she got the cookie taste out of her mouth.

The whole thing was taking its toll. Miss Jessica was becoming harder to host. Her commitment to being wronged and getting revenge, even the most petty revenge, was both tiring and also weirdly attractive. Evelyn found herself at odd moments burning with random resentments.

The ladies met at Star Seed to chew over the situation. It was 2 am, and they were the only patrons. The cook was their waiter and cashier.

"I'm not going back," Evelyn told them. "She's narcissistic and dangerous." She shuddered. "I'm not a delicate flower, but this isn't worth it."

"We're close, though," Margie said. "When she's not inside you, when it's just us, I keep getting images of strongboxes."

"Well, I'm not," Evelyn said. "She just giggles over the fact that she mentally tortured her children when they were little."

"Well, that's just it," Margie said. "I think you're distracting her. Maybe try not to be so judgy when she's in there."

"Oh, you try not judging her," Evelyn said.

"I'm just saying, what are you doing in there? Just rummage around a little. That's the whole point."

"She wants my body." Evelyn's voice was rising. They all looked at her, and she shushed, but she went on. "She's getting harder to evict, too."

Carol raised a hand. "Ev, I trust your analysis. But from everything I'm hearing, is it possible we've got the wrong target? I mean, maybe we need to be working Jimmy, and pushing Jessica."

It made sense. Jimmy knew something was up. Sure he was taking the household goods, but he ended up in the back rooms all the time, rummaging around. He knew there was something else.

"It's harder to let a man in," Evelyn said, but speculatively. "And doubtful he'll tell us anything useful, if she won't."

"We're not getting anything useful now," Margie said. "Carol should be doing this."

Her words fell into the sudden silence around the table. "Jesus, Margie," Evelyn said, disgusted. Ginger made a sour noise through flaccid lips. Carol smiled, her dark eyes damp.

"Oh, don't worry. She's just saying what we're all thinking."

I wasn't, Evelyn thought, even though she was. And then she had a sudden flash of something ugly, something spiteful. *Sure, Carol gets to be the noble one, but she's just like us. Hypocrite.*

"I'll do it," Evelyn said. "I'll ride Jimmy."

"No," Ginger said at once, her words both mushy and clear. "You already have a rapport with Miss Jessica. I'll ride Jimmy, push him to confront her. You pick up on the strongbox." She looked around at them, face like a wrinkled apple doll. "And once we learn where the money is, then –" She made a gesture, like reining in a horse. "Heigh-ho, Silver."

They all looked around. It was quiet in the diner, and the cook was in the back, washing up. As one, they all smiled.

"Brought more friends, eh?" Jimmy said, as he came in to see his mother, Margie, Evelyn, and Ginger. Ginger smiled, a professional therapist's smile, flashing perfect teeth, her frizzy hair calmed under an ash-blond bobbed wig, her lean form in a Dress Barn pantsuit. She stretched out her hand.

"Mr. Bertram, so nice to meet you. I'm from the home health agency, and Margie called me in to discuss what's going on. As you know from the contract you signed, the agency is required to step in when there's evidence of elder abuse."

He grew red and closed in on her. "The only people abusing my mother are your aides! I've suspected for a long time that they've been stealing things from her house, and I have proof –"

Ginger reached out and touched his hand, tapping the inside of his wrist twice. At once, Jimmy fell still and silent.

At the same time, Evelyn opened herself up to Jessica.

"What's happening? What's going on?" Jessica demanded.

"Ginger here is a licensed therapist," Margie said. "She's going to facilitate a conversation between you and your son." She sat back on one of the end tables. "And I'm going to listen."

Evelyn and Jimmy faced off against one another. Jimmy was immobilised under Ginger's influence. Only his lips moved.

"Well," Jessica-Evelyn said. "Look at you." The sarcasm came through loud and clear.

"What – what's going on, Ma?" His voice – Ginger's voice – was full of fear.

"These nice ladies want us to talk, I think, mother to son. Open up, tell family secrets. Don't you, ladies? Isn't that why you're here?"

A twinge of panic shivered down Evelyn's spine. Shit. Jessica Bertram wasn't stupid.

"Why should I listen to anything you have to say?" Ginger's voice came out of Jimmy's mouth. "After freezing me out since I was ten years old." Jessica turned Evelyn's body, looking past him, archly ignoring her son. "Of course. Good old Mom, always got to stick it to me."

Self-righteousness flooded through Evelyn.

"Do you think I wanted to? You gave me no choice," Jessica said. "You and your sister – you, you – it was the only way to make you be respectful."

"We were kids, Ma. We didn't know what was going on. You made me and Ellen feel like shit."

"Oh did you?" Jessica said. This was going all wrong, Evelyn thought. What was Ginger doing? She tried to reach out to Ginger, to Margie, but the old woman was having none of it, her spite and self-satisfaction a greasy river smothering Evelyn's initiative. "How sad for you. But when you chose to disrespect your mother, those were the consequences. You knew what you were getting into."

"You never talked to us! How could we know anything?" Jimmy was crying, Ginger's voice thick with tears.

"Do you remember when I stopped? Do you remember when I finally gave up?" Jessica said, with righteous tears of her own. "That night your father tripped me coming out of the kitchen into the dining room with a roast chicken. Then he laughed. And you laughed too, you both did. And your father took you out to dinner at Roy's while I cleaned up."

Jimmy was quiet for a long time. And then he said, in Ginger's monotone, "We were so scared, Ellen and me. It was all so wrong. When we came home that night, we tried to say we were sorry. But you turned away. We begged and begged you to forgive us. But you just didn't say anything."

"You wanted to be just like him and you got what you wanted."

"We were scared, Ma. We were so scared of him, and you acted so different. I didn't know a person could be that way. You were like a ghost in the house." He was crying. "I begged you, Ma. We both begged you."

"Well, and see where it got you," she said. "Not yet," she added at Evelyn's attempt to throw her. "I'm not done."

"Don't you see, Ma? We would have done anything for you, but you turned us both away."

"You chose him," Jessica said.

"You gave us no choice," Jimmy said, echoing her words. "You drove us away, Ma. You pushed us right toward him."

"*You wanted to go,*" she said. There it was, the willingness to be hard done by, to be put upon, the sick need to be wronged. It was her world view, her identity. She wanted nothing more than to show the world how hurt she was.

Again, there was a long silence, so long that Evelyn began to wonder what was going on inside Jimmy's head, and what had happened to Ginger. He finally sighed.

"Well, you're wrong," he said. "But this is where it ends. I'm not coming back." His voice changed, became tired. "Let me go. You ladies can do what you want, but I want to go."

"You think it's that easy? You get to leave, just like that, and leave me here?"

"Let. Me. Go." It was Ginger's voice but it took on a rasp of desperation.

"NO! Don't you dare leave me!" With a strength that took Evelyn by surprise, Jessica Bertram ran forward at her son's immobile body, and pushed as hard as she could. Evelyn's hands connected with Jimmy's chest, and the body went over backwards, the back of his head landing on the marble-topped end table.

The sickening dull crunch was a sound Evelyn would never forget. Ginger jerked as Jimmy died, and she went to her knees. Evelyn struggled against Jessica, and this time the old lady was so shocked at what she had done that she left easily.

They looked at the dead man and his mother the murderer, who would never be charged with the crime, since she was wheelchair-bound and frail.

"We are so fucked," Margie said.

*

The newspapers were full of the crime. Investigators found that Jimmy Bertram had been robbing his mother ever since her stroke, and that an unknown accomplice had come in and likely had a fight with him over her belongings. The only prints in the house were Margie's, Jimmy's, and Jessica's, and the witches made sure that the investigators were inclined away from Margie, who 'discovered' the body when she came on shift.

Investigators never found the silver, which was probably a good thing.

Carol went into hospice care and died, which wasn't.

The witches kept meeting at Star Seed Café each week, Carol's empty chair a silent reminder. Margie got a job cleaning office buildings, prowling dimly lit hallways with a rolling trash can and an attitude worse than usual. Ginger kept her teeth in, but still ate hardly anything and spoke less. They had asked her what happened, and she just shook her head, a little less witch-like and more just …tired. Maybe Jimmy's last words had been Ginger's after all.

Evelyn's dreams had grown strange. She kept seeing children she didn't have, a husband she didn't know. She woke with a belly full of acid and strange resentments taking control over her at random moments. Something had to be done.

At the next Star Seed, Evelyn blew across her coffee, and said, "Hey Margie, whatever happened to Jessica anyway?"

Margie just snorted.

"She's in assisted living over there on 45th St, where she should have been in the first place."

So Evelyn went to visit, a packet of Nutter Butters in hand. The administrators were glad to see poor Miss Jessica had a visitor so they let her in. Evelyn sat down with the old lady in her room, door closed, and held her hand. She began the chant, and in an instant she had company.

"What do you want?" Miss Jessica said resentfully. "You gonna give me those?" She made to grab the cookies, but Evelyn was strong, and kept her hand down. She knew better than to give Jessica Bertram even the slightest bit of control. She knew what the old woman could do.

"Not until you tell me where the silver is."

There was a long silence. Then, a laugh. "Why should I tell you?"
"You want to get out of here, don't you?"

The silver coins were in a strongbox in the backyard, inside the old greenhouse. The house, with a 'for sale' sign out front, was vacant, waiting to be sold, knocked down, and the lot repurposed for a gigantic fourplex. Jessica-Evelyn found the key to the chain-link fence gate under the old flower pot, and they unlocked the gate and went into the greenhouse. It was dark and full of spiders, but Jessica told Evelyn where to dig, and the dirt, compacted though it was, came up after chipping away at it, and there was a box, buried shallowly. It was heavy, and it was full.

She made a half-hearted attempt to evict Jessica, but the old woman just laughed, and whispered her secrets in Evelyn's ear.

The diner was hopping that night. Evelyn drove up in her little car and parked. It was a clear night, no rain, and bright lights of the café illuminated Margie and Ginger at their favourite table. There were a few more patrons; the university term was in session, so there were students studying or talking. All very normal.

Evelyn had come with a peace offering and plan – a pile of silver and a new recruit. But she saw Margie and Ginger, heads together, in close conversation, and her stomach burned.

They just had to start without us, she thought. They never wait. They're probably talking about us right now. Well, maybe we'll just give them the silent treatment. See what they think of that. Especially Margie. She thought about the strongbox in the trunk of her car. *Who's the smart one now, Margie?*

With a thin smile, they got out of her car and went in to meet their friends.

Pilot's Forge

An unabashed science fiction romance. There's a whole series in this little story, a space opera love story that spans generations. Maybe someday, I'll write it all down.

The Hatch-registered freighter *Godolphin* drifted in space, about two hundred thousand kilometres from Merritt's skiff, the *Crane*. The *Crane*'s sensors reported the details. The *Godolphin*'s hull was breached and the ship had lost propulsion, engines, most life support. The distress call was on auto and getting weaker. No one could be alive. Merritt flipped the readouts to visual and zoomed in to see for himself, and sure enough, the freighter was dark.

Likely raiders had cleaned her out and taken the crew as captives for ransom.

"So why didn't they tow the boat in for salvage?" he said out loud. He was the only one on board the *Crane*, but it didn't stop him from talking. He thought better that way, and right now he had a puzzle. The ship had been left to drift when arguably she was the biggest prize of all. He flipped back to the datastream, sat back in his chair and considered. He could tow the freighter in to Crowe's World to one of their notorious chop shops, or play it the other way, tow her into Hatch station for the reward or stake a salvage claim. All without firing a shot. He let himself dream for a bit. If the ship were still sound, he could set himself up as a skipper, hire a crew, and get ahead of sector police. "You know, go straight," he told the datastream, running in heads up display in front of him. "Settle down somewhere." Make the family proud.

It was a nice dream. He indulged it for a few seconds more, then turned down the datastream. More likely, if he towed that ship in, he'd find sector cops just waiting to bust him one more time and he would never see space again.

The *Godolphin* would have to continue her solitary journey through the galaxy's spiral arm, and Merritt would be the last one to see her. That didn't mean he shouldn't at least board her and confirm she was derelict. It was the charitable thing to do. And if he happened to pick up anything of value that might have been left over, well, even a good Samaritan deserved something for his trouble. He went to suit up.

He was surprised to see that the *Godolphin* still had atmosphere when the airlock whooshed and opened up for him, but with a hull breach the ship could vent at any time, so Merritt left his faceplate closed. His breathing was loud in the confined space of his helmet, and for a moment his readouts flashed that he had elevated pulse and respiration. The ship's interior was dark and his headlamp flashed through the smoky darkness. He needed to get some lights working on the old girl. That was confirmed when he tripped over the first body, killed with a pulse weapon. The woman's uniform had the Beauchamps logo on it. Beauchamps – one of the smaller merchant clans. Merritt's own clan was Crane, though he was only a distant relative of the great family and he didn't doubt they had as little care for him as he did for them. A Crane ship would not have been attacked. Raiders were smart enough to go for easier meat.

He counted three more bodies, scanning slowly. There had been a running gun fight, and there was plenty of scarring along the bulkhead.

Merritt tamped down his sudden desire to get the hell out of there. His suit sensors kept up a data feed, along with a ship schematic, displayed on the inside of his helmet. The hatch to the bridge was down the corridor, and Merritt headed that way, sidestepping the dead. There's not gonna be any salvage, he told himself, but he kept going anyway, knowing it was sheer stubbornness that drove him. His helmet readout flashed a single dot, signifying his position along the schematic, and then, faintly, another dot flashed out of the corner of his eye.

There was someone else alive on the *Godolphin*.

Merritt stopped. With great care he thumbed the button on his suit to replay. The dot flashed again, flickered, came back. With his other hand he unholstered his pistol. Whoever it was might be dying, might not be human, might be trying to shield from his suit. He got a lock on the other dot and saw that it emanated from the bridge. A hatch lay about twenty meters ahead. He found it, and climbed up, his boots clicking on the rungs. He was sweating by the time he got into the control room, and he found the body, suited up with the helmet latched. He muscled between overturned chairs and broken panels and knelt stiffly next to the body. The man opened his eyes and muttered something that Merritt couldn't catch. Under his faceplate, blood crusted around his mouth and nose.

"What happened?" Merritt said, hardly expecting an answer. "Raiders?"

The Beauchamps captain moved his head slightly inside the helmet. *Yes.*

Merritt's suit beeped, letting him know he was running low on air. "I need to get you to my ship," he said. "I can't carry you – is there a float?"

The captain shook his head. He tried to say something, spoke hoarsely. "Get off my ship."

Merritt kept from rolling his eyes. *Man's dying, and he's still pushy.* "Sorry, captain. Looks like this is a rescue."

"Damn fool," The Beauchamps captain said, and that came through clearly. "You. Are. In. Danger." He grabbed Merritt's arm, his bloody fingers leaving prints. "Jumped by raiders, and disabled. But they hit the D-space navigator." He stopped, gulped a lot of air. "We've been cycling in and out of space-time, each time it's getting worse. We're due for another cycle any second, and if you don't get out of here, you're dead too."

Merritt's status sensors told him what he already knew – respiration, heart rate, adrenal glands, all pouring forth accelerated data. He holstered his gun and knelt, trying to lift the Beauchamps captain. He grunted under the effort; his suit didn't make things easy. "Then I guess we better be going."

47

Beauchamps cried out in agony. "No time. I'm cycling too."

Merritt looked down and almost dropped him. Beauchamps was *fading*. D-space was happening all around them. Great for getting from place to place without having to take, say, 100 years to make the next star. Not so great when a wormhole opened up inside you. Beauchamps got a lot heavier and Merritt saw that he was dead. He set the man down and backed away, then ran for the ladder. He slid rather than climbed down.

The ship shook all around him, coming in and out of reality. The central corridor seemed longer this time, even though he was sprinting. The heads-up display flared and shook, transmitting streams of unintelligible data. Merritt kept running, hit the controls for the airlock, and froze. The door had *changed*. It was made of wood and iron and had an old-fashioned doorknob. Tentative, he touched the doorknob and the door whooshed open, an airlock once again. He stepped in and reflexively slapped at the side of the door to close it.

His glove hit wood and something fell to the floor. An old-fashioned key, an iron skeleton key, lay at his feet. It's not really there, he told himself. It was a ghost of the D-space nav malfunction. His brain was making sense of what it couldn't understand, creating familiar images out of multispace. The ship was coming apart at the subatomic level, and so would he. He saw the great gathering darkness rushing toward him, pulling him into the wormhole that gathered at the bow of the ship. Breathing hard, Merritt pulled the door closed.

"Come on, come on," he muttered, sweat slicking down his back. Would the airlock work, or would he be trapped inside the wormhole forever? With agonising slowness the rising whine indicated the airlock begin to pressurise. Merritt heard a noise and looked out the tiny window in the wooden door.

A face filled it, a face contorted in hatred and fear.

"Shit!" Merritt flung himself backward, fumbling to pull up his weapon. The man was snarling, his teeth showing like spikes through his beard. That's not the captain, he thought crazily. What the hell was going on?

The power whine stopped and the airlock stopped pressurising. The man continued to snarl like an animal, and he was pulling the door open. *Shit shit shit.* Merritt knelt and scrabbled for the key, fumbling it in his panic and haste. He held the door closed, desperation giving him strength, and pushed the key in the lock, turning it. The door locked with a click. Again the slow rising whine, again the long wait as the airlock pressurised. The face dropped away and Merritt allowed himself a slow breath.

With a shuddering crash the man threw himself against the door, teeth bared, eyes bulging. The small compartment was rocked again and again as the creature threw itself at him, and Merritt drew his gun, faced the door, and waited for the moment when the creature burst through. If the explosive decompression didn't get him, he might survive.

A polite chime sounded, signalling the atmosphere had stabilised, and the airlock opened behind him.

Billy's was crowded that night, the little roadhouse bar spilling music and laughter out into the parking lot. Edith parked her battered old work truck, with Crane Farrier and Blacksmithing stencilled on the side, at the end of the parking lot, and got out, stretching. It had been a long day. She had shoed five horses. Her business was picking up, but it meant that she had spent a lot of time bent over double, and some horses were lazy about supporting their own weight.

"Edith Crane!" shouted Melissa Andrews from over by the front deck with a bunch of friends. "'Bout time you got here!"

Edith made her way over to the group and slid into an empty space on the bench. Melissa poured her a beer from the pitcher and Edith sipped and relaxed.

"Oh my, that's good." She looked around at all of her friends. There was Melissa and her boyfriend Brian, and a half-dozen people her age, all young, all making their way in the little Tennessee town of Pilot's Forge.

Melissa leaned across the table at Edith and spoke low. "Listen, Edith, have you heard from Sam Grenady?"

Edith felt a shiver of unease. She and Sam had dated briefly when she came to town. She was drawn by his rough good looks and a kindred liking for physical labour. He was a carpenter and jack of all trades, and had an easy smile that, she realised after about a month, he could put on and take off as easy as a jacket. The smile and the charm hid a sizeable chip on his shoulder which came out when he drank, and he drank a lot. He had lots of plans for her, he told her. Big plans that she had no say in. After three dates she made sure they were at Billy's when she told him she wasn't the girl for him, and the expression he gave her was cold and empty. And then he smiled, gave her a kiss on the cheek, paid for their beer, and walked away. She hadn't talked to him since.

"Why, what's up?" She asked it carefully.

Melissa said, "He's been heard making noise about you. Says you lamed Cindy Dupre's warmblood with lousy shoeing."

Edith's heart sank. Pilot's Forge was a small town and Sam was an old-timer. He could sink her business in no time. "That son of a bitch."

Melissa snorted. "Don't I know it. He sweet talks plenty, but the minute he doesn't get his way, he goes ballistic. He was always like that, even when we were in high school."

Edith was reminded again that she was the newcomer. It didn't matter that her grandparents farmed here eighty years ago. If Sam Grenady wanted her out of Pilot's Forge, all he had to do was spread a few rumours. Well, she wasn't going to go without a fight. She'd call Cindy Dupre and all of her clients and let them know that Sam was full of it. She looked straight at Melissa.

"If you hear anything else, you let me know."

"Will do, California girl. I've been telling everyone that this town has always needed someone to put it on the map, and that's going to have to be you."

Edith laughed. "Melissa, I shoe horses. That's not glamorous,"

"Oh honey, in these small towns you have to make your own fun."

It was late when Edith drove up the mountain road to her old farmhouse, her Ford F-150 growling in low gear as it rounded the turns toward home. Trees massed around her, and now and again her headlights reflected on the eyes of animals in the dark. A whitetail bounded on stick-thin legs across the road in front of her, its twin fawns leaping behind it. She was glad to be heading home but Sam's lies made her uneasy. She remembered his expression when she broke up with him. Should have known it wouldn't be that simple, she thought. She would have to look out for him.

Her porch light was a welcome sight as she pulled into her driveway. She got out, locking her truck, and the cool summer air swept over her. Overhead the stars glittered between the trees. She hadn't even seen the Milky Way before she moved out here from smog-filled Los Angeles. The swathe of stars filled her with peace and awe.

Edith yawned. Straight to bed for me, she thought, but she needed to check on her own horses. She let herself in, turning on lights, and went through her kitchen, with its jumble of mismatched crockery, Formica table and chairs, and old stove that came with the house when it was remodelled in the 1950s. Out back was the old barn, well over one hundred years old and still sound.

The only light came from the dusty night light by the door. Katahdin, her big seventeen-hand retired show horse, nickered, but Cowboy and Blackjack both slept, Cowboy curled up like a foal. Edith made sure he wasn't cast in his stall; a cast horse could break a leg trying to get to his feet. Cowboy had plenty of room. Edith was about to leave when she heard the noise.

She turned toward her tack room door. It sounded like a machine was in there; she could feel the thrumming of an engine deep in her bones. Edith backed away, fumbling for the iron prybar she left in the corner of the barn. Behind her Blackjack snorted and whinnied, and Cowboy lunged to his feet.

Katahdin kicked at the back of his stall, shaking the wall of the barn. Edith jumped. The tack room door jerked open and someone stumbled out.

She had little time to register before whoever it was, in a streamlined G-suit, collapsed in front of her.

Oh my God. There's a dead astronaut in my barn.

*

Merritt opened his eyes and wondered if he was still cycling in D-space. A woman stood over him with dark curly hair, dark eyes, and a long metal bar poised to strike. She was good-looking too, he noted; trim figure in a simple shirt and trousers. And scared and determined enough to take the prybar and smash him with it. She didn't look like Beauchamps crew – where the hell was he? And where was the man from the freighter?

He stayed as still as he could. Sometimes the best thing to do was to play dead and hope for the best. With her free hand the woman fumbled for something in her pocket.

"Don't move," she said, her voice coming through his helmet's comm. "I'm calling the police."

Crap. That was all he needed. He started to get up.

"I said, don't move!" Her voice rose.

He didn't have time for this. He might only have a few minutes before whoever was chasing him on the *Godolphin* came through the airlock after him. He pulled his gun and trained it on her. Her eyes got big and she back away.

"Lady, the way I see it, you just brought the wrong weapon to a gunfight." He nodded at the prybar. "Drop it." She hesitated and set it down. "Now the comm."

She frowned in confusion, but he held out his hand for the strange little comm, and she handed it over. He tucked it into his suit pouch.

"What do you want?" she said, swallowing to get her voice going.

"Same thing you do. To get out of your hair." He gestured with the gun. "Move."

She didn't. She stood her ground. "Who are you? Did Sam Grenady put you up to this? What did you put in my tack room?"

What? He followed her gaze, turning his head. There was the door, and behind it, the *Godolphin*. The woman started toward the door, which had fallen ajar. For an instant he was back inside the scuttled freighter, the wormhole chasing him down and drawing him in, toward the crazy screaming man.

"NO!" Merritt shouted, as she pushed it open.

She flicked on the light.

Without thought Merritt plastered himself up against the opposite wall, aiming at the door, his heart hammering, as he registered what he was looking at. There was no D-space, no wormhole, no freighter, no madman, just a tidy room lined with gear, harness, and metal grain bins. Stand down, he told himself, just as something big snorted just behind his ear. Merritt whirled around and almost screamed. An enormous quadruped stood there, long-necked and big-headed. It eyed him and snorted again.

"What the hell is that thing!?"

"Don't shoot him!" the woman said, and she threw herself at Merritt, grappling for the gun.

They wrestled. The suit gave him extra weight and boosted his strength and he soon had her pinned to the floor.

"I swear to God, if Sam Grenady is behind this I will kill you both!" she shouted, still trying to squirm free.

"Stop," he said. "*Stop*. You keep fighting, the suit will keep compensating, and I can sit on you all day, and you'll never get up." She listened to him, sullenly, fury still in her eyes. Merritt was suddenly enjoying himself. Finally, something was going his way. And even through the suit he could get a sense of how it felt to be straddling her.

"Now. I'm going to get up and I'm going to let you up. You're not going to try that again, right?"

He waited. She didn't want to, but she nodded. He got up, and held out his hand to help her up. She ignored it and got to her feet.

"Like I said, I just want out of here. I need to know where the nearest port is. What world is this?"

She looked as if she were trying to come up with the right thing to say, and one of her choices was not going to be complimentary. Finally, she settled on, "Get the hell out of my barn."

"My pleasure. After you." He gestured with the gun and she went in front of him. He followed. One of the quadrupeds stuck its long neck out and eyed him with interest. Merritt scraped along the opposite wall, but she reached out and stroked the animal's neck. A pet? A thing that size was a pet?

Outside the barn the skies above the trees were filled with unfamiliar stars. Merritt stopped, enjoying the rush of wind against his face, and wishing he had the Crane's nav service to tell him where he was. There was a swathe of galaxy above him, but he couldn't tell which spiral arm he was marooned on from here.

She led the way through an ornate gate that swung silently on oiled hinges, past a small stone house and pointed down the mountain. In the pale starlight a road shimmered faintly before him. "That road leads to town. I don't know who you are, or what you are doing here, but I would appreciate it if you didn't come back."

"You and me both," Merritt said. The sooner he got off this rock and back to civilised space – well, the sooner he would be back to dodging the police and trying to hustle a living. He remembered the key and opened his glove. With a sudden surety that took him by surprise, he said, "I think this is yours."

She stared at it in the faint light from the stars. It lay in his glove, flat and heavy, and he waited patiently. She took it finally, and through the extra sensitive glove material he felt the gentleness and warmth of her fingers. He turned and began to walk down the road.

In the warm light of the kitchen, her heart still pounding, Edith began to dial 9-1-1, then hung up before the call connected. What the hell was Sam up to? If he had put this guy up to it, what could he mean by it? To make her sound crazy when she called the cops and said there was an astronaut in her barn. She got up and paced.

What if Sam wasn't behind it? What was crazier, that there was a guy pretending to be a spaceman in her barn –

Or that there was a spaceman in her barn?

Her gaze fell on the key. It was an old-fashioned skeleton key. A shiver ran down her spine. The old farmhouse had been modernised more than fifty years ago, but before that, it had a key very much like this one. And that key had been lost for generations, she knew that for a fact.

She should have called the cops on him. She could still call the cops. She looked over at her phone, but she didn't call.

Crazy guy hides out in my barn wearing a spacesuit, pretends he's an ET who doesn't know what a horse is. Yeah, she should have called the police.

Except. She remembered the sound coming from the tack room. That hadn't sounded like anything she had ever heard. And he was terrified when she pushed the door open.

And then there was the feel of his gloves when she reached out and took the key. Thick gloves, yet so sensitive that she could feel his hand beneath them. Her hair rose at the memory, even as she scoffed.

So, you are out here in the back end of nowhere, making a living at a centuries-old craft. What do you know from new technology?

Edith got up. She went around her house, closing windows and turning locks. She went upstairs to bed, and looked out the window at her barn. The building was dark and peaceful, the small glow from the night light a comforting sight. For the first time since she moved here she felt unsettled by the loneliness of the mountain.

It took her a long time to fall asleep.

One-gee normal, his suit told him, and Merritt could feel every bit of it as he trudged down the mountain road, helmet in his hand. The cool mountain air felt good against his face. As the road curved down the mountain he could glimpse the lights of a small settlement in the valley below, and, further away, a much larger city. There was no sign of an air transport grid, though, and surely he'd be able to see port gantries from here. He craned his neck to look up at the stars again. Through the trees he could see a tiny, fast-moving point of light. Too small to be a space station, though. Most planets were orbited by the wheel-and-spoke standard stations that could be seen even in daylight.

Wouldn't that be his luck, to come out of D-space on one of the lost worlds.

Merritt stopped. He wiped sweat from his eyes. Night noises rose up around him. A faint wind rustled through the leaves, and in the distance he could hear hooting, a rippling cry, and a rhythmic call. Animals, he told himself nervously. Just basic animals. He didn't get dirtside on too many worlds, but most terraformed planets were rife with flora and fauna. This one looked to be well along in the process. Merritt checked his sidearm. It was fully charged.

The sound of an engine caught his attention. Merritt looked down the road. Someone was coming up in a groundcar, and whoever it was wasn't running their lights.

Had the woman called for reinforcements after she sent him on his way? Merritt melted back into the woods, and touched his suit controls. The suit obligingly made itself match the shadows in the woods. The smell of low-tech fuel made him gag. Internal combustion? What the hell?

When the car was swallowed up into the night he played back the recording made by the suit.

A cargo vehicle much like the one he saw at the woman's house. The man driving it was shaggy, bearded. Angry. Obviously racing up the mountain to help out a friend who was in trouble. *I'd better get the hell out of here before he comes looking for me on the way back.*

Still, Merritt hesitated. He stopped the video, zoomed in on the truck. There was lettering – his suit chittered as it ran itself through standard transliteration modes and finally settled on one he recognised.

Grenady Construction.

Did Sam Grenady send you?

Merritt cursed under his breath. The last time he tried to help someone he had been kicked through D-space to a lost world and would likely never see his ship again. Forget it. She could handle herself. He actually took two steps down the mountain before he stopped, cursed again, and charged back up the road.

The sound of breaking glass jolted Edith out of her uneasy sleep. She sat upright. There was another crash of glass, and Edith threw aside the covers. She grabbed for her phone and remembered. The guy in the tack room had taken it. Edith ran down the stairs in her T shirt and shorts, getting into her boots along the way. She hit the light switch and flooded her front yard with light. Sam stopped only for seconds and looked toward the house, then took another swing at her truck, battering the hood.

"I'm calling the police!" she screamed. "I see you, Sam Grenady! You will go to hell for this!"

"Screw you, bitch! I'm just giving you what you deserve!"

He swung the sledgehammer once again into her windshield. Edith ran for her kitchen phone. Nothing. No dial tone. Son of a bitch, she thought. He cut the wires. She would have to stop him herself.

Sam was sledgehammering at the back of her camper shell and had got the door open. He pulled out her tools and supply of keg shoes and had begun to dump gasoline all over them. Dear God, nothing would stop a fire that caught up here. Her house, her barn. Her horses. She burst from the house with a wild scream, brandishing the fire extinguisher.

"Get away from my house!"

He looked up just as she sprayed him full in the face. He staggered back, scraping foam from his eyes. Then he roared, and swung the gasoline at her. It spattered over her, and she stumbled backward, the smell of gas overwhelming. She kept spraying at him until the fire extinguisher was out and she threw the empty canister at him, screaming a wordless war cry to meet his howls of rage and pain as the extinguisher struck him.

"Hold it!" came a voice from outside the pool of light. They looked up into the darkness, Sam with blood and foam cascading down him, Edith wild-eyed, reeking of gasoline. A glowing red light began to gather to a point. It was her spaceman, and he had his raygun.

"Don't move!" he ordered and came into the light.

With a curse Sam grabbed Edith and threw her at the man, then bolted for his truck. The man pushed Edith away and ran after him, but Sam was lost to the darkness. An instant later they heard the engine roar and he peeled out down the mountain. Edith looked at the destruction of her truck. Her yard was full of glass and tools, and her truck listed to the side.

The spaceman came back. "He's gone," he said, his voice grim. "I couldn't get off a clear shot."

Edith turned to him. She ached and stung all over. Adrenalin was fading, leaving her with anger. She looked at him and shook her head and then slapped him as hard as she could. He staggered back, shock turning to anger, but she didn't care.

"You stupid –" she said, her throat so thick she could hardly get the words out. "You took my phone."

The police came, their blue and red flashing lights washing over her yard and the damaged truck. They took down her account and took pictures, and promised they would look for Sam, though at least two of the cops were related to him. Yeah right, thought Edith, bitter and cynical now. One of the cops looked at the spaceman. He was no longer in his suit. He had stowed it and his gun inside the house, upstairs in her bedroom. Now he just looked like a normal guy, though his shorts and T shirt were made out of an odd material that she almost wanted to touch, just to see if it felt as strange as it looked.

She hadn't wanted to cover for him, but if the police thought he was a crazy spaceman they might be distracted from Sam. Better not to confuse things any more than they already were.

"How are you involved?" the cop said.

"He's a friend," Edith put in. "He's here visiting." The man nodded, his expression showing no surprise at her explanation, as if he was used to lying about who he was and what he was doing. She hoped like hell they didn't ask her for his name.

"He can talk for himself, can't he?" the cop said. "You have a name?"

The man closed down a little. "Merritt Crane." His voice was cautious.

Edith tried to keep surprise off her face. What was he playing at? The cop caught it too.

"So let me get this straight – you a friend or a relative?" he asked, suspicious now.

"Friend," she hastened. "Just a coincidence."

Now the man looked at her, his expression guarded. Secrets, she thought. There are too many secrets for one front yard to handle. The cop went on.

"So you were here for the attack?"

Merritt nodded, a helpful easy attitude. "I just went for a walk down the road a bit, to stretch my legs. I saw him drive up in his ground vehicle, and thought that looked suspicious. Especially after – my friend – here said she was worried he'd try something."

Ground vehicle. My friend. The cops looked from one to the other. "Right," one said. "All right, that's it then. We'll keep up patrols for the rest of the night. We'll find him. He won't go far."

Edith sat back in the kitchen chair and looked at the stranger. She was exhausted. She smelled of gas and she was covered with bruises. Tears bubbled up just under the surface and with the last of her effort she kept from breaking down into sobs.

"Won't this night end?" she said. "I don't think I can take any more." She looked at him, the crazy stranger who wasn't so crazy any more. He watched her with concern. She got a good look at him, finally, in the light. Handsome, with a lean face and dark eyes, short dark hair. He looked to be around her age, early thirties. Her voice shook a little as she asked,

"Who are you? Is your last name really Crane? What are you doing here?"

He hesitated and then said, "Yeah. I'm really a Crane. As for what I'm doing here – I don't know."

"Why did you come back?" she said.

A muscle twitched in his cheek. "Something didn't feel right."

If he hadn't come... if Sam hadn't been outnumbered... The tears came at last and she covered her face and sobbed, her shoulders heaving. He reached out and put his hand over hers, and squeezed.

"Hey," he said. "Glad I could help. You did good by yourself."

"My livelihood – my truck. I don't know how I can repay you."

"You don't have to repay me," he said, but it sounded as if he had to force the words out. "You just need to tell me. What world is this?"

She was silent for a long time, the ticking of the clock the only sound in the kitchen. If she answered his question, it meant she took him seriously. Edith shook her head. She was too tired to second-guess any more.

"It's Earth," she said. "You're on Earth."

She watched as comprehension dawned – comprehension and something else. Wonder. Disbelief. Fear. She expected him to say something but he only said, gently, "Go clean up. I'll keep watch."

"Aren't you tired too?" she said. He smiled, and it lightened his expression.

"The suit's been stimming me till I took it off. I can push it for a few more hours."

She couldn't even protest, just got up and pushed herself away from the table. Then she stopped, remembering something.

"Merritt. I'm really sorry I hit you."

He gave a rueful grin and rubbed his cheek. "I'm sorry I sat on you."

She laughed despite herself. "We're even then."

"Even."

Earth. He was on Earth. The Earth Merritt knew was a wasted planet, with seas of glass and dead cities, its oceans boiled away, the losing side in a war with an unstable sun that had gone from even-tempered to angry giant in the cosmic blink of an eye. The arks had left Earth for other star systems eons before. There were about twenty planets that called themselves Earth, but he didn't think she meant one of those. She meant *Earth*.

First things first, he told himself. Secure the house. Merritt started on the top floor, making his way up the narrow wooden stairs. There were two rooms. He opened the door to the first one. It was a sleeping room neat and tidy, sparsely furnished, its ceiling slanting down over the window. He looked into the second one. This was where she slept. The bed was untidy, the covers thrown back. Clothes were piled on a round-armed chair under the window, and there was a closet full of more clothes, its door ajar. The room smelled of her, warm and clean.

He went down the stairs, hearing the water running as she washed up in the bathroom. He imagined himself in there with her, grinned and shook his head. Need to keep my mind on what I'm doing, he thought. The downstairs held two rooms in front and the kitchen in the back of the house. He figured out the controls for the lights and he flipped the switch. Light came on to show another tidy room, not used very much. A word came to him, dredged up from distant memory. This was a parlour, for guests.

He heard the water shut off. There was one more door, at the end of the hall. He opened it and stumbled back. It opened on to a black hole, a void, and for an instant he thought that he had come upon another wormhole. He realised that he had stopped breathing, and forced himself to take a breath. He fumbled at the wall, but there was no switch. So he turned on his torch and pointed it downward. Now he could see stairs going down.

"What are you looking at?" she said from behind him. He turned, absurdly relieved that she was there. She still smelled faintly of gasoline, but she was in a clean sleeveless shirt and drawstring trousers, and towelled at her hair. His heart stuttered again but not from fear. He tried not to stare at the way she filled out her plain white shirt.

"What's down there?"

"The old cellar. The foundation of this house dates to the 1800s, and they gutted it and modernised it, oh, about sixty years ago. That's the root cellar." She wrinkled her nose self-deprecatingly. "It creeps me out. I don't go down there much."

Funny how he knew exactly what she meant without knowing the words. He nodded and closed the door and they both breathed a sigh of relief.

"All right. It looks all clear. Sleep sound. I'll take the downstairs."

"Thanks." She hesitated, and a bit of colour touched her cheeks. "I mean. I don't know how to thank you."

"It's all right. I'm glad to help."

He watched her go, and shook his head. Merritt, don't even think it, he told himself, but it was too late. He was already thinking it.

Sam Grenady holed up in a swale off the road. He was covered with dried foam and blood, and smelled of the gas he had used to douse her truck. Crazy bitch, he thought. He shivered in the night air, and tried to cover himself with leaves. She found herself another guy in record time, and he had some kind of taser thing. It glared in Sam's eyes, and he couldn't see, couldn't think. Well, if she thought she could get away with dumping Sam and taking up with someone else, bitch had another think coming. It was time to finish the job he started.

He'd have to do it quick, though. He heard the police cars screaming up the road after he drove off into the underbrush near her place. Come daylight, they would be able to find his tire tracks easily enough.

"Don't underestimate Sam Grenady," he muttered. This was his town, his mountain. He'd been hunting on Crane land ever since he was a boy, and he knew its secrets. Sam kicked his feet into the soft dirt at the end of the swale. His boots banged against wood, and he kicked again and again till he smashed it in.

There were tunnels and caves all over this mountain, some natural, some manmade from when the locals ran moonshine. Sam slid inside as cold wet air rushed at him from under the ground and wormed his way through the low tunnel into the pitch-black underground. He'd teach Edith Crane a thing or two about her family history.

Birdsong and sunlight woke her, and Edith got up and dressed quickly in jeans and a T shirt, throwing on a plaid work shirt to ward off the morning chill. It was already eight o'clock. She never slept in this late. She paused before going downstairs, looking out the window. She loved this view. Beyond the barn and her forge, the green mountain rose up over the homestead, culminating in the bare granite mountaintop. From here she could see her meadow, blanketed in low morning mist, and dotting her land were the sculptures that she had made of iron and steel. Some she meant to sell, and she was starting to get clients from the big cities, even a few museums interested in her work. Others were just for this place, and had meaning only for her.

Her gaze fell on the key and she picked it up. Someone had hammered it out of pig iron. Not a method she would have used – she would have gone with an alloy and moulded the molten metal into the right shape. It was made out of old iron, heavy and anachronistic. A mystery, she thought, part of a bigger one downstairs.

She padded down the steps as quietly as she could. Her spaceman dozed in the chair by the window, the gun lying in his lap. He didn't wake, and she just took him in for a minute. Tall and lean, with dark hair, stubble on his face. Not classically handsome – someone had broken his nose at one point and it set awry, and she bet he had been teased about his ears when he was a kid – but oh, nice just the same. She took another step down the stairs, hitting the step that always creaked. He jerked awake, handgun up, then relaxed as he took in his surroundings. He looked at her.

"Damn it," he said. "The stim wore off. I didn't mean to sleep."

"It's okay. We both needed it." She bit her lip. "Look, if you want to wash up, the bathroom's through there. I'll make breakfast, but I have to tend to the animals first."

He went off to the bathroom and she waited, wondering if he was going to need help with her old-fashioned fitments. Hmmm, that might be kind of fun, she thought, then scolded herself. Bad girl, Edith, but she was grinning as she went out to feed her horses. Katahdin had his nose out the door of his stall, neighing furiously at her, kicking the walls of his box for good measure, irked at his late breakfast.

"Get over it," she told him, as she shook out flakes of hay and freshened their water. She left their stall doors open. When they were finished eating they knew enough to take themselves out into the meadow.

She stood at the split rail fence, breathing in the clean mountain air. It stayed cool up here even in summer, and the birds sang their hearts out in the clean sunshine. It was so peaceful, she could pretend that nothing had happened last night. Only the faint smell of petrol told her otherwise.

Instead of tears, anger welled up. She was through crying. The police had better find Sam first, because if she did, she was going to make him pay.

Her kitchen door opened and Merritt came out. He looked freshly washed, his hair wet. Her mood rose.

"Figured it out?" she said.

He nodded. "I haven't washed with water for a long time. Felt good."

She couldn't help it; she laughed. "Merritt, are you bullshitting me?"

He laughed too, but a little uncertainly. "I don't –"

It didn't matter. She was suddenly happy. Sam had done his best but he hadn't broken her spirit. She put a hand on his arm, and nodded at the barn. "Watch."

He followed her gaze. Led by Katahdin the horses filed out of the barn, their heads nodding peacefully as they walked out to meadow. On reaching their pasture they began to trot, and then to canter and buck. Merritt tensed. "Watch," she whispered again. Katahdin moved in a floating trot, the big bay horse lifting each hoof as if he were in a dressage test, his neck arched. The horses circled the pasture, disappearing down the hill and then came the sound of thudding hooves as they galloped back up.

When they settled to graze, Edith finally stirred.

"Gets me every time," she said.

For a second a flash of sadness shadowed his eyes. "That was… that was incredible."

She still had her hand on his arm and blushed. She turned the caress into a comradely slap on the shoulder. "Come on, I'll make you breakfast."

*

She made him scrambled eggs, grits, toast, and strong coffee and they sat at her kitchen table. Earth food tasted pretty damn good, Merritt decided after the first few cautious bites. He hadn't had a home-cooked meal in pretty much forever. He was so deep into his breakfast, he was almost surprised when she spoke.

"That key you gave me last night. How did you get it?"

"I doubt you'll believe me," he said. "I hardly believe it myself."

"Try me."

She listened as he gave her the whole story, and when he was finished, she was silent for a long time, swirling her spoon in her grits. "You're right," she said at last. "I don't believe you. But that key you gave me last night? In the Great Depression, when my family left Tennessee for California, they brought that key with them. It was a symbol of this place. That key went missing in my grandparents' day."

He thought of how the key landed at his feet, with the wormhole behind him and closing fast, drawing him toward the attacking madman. At first he thought it was a figment of his brain, trying to make sense of the collapse of space-time. Had he conjured that key out of the past – their past? But his past was her future, and maybe in more ways than one.

"I told you I was Crane, right?" he said. "Well, I'm part of the Crane clan, though I doubt we share much of the same DNA."

"Distant cousins," she said, her voice dry.

He laughed. "Really distant. Yeah. In my time, the Cranes became one of the greatest clans in the galaxy. Three hundred years ago, the Cranes built the arks to take humanity off Earth, and we settled the known worlds, terraforming and transforming as we went."

She looked puzzled. "What? Why would we leave?"

"Because Earth died. The sun grew unstable and became a red giant, way sooner than anyone expected."

Watching her absorb the news was like watching someone get kicked in the stomach in slow motion. She looked out the window and he knew what she was thinking. This beautiful country with its horses, her home, her land – consumed by an angry sun.

"All of it?" she said. "I mean, it's all gone?" She turned to him. "How do you stand it, knowing that Earth is gone?"

He surprised himself with his own answer, because until she asked him he never knew that it was something he had to stand.

"We spend our lives looking for her," he said. "No matter where we live, no matter what station or what planet, no one ever stops looking."

She looked stricken. "I wish you hadn't told me. I wish I never knew. I'll never be able to stand it, never."

Merritt got up and went to her. He meant only to comfort her, and he put his arms around her but she lifted her face to his and they kissed. Her lips were soft and he pulled her close, letting his hands fall to her waist and then smoothing over her hips. She put her arms around his neck, and their kiss deepened.

Somehow they made it upstairs to her bedroom, scattering clothes along the way, and in the cool breeze from the open window they made love on her rumpled bed.

It was afternoon before Edith woke from her doze. The room had grown chilly. Merritt had both his arms around her as if he didn't intend to let her go, but he dozed too, and when she stirred, he muttered a protest.

She kissed him. "Not going anywhere." She didn't want to. It felt good, lying in his arms, their legs entwined, but there was a residual sadness too. The iron key lay on the bedside table where she had put it the night before. She sat up to pick it up. It was cool and heavy in her hand.

Merritt sat up behind her, wrapping his legs around her, nibbling along her neck. "What is it?" he said, between kisses, keeping his hands around her waist. She shivered, losing her concentration for a moment.

"I think this key is the crux," she said. "Somehow this key got lost so it could bring you here. But a key is nothing without a lock." Edith pulled away and started to get into her clothes. She tossed Merritt's to him. "If this is my grandparents' key – what is it the key to?"

They both hesitated at the top of the stairs to the cellar, shining their flashlights into the dark. The stairs weren't steep but they were in darkness by the bottom. Merritt got the impression of an earthen room, supported by timbers. Trash hulked in the corners, old ceramic jugs and rusty washtubs, and a tangle of copper tubing in one corner.

"What's all that stuff?" Merritt asked.

Edith laughed. "It's our sordid past. The Cranes were bootleggers back in the day. You'd never believe it by my grandmother, but the Cranes ran on the wrong side of the law now and again."

Merritt gave a short laugh. Some things never changed.

They picked their way down the stairs, brushing away cobwebs. At the far end of the cellar was a wooden door, its threshold dull with dust. Edith put the key in the lock. It fit but resisted her attempts to turn it.

"Damn," she said. "Here, hold this." She handed him the key while she rummaged through the junk piled up by the stairs, her flashlight shining wildly. She held up a can. "I knew I saw some down here. WD-40. This and duct tape – keeps the universe together." While Merritt kept the light steady, she sprayed the lock and tried again. Sluggishly it turned. They both pulled the door open and it shrieked on stiff hinges as it came open.

With a scream of fury, Sam Grenady burst through the door.

For a second Merritt was back on the Godolphin, watching the wormhole close in, the figure of the man rushing toward him. It was him, he thought dazedly. The cycling of the Godolphin had brought him here, through time and space, to this moment, and sent him the key to save himself.

He realised all this even as Sam threw himself at Edith. Merritt jumped on Sam's back and pulled him off. He grabbed the man under his arms and held on. The flashlights rolled away, illuminating useless corners of the cellar, so the only light came from the stairs. Sam screamed and fought, and Merritt wished he had brought his gun.

Light began to grow from behind them, and Merritt heard a familiar noise, the gathering sound and energy of a ship's mechanics. He could see the dawning wonder on Edith's face and he knew what was happening behind him. The airlock had returned, and behind it the Godolphin corridor. He probably even had time to get to his ship and cast off from the freighter, bolting before the Godolphin's final destruction. He could pull Sam through too, and the man would remain in the stasis forever on the edge of the wormhole exactly as Merritt found him.

Merritt dragged Sam toward the airlock. The whining noise rose and the soft chime of the warning system told him he was running out of time. He backed into the open door, the white light of the Godolphin airlock all around him. Sam struggled and fought, screaming and cursing, and Merritt tightened his hold even as the man threw himself backward, trying to break Merritt's nose with the back of his head. Over Sam's head Merritt could see Edith struggle to her feet.

The airlock whooshed shut. As he waited for the atmosphere to balance, he could see Edith through the tiny airlock window, impossibly far away. They stared at each other, and in the split seconds that remained, he could see her dawning despair, and knew it mirrored his own.

*

Edith worked steadily at the forge on her land, coaxing the iron into shape with fire and hammer. It was a facsimile of the airlock that had appeared in her cellar weeks before, made out of iron, to match the key and the lock. Crazy, she thought to herself, more than once, but the concentric rings were beautiful. Looking through, you had the impression you could see an infinite distance.

Edith took off her goggles and wiped back her hair with gloved hands that smelled of metal. As far as the police knew, Sam had left town. They found his truck off the side of the mountain, but he had disappeared. They promised Edith they would make sure they caught him if he tried to sneak back into town. They never asked about Merritt. It was as if he had never been there. She had tried the key a couple of times, but the broken door always opened on the dark tunnel leading up the mountain, and never into the airlock. So she decided to build a new one, forged of iron and hope.

It took her all day to haul the pieces of the new door down into her cellar, and almost all night to set it up, under a rig of lights that illuminated the dirt cellar and the remains of an old life. The lights shed plenty of heat and Edith was drenched with sweat. The close cellar smelled of it, along with metal and warm dirt.

Finished, she stepped back and looked at her handiwork. The iron door with its concentric rings fit in the opening, almost filling the cellar. Merritt said he spent his lifetime looking for Earth. It didn't seem fair that he should find his home planet, just to lose her again less than a day later. The key brought him here once before. It would just have to do it again. Plus, if she were going to found the clan that built the arks, she couldn't do it alone.

She took a breath and fit the key in the new lock. It turned without resistance. There was a pause, and then she heard a rising whine of power gathering behind the door. A chime signalled that the atmosphere stabilised, and the door swung inward.

Joe Fledge's Jump

If we do it right, our children leave us. If we do it really right, they evolve into something better and take the world with them. No one ever said parenting is easy.

The chatter over my commlink was faint, constant, and easily ignored. My helmet limited my view, but if I turned my head I could see the rest of the crew in our white suits, locking together each metal and plastic section of the new bridge that connected to the space elevator terminus. It was as deceptively flimsy as a rope bridge, only instead of crossing a jungle ravine, it crossed space.

I took a moment to look out at the work so far, leaning back against the safety netting, my boots secure against the strut I was working on. The bridge soared above me, the arc unfinished, its jagged ends waiting for the next segment. The structure was stark against the blackness of space, catching and reflecting the sunlight. I tapped the image capture button on the side of my helmet, snapping a picture. I'd send it to Alex when I went off shift.

The crew hab was a turning tin can that provided a semblance of gravity. There were eighteen of us, all on two-year contracts. I had another year to go.

"Hey Randy," said Devin Fisher, crew chief and station head. I looked up at him from my terminal, in the middle of a letter to my son. Devin slid into the chair next to me. "Head's up. We're telling everyone not to go public, and that includes family." Devin was a tall black man, a seasoned crew member, who had made the career change from ironworker on some of the tallest skyscrapers on Earth to space bridge builder without much of a hiccup.

"Okay," I said, confused. "And why is that?"

He gave me a hard look. "Some newbie tried to space himself. He survived and we're sending him home, but the less it's talked about the better. We need to stay on schedule."

There were easier ways to commit suicide. I was glad the guy was okay, but a shiver went down my spine at the thought. Decompression wasn't quick or painless. Those would be the longest last twenty seconds of a person's life.

He let me take it in, and then said, "From now on, keep your radio turned up, man."

It was like all of Devin's rebukes – to the point, not a word wasted about *why*, but no less of a direct order.

"Got it," I said. I would miss the silence but I didn't want to cause trouble. I went back to my letter to my son. *Hey Alex*, I wrote. *Check out the latest on the bridge project. When you're older, you can see it for yourself. That's why we're building this thing, you know? Someday, you will think nothing of taking the space elevator up from Earth Terminus to NE-Terminus, and then suiting up and walking the bridge out to the hub, where the ships will dock. Love you, kiddo. Dad.*

I attached the image and sent the letter.

Archie, the communications tech, pinged me a few hours later, just before I was turning in. "Incoming, Rand," he said. "Real-time from your wife."

My first thought was dire; Melissa hated calling because she could never get used to the very slight time delay.

I took the call. "Hey babe. Everything okay?"

"Randy, what the hell? What kind of joke was that?"

It got my back up. "No, 'hello, sweetheart, nice to see you'?" I said.

To her credit, once she got the message, she looked rueful. "Sorry. No, it's the photo. What the hell was that about?"

"I send Alex a picture of the bridge every day, Mel. I have no idea what was wrong this time."

"Look at the picture, Rand. Tell me what is going on. Alex asked if that was you."

I pulled up the picture from my file, still not sure what she was talking about. The image was exactly as I remembered it – stark, bright metal and plastic against the black of space, rising up in an unfinished arc. Then I saw it.

At the lower left of the image, just exiting the airlock on the elevator terminus, was the newbie, arms outstretched in a swan dive, caught in the act of jumping away from the structure.

*

I didn't know Joe Fledge. He had come up a week before, rotated in with a group of new riggers. They were still in training and wouldn't be in-filled into the crews until they acclimatised to near-Earth orbit. Apparently Fledge had not acclimatised.

Fledge was rescued by a quick-thinking rigger who was fully suited and waiting his turn in the airlock. Fledge might have thought death would be instantaneous, or more likely that his momentum away from the station would be enough to keep him out of reach until he expired. Anyway, he was brought back in, and given meds and revived in a bends chamber. He survived his walkabout with nothing more than some burn and was sent home.

That should have been that.

Months later, the commotion over the radio was loud, chaotic, and against protocol. I turned my commlink to private and direct lined to Devin, who was out on shift with me. We were behind schedule, the only reason Devin suited up any more.

"What now?" I said.

"Another walker," he said, terse as always. "Hang on. I'm finding out what's going on."

Some people see somebody do something stupid and they don't think, *that idiot.* Joe Fledge had set a record for surviving the longest unsuited spacewalk. The chatter on the Net had all been speculation about how long a person could survive, and what someone needed to do to stretch that survival time to its maximum.

Two newbies had joined the rigger program specifically to recreate Joe Fledge's jump. They took advantage of the accelerated training program, put in place to keep the project on schedule and at its target budget. They had practiced beforehand, learning how to expel all the air in their lungs to slow de-oxygenation
. They smuggled up drugs to pre-treat themselves to prevent ebullism. One – Tandy Rollings – went out unsuited. She held the hand of her partner, fully suited, who timed her.

Twenty-five and a half seconds. Give or take a millisecond.

On my last shift on Terminus, I took a long look at the bridge. It was a massive structure, a complex lattice of steel and plastic. And yet, this triumph of human ingenuity was impossibly spindly and fragile, no match for the hostile environment of space. We can't survive out here, I thought. We're Earth-bound, not meant for space. One fire or explosion, and small bodies would be propelled outward with the rest of the debris.

I was glad I was never coming back.

I opened my son's bedroom door and peered in. White moonlight came in through the window. I could see his small body, a lump under the covers, facing straight up. The moonlight reflected in his open eyes. I listened for breathing, and heard none.

"Alex?" I said. My voice was sharper than I mean it to be, and I was acutely conscious of my respiration and heartrate.

After a moment he turned his head, and then I heard him take a deep breath and expel all the air from his lungs.

"I'm practicing, Daddy," he said.

"It's late, kiddo," I managed. "You can practice another time."

Another deep breath and long, measured exhale.

"Okay, Daddy."

"Good night, son."

I closed the door, a sinking feeling in the pit of my stomach, and went down the stairs to the dark living room, where Melissa was curled up on the sofa watching a movie, her face illuminated by the display, inchoate dialog like the chatter over a commlink. She glanced up at me.

"Everything okay?"

"Yeah," I said. "He's good."

Thirty-three and three-quarters seconds, the news reports said. Tandy Rollings and her latest accomplice were arrested, and there was another flurry of excitement before the news died down. I didn't know how much Alex was aware of the latest skinwalk, as the stunt was being called. I thought about my son's deep exhales, and pushed the fear away. I didn't ask him about it, and whatever secrets he had in his baby-faced way, he held them close.

Years passed and my son grew up, quiet like me, intense like his mother. Our marriage fractured under the stresses of our distinct natures, like a badly engineered superstructure. Alex shuttled between us, strewing books and papers and dumping his backpack by the front door, some days an emotional firestorm, other days content to just be. He changed imperceptibly, until I took the time to really look at him, and then I could see the lengthening of his bones under his skin, indicating the shape of the man he was becoming.

Once I picked up his papers, trying to put some order into the chaos, and stopped at a picture he had coloured. It took me a second to recognise it. Terminus, the unfinished bridge, and a figure with arms outstretched floating off to one side.

Melissa called. We hardly ever spoke any more, now that Alex was in college and our co-parenting duties discharged.

"Hi," I said, mildly surprised.

She jumped right in. "Alex is a skinwalker. And before you say anything, I just want you to know that I don't blame you."

"Yes you do."

There was a pause, like our old Earth to Terminus conversations. Then, "Yes. I do."

"He doesn't talk to me," I said. I felt a deep pang of envy. How had I missed this? My son didn't tell me about the most important things in his life?

"Well, he doesn't talk to me either," she said. "I saw it in the news. He's with a group who are pushing for the record – and other things."

My worst fear, confirmed. "What other things?"

"I'll send you the article." She paused. "Rand. I think we're losing him."

An interview with: Alex Mulvaney, Skinwalker

Hi Alex. Let's jump in. How did you get involved in skinwalking?
My dad was a rigger on Terminus when I was a little kid. He used to send me images of the bridgeway as he was working on it, and one of them caught Joe Fledge as he went out the airlock, and I thought, wow, I want to do that.

Joe Fledge. He tried to commit suicide by EVA without a suit, correct?
Yeah. He found out that you can actually survive a pretty long time in hard vacuum. He –

But he wanted to commit suicide, and you didn't want to emulate that, right?

(Laughs) No, of course not. But Joe Fledge, he exhaled real hard when he stepped out, and that saved his life. He lasted twenty seconds and they pulled him in and revived him. It was hushed up, but we had the picture, and when I was little I looked at it all the time. I thought, man, I could do that.

What's the attraction?

Pushing yourself. People used to think you could only go fifteen seconds at most, before decompression sickness, arterial gas embolism, all that shit, kills you. Barebacking it now, people can go forty seconds, easy. I went forty-seven but had to be resuscitated.

Explain barebacking for our audience.

Mostly us Skins, we use a skinsuit. It's basically a wetsuit, and adds extra compression, but it's not a pressure suit or anything like that. Barebacking is hardcore. That's when you go out with nothing. No clothes. Just you and space.

You've gone much longer than forty-seven seconds. You're the recordholder for a three-minute skinsuit spacewalk. What was the difference?

(Laughs) Drugs, man. We take a few different drugs that mitigate the effects of ebullism. Pentoxifylline, NMDA antagonists, a few others.

Which do you prefer, skinwalking or barebacking?

They each serve different purposes. Skinwalking now, that's to break records and to test the science. Barebacking is just *pure*. Raw.

What does it feel like to go out there? No suit. Just skin. Isn't it cold?

Hot, actually, but cold too. We call it old cold. You can practically feel the solar radiation zapping your cells. But inside, everything is trying to boil away and bust out. It's – euphoric. You just fall and fall and fall.

Yes, the Sun, and the solar radiation – you know you've basically signed your death sentence, right?

I guess.

That doesn't bother you?

Listen. It's not about the minutes or the radiation. Humanity occupies a fingernail-thin slice of the surface of the planet. Everywhere else on

Earth – underground, the ocean, the upper atmosphere – is hostile to human life. It's insane that we think that's the only space we should ever occupy and that's the environment we should bring with us off-planet. Skinwalking isn't about setting records. That radiation you say is going to kill me – that radiation is going to *change* me, just like oxygen changed life on Earth. You can keep building your habitats and stations. You can keep your razor-thin environment that's already been poisoned almost to death. Us Skins – give us a few generations and we can survive anywhere. We're the future of the human race.

When Alex sent me and Melissa a terse message that he had dropped out of college, I called her.

"Wow," she said, looking up from her handheld to take the call. "He's cheating death on a regular basis but for this you call?"

"Have you talked to him?" I asked.

"Randy, he doesn't talk to me. He's like you – no words, just shutting people out."

The same argument, the same accusation. "He's like you," I corrected her, my voice like ice. "He is. You saw the article. That was all you."

For a moment, Melissa paused. Then she sighed. "Oh, Randy. What have we done? Is he trying to kill himself? Is he punishing us? Is this our son's way of saying, you two never should have got together and made me?"

I licked my lips, tried to get my voice to work. "I think – he's evolving."

Alex and I agreed to meet at a café at Earth Terminus base. The space city that sprang up at the foot of the massive looming elevator was a combination of shipping containers and man camp shantytowns, cheek by jowl with state-of-the-art light rail and sleek new construction. It was mid-January: the sun was a glare of light and the sky was parched and white.

I watched from across the table as Alex scanned the crowd. He looked so much like his mother. It was more than just the dark eyes and dark hair. It was the expressions that swept across his face, the way he held the coffee in his hands, the way he set his shoulders and jiggled his leg with impatience. He was nineteen now, and he had filled out, and he was tall. He wore jeans and a hoodie, a ball cap drawn down over his face. But the camouflage couldn't hide everything from the merciless equatorial sun.

His face was mottled with bruises from the broken blood vessels under the skin. The whites of his eyes were shadowed and red, and the tiny capillaries around his nose made him look like a forty-year drunk.

He felt my observation and turned to look at me. He gave a wry, twisted smile, and fished for his sunglasses and put them on, hiding his red eyes.

The waitress brought us our burgers, and I saw that when he took a bite, he had to eat carefully, as if it were painful to chew.

"Do you – do you need anything? Money?" I was grasping at straws.

His mouth quirked again. "Nah. I'm good. Cheap rent out here."

He lived with a group of friends, but he refused to let us visit him, and I suspected that they were all Skins. I knew someone was bankrolling them, because it cost money to ride the elevator, and it cost money to defy the procedures that were established to prevent Skins from making their jumps. Every jump was followed by a flurry of announcements from the Terminus authorities that anybody making an unsuited spacewalk would be arrested and fined. It had not been much of a deterrent.

"You need to stop," I said.

He looked at me from behind his sunglasses. "You know I'm not going to stop."

"You mean you'd rather die out there than stop for us."

"That's Mom talking," he said. "This isn't about you or her."

"Then what is it?" I challenged. "You're going to die, Alex. Doesn't that –" My voice broke. Alex knew what I was going to say, or thought he did. He leaned forward.

"Frighten me? No. You don't understand. I'm not frightened of anything. This is what I've been meant to do, ever since you sent that image. This is the future, Dad, of all humanity."

Anger flared. "You aren't evolving. It doesn't work that way."

His expression changed, and he dropped his head to concentrate on his burger, and in that moment he reminded me so much of his mother that I knew that he was hiding something.

"Jesus Christ, Alex," I said. "What have you done?"

He was silent for a long time. He set down his burger. I saw a smear of something on his cheek until he wiped it away. He stood up, his skinny, angular frame looming over me. "I'm sorry," he said finally. "I can't be what you want." He looked as if he was going to say something else, but instead just picked up his backpack, hiked it over his shoulder, and walked away, toward Terminus. I watched until he disappeared into the crowd.

When I could no longer see my son, I leaned forward and touched a smear on the bun, where Alex had bitten into the burger. It wasn't blood red; it was closer to purple. I knew it was blood, though, blood from gum tissue that had been compromised by vacuum.

The waitress came back, a bit surprised that we had barely touched our burgers. "Do you want a to-go box?" she said kindly.

"Yes please," I said. When she brought it, I wrapped Alex's burger in its paper and put it in the box, leaving my untouched meal behind.

It took weeks before the genelab came back with results. Alex's blood was awash with genetic code that altered the effect of hard vacuum on oxygen-carrying blood cells. They weren't waiting for evolution. Skins were becoming something other than human, other than Earth-bound, skipping thousands of years of genetic progress.

That was the last time I saw my son alive.

I watched the video over and again. The airlock opened, and Alex pushed out, a graceful swan dive into the abyss. The camera zoomed in on him, and his eyes were open, reflecting Earthlight. He somersaulted, and I could see the exuberant grin, and behind the alien creature swimming in near-Earth space, I could see my son, both the man he had become and the boy he once was.

Then his grin changed, and the light went out, first in his eyes, and then in his body. And he fell, endlessly. Endlessly he fell.

Months later, I found the drawing again, crumpled at the bottom of Alex's desk drawer in his bedroom. I thought I had tossed it but no. I smoothed it out, and something struck me. I called up my image files from almost twenty years before. It took a while before I could find the photo of Joe Fledge.

If you didn't know what to look for, you could miss it. The focus of the image is the bridge, a soaring arc in space, against a backdrop of stars. Down in the corner was the figure of Joe Fledge. Behind him is his rescuer, reaching out.

I looked again at Alex's crumpled drawing. It was a ten-year-old boy's self-portrait. He had captured his own cheeky grin. And behind him was a meticulously detailed figure waving him on from the airlock.

I looked at the image. I looked back at the drawing.

Alex had drawn me, waving him on.

Devin Fisher called me out of the blue. He said that Terminus One was expanding the bridgeway, and they wanted to bring in experienced riggers for a fast ramp-up.

"There's a spot for you. If you want." He paused, and then said, "I heard about your son. I'm sorry."

"Thanks," I said.

I took him up on it. It's quiet up there. My helmet restricts my view, and I can be alone with my thoughts and the routine work. I keep away from the Skins, who continue to make their jumps, setting records previously unthinkable. News reports say that in twenty years, cellular modification may successfully be used to prevent decompression and radiation exposure, and to facilitate adaptation to the most alien of environments – Mars, say, or Venus. Humans would no longer be limited to the sliver of Earth's surface. We would no longer be a single species. All because of Joe Fledge's jump.

The bridge is almost complete. When it's finished, I'll suit up and take the long walk out to the hub where the ships will dock. I will look out over Earth and space and scan the heavens for my son. And when I spot him on his long journey, I will lift my hand and wave him on.

The Night of Their Conversion

The craziest thing about this story? I dreamed it. When I woke up, I had the most vivid memory of the scene at the end. I couldn't write it all down fast enough.

Susan wanted to go to the airport, so Uncle Walter took her. When he came back, he said that it was packed.

"People were waiting in line at the ticket counters with their luggage and strollers. You know how the ropes make you snake back and forth? Every inch of it was full. Makes you think it was Thanksgiving, that crowd."

Bobby laughed and asked if the airline attendants were taking tickets and tagging luggage. Uncle Walter said sharply that yes, they were. "It's a kind thing, Bobby, and don't you forget it. They were swiping credit cards and everything. The only thing different is that there were seats on every flight and flights to everywhere."

So that shut Bobby up. I asked Uncle Walter which gate he dropped Susan at, and he said twenty-seven, and then he kind of got sad again and I let him be. I was a little surprised that Susan wanted to be at the airport because even though it sounded like the airlines were doing everything they could to make it seem normal, it couldn't be normal, ever. The whole thing about the seats on every flight for instance – they weren't fooling anybody with that.

Uncle Walter flipped through the paper from the fifteenth, even though it had been read to tatters. Susan had done the crossword in pen, and if we had known then we would have stopped her. At least we could have erased the answers and played it a few times before it got easy. I tried to make one but gave up – they are harder than they look.

Bobby sat in the La-Z-Boy by the window, hands over his face. He might have been crying, but he didn't make a sound.

I decided to go for a run. That hadn't changed. I went upstairs and dug out my running tights and sweatshirt and laced up my sneakers. I put on a hat and gloves while I trotted down the stairs. Bobby never moved but Uncle Walter looked up and watched me go. I thought he would say something but he didn't, and I let myself out.

The cold January air hit me hard, and I jogged down the front stairs, careful of the ice on the stoop. I took a hard left and headed toward the park, my eyes tearing from the cold wind. Frozen bits of icy snow piled up in the corners of the dirty street. No one was out – okay, it was freezing, so that made sense, but really it was because either everyone else had converted or was indoors waiting for the next wave.

My heart pounded in my chest and my lungs rasped in and out. I hadn't yet warmed up so every step hit the ground hard, thudding up my spine. I concentrated grimly on the discomfort, because I didn't want to think of anything else, but it was no use. The idea of Susan at the airport, waiting there instead of at the house, made me – I don't know... Disappointed.

I had the empty street to myself, the buildings looming on either side of me, the staircased towers of the city centre rising in the distance. Most of the stores had been looted, their windows jagged starbursts of broken glass. Graffiti everywhere. Someone's idea of fun, destruction for its own sake.

I thought about that, doing all the things I never had the guts to do when it was against the rules, but it seemed most people were either just having lots of sex or stealing stuff. And since people did that anyway, it didn't seem special to do it now. So I just ran, although now I ran down the middle of the street. That was different at least.

It was funny, though. If someone told you this was your last night to be human, what would you do? It turned out that all I wanted was the same old. Those people at the airport, that's all they wanted too. I heard there were lines at the bank, and people getting their dry cleaning done and grocery shopping.

Then it happened. My muscles warmed up, my lungs adapted, my pulse smoothed out, and endorphins flooded my bloodstream. Just like that, I had become an effortless running machine. My breathing was steady, barely puffing out through my lips. I was euphoric. I thought: I could convert this way. I didn't know what that would make me, but running converted me anyway, or so I thought of it.

The street settled into a long uphill climb, but I was ready for it and I lengthened my stride, my heart and lungs adjusting to the demand. The sky was grey but there was a pale-ish aura behind the clouds to the west where the sun tried to shine through. It would set before the clouds cleared, and that would be that. Tomorrow if the sun shone, I wouldn't see it.

Well, I would see it, but I wouldn't know it. Or something like that. Uncle Walter tried to explain what happened when we convert, but I didn't understand. I mean I got the part how we weren't human any more, but I didn't know what that meant. I figured I wouldn't until I converted, and then it wouldn't matter any more.

The hill flattened out, and I could see the city spread out before me. The wind was fierce here, blasting me from the side, but that wasn't why I almost stopped. I had jogged right into a network.

After my initial surprise, I kept going, threading my way through them as they walked along on their own mission. I could see at once they had converted – they had that look. It was as if they were thinking faster or living faster. Their faces were alive, the emotions flickering faster than I could keep up. I could hear my own breathing, my own footsteps, but I think I was the ghost.

Even though I was careful, I bumped shoulders or jostled one, but aside from a vague gesture, as if to brush me away, nobody looked at me or acknowledged me. I guess it was like Uncle Walter had said, they didn't see the connection between us anymore. They were more in focus to me, but I was a blur to them.

It didn't seem to bother them at all that they had converted. Every time I ran into a network, I checked to see if they looked sad or in pain, but it wasn't like that. They were just more there.

I kept jogging, keeping an eye on them all the while, until I left them behind. Without knowing it I had turned down a familiar street, my feet taking the usual route. I had begun to breathe hard, but I still ran steadily, all systems go. I had a choice – I could either run a longer distance, which is what I usually did when I reached this point and I still felt this good. Or I could let myself loose, and run my heart out, sprinting the last mile toward home.

You'd think it would be an easy choice. The long run of course. I didn't want to leave my city's empty streets too soon on what was my last run. But even while I thought that, my body decided for me. I began to sprint, pushing myself with every stride. Just like before, heart, lungs, muscles answered the call and I began to play myself. A little faster? Why not? How about faster? Every time I asked I ran harder, and it was all effortless.

Was this conversion?

I skidded to a halt, gasping, my heart beating so hard that I blacked out for a moment, bright dots in front of my eyes. I groped the air as my knees buckled, finally clutching the cold points of a wrought-iron fence. Finally my heart slowed, my breathing slowed, and the dots faded and I could see. I let go shakily and looked around.

It was almost twilight. The sun was a line of gold on the horizon, or the bits I could see on the skyline. My legs aching, I stumbled back to the house. It was dark when I got there, and I let myself in. A small candle glowed in the kitchen, and Uncle Walter sat at the table in the darkness.

"Where's Bobby?" I asked.

"Bobby went on ahead. What happened to you?"

"I ran longer than I thought. I didn't mean to keep you waiting."

"You didn't. It wasn't time yet. Bobby just couldn't stand to wait around."

I nodded though I doubted he saw me. I wished I had some water but there wasn't anything from the faucets. I would have to break off some crusty snow from the windowsill or something. Then Uncle Walter surprised me and pulled out a bottle of water. I took it and broke the seal and drank. It tasted plasticky. It was wonderful. I drank half and handed him the rest but he waved it away, so I finished the bottle.

Thanks," I said. "Where did you get it?" I wondered if he had saved it for a special occasion. Like tonight.

"I liberated it from the corner store. I thought there might be some water left and sure enough."

He couldn't see my face but he had to know I was surprised. Uncle Walter took an almost perverse pride in keeping the customs of civilisation now that it had broken all around us. I set the empty bottle down on the table, the little drops of water inside reflecting in the candlelight.

"Well," Uncle Walter said. He got up, bulky in his big overcoat. "Are you ready?" What could I say? Of course I wasn't. I followed him out of the house and he locked the door behind him. Night had fallen and the temperature dropped, and my running clothes did little to keep me warm. I crammed my hat back on my head and shivered after him.

We went down to the little gazebo in the park. A crowd had gathered there, some people carrying candles, and a bonfire burned off to one side. I made for the fire. I was freezing.

A woman in a heavy coat and scarf came up to me, holding out a sheaf of papers and a pencil in her gloved hands. She asked me if I could write, and I said yes, though I was shivering so hard that I wasn't sure how legible it would be.

"It's for the archives," she said. "We don't know how much time we have so everyone is going to write something, some bit of knowledge, to keep for later. You know, just in case," she faltered. "They're still us," she said finally and her voice was pleading. "They should know what we know. They should know who we are."

I just nodded, and she went on to someone else, leaving me with a couple of pieces of paper and a pencil. I had to warm up my hands in front of the bonfire before I could get started, and then it was hard to think of something to write. So I began to write everything I knew about running. Stretching, breathing, interval training, improving distance, all of it. I wrote and wrote and didn't notice that the crowd had thinned and the bonfire burned low. Then the woman came back.

"Stuff it in the cracks in the rock," she said. I had no idea what she was talking about. I looked around and by the bonfire light I could see little bits of shadowy paper stuck in the rock wall. I put my notes in there, feeling a little stupid. I didn't know how this was going to help. And anyway, no one was going to need to know about running.

Some people started singing hymns, and I felt all sick to my stomach and burning hot, like I was coming down with something. I saw Bobby and Uncle Walter talking to someone and a jolt of recognition made my heart jump. It was Susan. I knew she wouldn't leave us.

She pulled four envelopes out of her pocket, boarding passes poking out of the top, and handed them out. "I booked us on a late flight," she said. "I hope everyone is packed, because we have to hurry. There's not a lot of time left." I just took one numbly, because I thought she was in denial and it was Susan, who always faced everything head on. She must have caught something in my attitude because she gave a little shake of her head. "It's not for leaving. It's for coming back. I have to believe we're coming back."

We held hands and I thought about my notes. My heart sank – I forgot the most important thing. When the time is right, when your muscles are warm and your brain begins the flood of chemicals into your bloodstream, let it go. Don't struggle. Don't think. Convert.

Spider

After writing about the events on the Hohmann, *I couldn't shake the idea that there was another story; namely, how did they get there? Well, it starts, like most crime stories do, with one last score.*

Bifrost Mining Station, June 2063

The plan

I knew the two miners were trouble as soon as they pulled themselves into the bar. They looked around and one, I think it was Carter but you try telling the brothers apart, nudged Rose and nodded his chin at me. They came over and slid next to me, one on either side. We floated there, me pulling at my bulb of cheap station whiskey, trying not to show my unease.

"Hawkes," said Carter. "Good to see you." He was close enough now to see the scar under his eye, a reminder of when Rose had tried to gouge his eye out. Family.

"Hmmm," I said.

Carter was unfazed and leaned closer. "We have a proposition."

My heart sank lower.

Carter said, "It's your share of five hundred million dollars and a way off Bifrost."

I gave him a sceptical side eye and took another drink. Carter and Rose were lifers – asteroid miners who had been out in the dark so long their bones would crumble upon re-entry. There was no chance they had access to the kind of money they were talking about. And I had many good reasons to leave Earth nearly a decade ago, and not so many to go back.

I took another suck at the drinking bulb and thought of whiskey – good whiskey – drunk out of a glass, the way God intended.

"If I were interested," I said, "and let me emphasise *if*, just what does this too-good-to-be true plan entail?"

They exchanged the merest smirks.

"Meet us in Rainbow, tomorrow night at 19:30," Carter said.

Rose spoke for the first time, "Hawkes – you better be there."

"Aw, come on, fellas. And miss movie night?" I said. They didn't answer. Instead, they pushed away from the bar and floated out through the hatch. I turned my back, hunched over my drink, my concern deepening. No one crossed the Goucher twins.

The Bifrost Corporation (registered Corporate Citizen Entity) Mining Station floated out in the middle of the asteroid field beyond Mars. We called its complex superstructure the spider – arms radiated out from a central wheel, a bulbous control system hanging below the main structure. It looked impossibly fragile, even from as close in as one hundred kilometres. Rainbow was the original arm of the station, used as storage now, where equipment, spare parts, and forgotten station amenities were secured and forgotten.

I watched as Carter diverted the corporate cameras to an empty section of the room and looked over my compatriots.

There was Evangeline Martinez. Chemo had not only taken her hair, it had rendered her once-brown complexion ashen and sickly, and the steroids and microgravity gave her an extra bloat. All of us dark-skinned people, so far from the Sun, tended to pale even with our extra melanin, but she looked like a ghost. I heard that she had given up her fight against the corporation for the right to die at home.

There was Asa Delacort. He had a better poker face than mine, helped no doubt by all the artificial scaffolding in his cheeks, nose, forehead, and chin. The drill he had been setting on a rock had bucked, boosting back into his face, cracking his faceplate and embedding itself into his cheekbone. Plastic bone under skin is all well and good, but the nerve damage was irreparable, so it was like looking at a real-life example of the uncanny valley.

With corporate eyes duped, Carter spoke. "So here's the deal," he said. "We have a buyer. We find a rock. All we need to do is spot it, set it, and boost it."

That's all?" Asa said. He couldn't lift an eyebrow, but you could hear it in his voice.

"What's the plan?" I said.

"Evangeline, you tell them," Carter said.

"There's a sector of the region that we haven't mapped yet, but we know there are a few big rocks. The Corporation doesn't know what they have – hell, they don't really know what they have in-sector, because it's not like the rocks stay still – and I've done a little bit of scoping on my own. There's a good-sized rock about 40 meters in diameter that we can boost with none the wiser."

"How far away?" I said.

"One hundred and seventy thousand kilometers from Region 5."

Not too far – maybe fourteen hours by shuttle.

"Evangeline, what's its roll?" Asa asked.

"It's a tumbler, but nothing you haven't handled before, Ace," she told him.

"That's where we come in," Carter said. "Hawkes flies us out to the rock, we set our boosters, and we're back before anyone knows the difference." The boosters would course-correct the rock so that eight months later or thereabouts it would show up where it was supposed to. Once the buyer released the funds into our bank accounts, the coordinates would be transmitted, and they would retrieve their rock. Was it stealing if the corporation didn't even know it had been robbed?

Evangeline's quarters were just big enough for Asa and me to join her. We squeezed around her screen, which displayed the datastream she had yanked from the asteroid scopes and downloaded to the (highly illegal) shadow server. Asa leaned over her shoulder, scanning the quick-running data that showed the asteroid's size and dimensions and its rough trajectory through the solar system. Evangeline was the best spotter on the station. I wondered how long she had known about this rock. We all had secrets on Bifrost, and this was a big one.

Asa sat down at her monitor, brought up another display, logged in, and began tapping queries. Asa and Evangeline were using a subsection of the server to run their calculations, via an ancient drive with a jerry-rigged connector to the main plant.

"Here," Asa said at last, and we peered at the still image of an asteroid in a high-res greyscale that showed the pockmarked surface. My heart leaped – and almost immediately sank.

M-class, a big, heavy, metal motherfucker. This would be a fortune in platinum, nickel, you name it. Five hundred million dollars for us was a drop in the bucket for whoever was funding this caper. If, and it was a big if, they were able to cut and sell, they would pull in billions. They could sell bits to buyers all over the world. Hell, they could sell shares to governments. And that was the problem. On the one hand, we were getting paid fuck-off money to pull off the biggest score of the 21st century. On the other, more realistic, hand, I wasn't sure I wanted to get any more involved in this. And on the third, more pragmatic, hand, I knew if I backed out now I would be out an airlock without a suit.

"Shit," Asa said. He must have come to the same conclusion I did, that we were in over our heads. Evangeline, curiously, had a little smile on her ravaged face. She glanced at Asa and he put a hand on her shoulder and squeezed it, a more intimate gesture than just that between thieves. I hadn't known they were together.

"All right," I said, abruptly, not wanting to be all sentimental in front of the dying woman and her plastic lover. "Do you have the coordinates?"

"All set," Asa said. He tapped a few more times, then disconnected the drive from the port and handed it to me. "Do your thing, Hawkes."

I pocketed the thumb drive, feeling their scrutiny. Evangeline had the same curious half smile. I couldn't tell what Asa was thinking. I knew what I was thinking though.

If we got caught, there would be no talking our way out of this. *Walk away. Risk the airlock. Walk away.*

Gravity has an attraction that goes beyond physics. If we pulled this off, I could go home.

How in the hell were we going to pull this off?

Bifrost had six shuttles and a fleet of rocket bots that we sent out to asteroids to scrape the surface and bag up material, anchoring the bags to the surface of the rock. Then shuttle crews would be deployed to dock with the asteroid, use the arm to unlock the anchor and pull the bag in, and then haul it back home. When things went wrong, crews would have to troubleshoot, sometimes with a pressurised jackhammer, sometimes with a blowtorch, and sometimes with explosives. Asa wasn't the only walking reminder of how dangerous it was.

Alone in my quarters, I fished out my own ancient drive and logged in to the shadow server using a cobbled together port connector. Technically I wasn't stealing a shuttle, I was just borrowing it. And when I brought it back, it couldn't look like I did anything wrong. The coordinates that Evangeline set were in a big empty part of space. I was searching for anything, any reason that would send me in that sector of the solar system.

I didn't find it. I found something better. *We might actually get away with this.*

The cop

Station security police Shane Harris pushed herself through the Bifrost Main Concourse on her way to the Security Station on Alpha Arm, orienting herself 'up' toward the station central complex by making a mental shift in her perspective. She was shaky and frazzled, a knot of anxiety in her stomach. It had been a bad night. When Shane first came to Bifrost a year before, her hind-brain had panicked at the approach to the spider-like structure. It took powerful anti-anxiety drugs, biofeedback techniques, and station-made vodka to prevent her from waking up screaming every night. If anything, the obsessive thoughts had grown worse, and Shane fretted that the governor on her brain wouldn't hold much longer.

Shane pulled herself inside Security HQ. Ray was already at his post with a bulb of coffee. Ray was Shane's foil – blond where she was dark, short and stout where she was thin and stringy. Calm and balanced where she was an explosive mess of nerves and energy.

Ray nodded at her and pointed at the screens that showed a steady stream of everything happening on the station in all the public areas. Black squares showed where workers had turned off the cameras in their quarters. It was a constant game, fixing cameras and hiding them, resourceful workers finding cameras and breaking them, and so on and so forth.

Shane didn't like the cameras, but the station was run by a registered Corporate Citizen Entity, and employees were told up front that their right to privacy was forfeit when they signed up.

She strapped in. "What am I looking at?"

"You know how I queried the AI to identify who blanked their cameras with a cross-reference of everyone they were in contact with on the station?" She nodded. "Last night Meredith Hawkes entered Evangeline Martinez's quarters with Asa Delacort. We couldn't see what they did, but they weren't online, according to computer records." He tapped the screen and slid the image sideways. "And look at this."

Shane leaned in closer. There were in quick succession still images of Hawkes, Martinez, Delacort, and the brother miners Carter and Rose Goucher. Carter and Rose sitting next to Hawkes at the bar. Carter and Asa Delacort in mining tech, where Asa worked. Evangeline and Rose in the infirmary waiting room. Evangeline sagged in her chair; Rose sat on the other side, his hand wrapped in a cloth. He had been fighting again. The Goucher twins were always starting fights, always in trouble. Ever since Shane had arrived on the station the twins ran roughshod and always got away with it. She had asked Ray about it once, but he was evasive and Shane was the rookie, so she didn't push.

All of it could have been coincidence. Shane knew that you could take any of Ray's interactions and find patterns, and if you put the data back in with all of the background noise, these interactions wouldn't rise to the level that pinged any alarms. Nevertheless, Shane felt a tingle raise the hair at the nape of her neck. Hawkes was a prickly loner. She did her job, but she didn't go out of her way to be friends with anyone. Shane looked at Ray. "How did you get the computer to come up with these interactions?"

He looked smug. "Once you train the AI to identify patterns it starts to recognise them on its own. I gave it Hawkes, and it fed me Evangeline; I gave it Evangeline, and it opened up the rest. Here." He swung the screen toward her and she saw the interconnected lines showing relationships between all the characters. "I hadn't even realised that Evangeline knew Rose."

Shane looked closer at the infirmary image. Evangeline wasn't looking at Rose, but the way their bodies were angled suggested they had just stopped talking to each other.

Shane sat back, calculating. "What could it be?" She was more thinking out loud than anything, but Ray answered anyway.

"Doesn't matter. They're up to something. And before you tell me that's not enough to base an investigation on, you know it's true. Everybody's hiding something, Shane. That's true back on Earth and Mars, and it's true here. Especially here."

It's the only reason anyone came to Bifrost. He didn't have to say as much out loud. They both knew it. Her stomach clenched, and reflexively she tapped at her wrist, releasing a dose of meds. If Ray noticed, he didn't give a sign.

"Just talk to them. Use your cop instincts," he said, with a reassuring smile.

"Okay," she said. "Okay."

Shane's unease only deepened as she approached Carter Goucher in the canteen, trying to ignore her rising heart rate, cursing Ray for his AI patterns. She was afraid of the brothers. They were dangerous. The Corporation didn't allow sidearms, which was just as well, since she had no doubt that Carter could disarm her easily, but she still wished she had a gun.

She coughed to get his attention. "Carter?"

The man gave Shane a narrow-eyed, considering look. His eyes were pale blue, and for a moment she was mesmerised. She struggled to look away.

"Rose," he said sourly. "What do you want?"

"Shane Harris, Bifrost PD," Shane said. "Sorry about that. Do you get that a lot?"

He just stared at her.

"Um, I wanted to ask a few questions?" she said. With an effort, she controlled her nervous upspeak. "Sorry, I thought you were your brother because his schedule has him off-shift right now."

He laughed, his mood changed in an instant. "Yeah, I'm Carter. Just messing with you."

"Well," Shane said, fighting the urge to smile back. "Since this is official business, can I see some I.D?"

Still with good humour, he pulled out his lanyard from his overalls and presented her with his dog tag. With a firm blink she activated her corneal display. The I.D. flashed its biometrics at her. It was Carter. She handed it back.

"So, Carter, I have a few questions," she began. "We're just doing a station audit." She ran through his considerable record ever since arriving at Bifrost seven years before. His expression was rueful, sheepish. Aw shucks, he seemed to be saying. Was that me?

His blue eyes were extraordinary. Pale. Icy. *Look away, Shane.*

Eyes were trouble.

She struggled to maintain her equilibrium, pretended to look into the distance as if accessing more data.

"So why?" she finished.

"Why what?"

"Sorry, I meant, all that assault and battery – what does it get you?"

He shrugged. "Respect. The station gets what it wants too. You think you're keeping the peace, but if it weren't for – for Rose and me, you guys would need a full-time department of a dozen cops to keep peace on this station. You should thank us."

Sweat trickled down the back of her uniform. She knew he could tell, by the way he smirked.

"Not going to do that," Shane said. "But we are watching you. You pull anything else, we will haul you in."

Carter snorted. His demeanour changed in an instant. "You? Word of advice, bitch. Keep your nose where it belongs."

Fear fuelled her anger, even as she struggled to regain control. *Don't antagonise; de-escalate.* But she was past Academy 101. "Is that a threat, Carter? Because from where I'm sitting, I can arrest you for that."

Now he full-on laughed. "Yeah, you? Go ahead. Try it." Her hands began to shake, and she fumbled to tap her wrist, but she had just dosed, and the device only buzzed a denial. They were so close she could see the striations in his ice-blue eyes, the silver in his crewcut hair. This was bad. She knew from experience it would be bad. She needed to get away fast. And despairing, unable to stop the reaction, she was overwhelmed by the image of taking the miner's shiv from his belt and stabbing it into his eye. She almost convulsed with release, with fear, with her own sickening attraction to the idea.

With difficulty she pushed away from the table, desperate.

"Remember what I said," she told him, the words coming harsh. She didn't wait for an answer, left him sitting in the canteen as she made it through the door into the corridor, sweating, heart thudding, her vision obscured by gathering darkness as she was overcome by vertigo. She knew she was getting curious looks but she pushed through the crowd, grabbing for handholds to propel her forward, until she could make it to security HQ by feel and routine. She slapped at the door controls and pulled herself inside, but the panic continued to rise, overwhelming her endocrine system. She was overdosing on adrenalin.

Shane let the door slide behind her and she flailed, her throat working. Ray's reaction was comical, his mouth and eyes 'O's of surprise and horror. He caught her and held onto her, but there was no gravity, and she could do nothing but float. God, that just made it worse, as if everything inside of her was going to explode outward in a violent decompression. He was saying something, asking what she wanted, and she couldn't speak. He pressed her wrist for her, and this time the pump released her meds. It was less a release than a dulling of extremity, but she was grateful for it. Her heart slowed. Her breathing slowed.

For a long time Ray held her close, even gave her a kiss on the top of her head. It wasn't sexual at all, and she was grateful for that too. In his arms, she could pretend she wasn't in zero gee. She felt sleepy now, as she always did after an attack.

"You want to strap in?" he asked, and she nodded. He helped her into a sleep sack in the office, swaddling her tight with an extra pull on the straps.

"I don't know what I would do without you," she said, almost asleep, hanging in the corner.

"Don't worry about it," he said.

She wanted to tell him what happened. She was distantly embarrassed that she had made a mistake, but now that was all a long way away. Shane slept.

The boost

I climbed into the cockpit and strapped in, the harness pressing against me. It was familiar and comforting. I ran through the rest of my pre-flight checklist, and then keyed my mic.

"Control, B-167 ready for takeoff."

"Clear for takeoff, B-167."

The deck crew cleared the shuttle bay and depressurised it. The bay doors opened, revealing the blackness of space, the brilliance of stars, and down below me and to my left, the bright star of Jupiter. I felt the slight tug as the locks holding the shuttle in place released. We floated together, the station and the shuttle, until Control gave the signal and I began thrust. It was so gentle as to be nearly imperceptible. Bifrost dropped away. My stomach roiled – not space sickness, but a remnant of fear. I had dropped my tether, the last connection to Earth out here in the black, and I would not have it again until I returned.

There's a phrase for it: *L'appel du vide*. The call of the void. Out here, you could fall forever, always a part of the velvet blackness of space, the roll of Mother Jupiter, distant Father Sol, jewels set in an immeasurable expanse. I felt a moment of yearning, and shivered at that sense of losing control, that one day the governor on my brain would fail, and I would open the airlock and step out.

Six hours later my computer signalled that I was approaching Asteroid ZG – 2048Bi179; Ziggy for short. We all had a lot of fondness for Ziggy. It was a carbon-rich rock that was one of the first asteroids Bifrost worked on, establishing the technology, protocol and procedures that made the station the trillion-dollar money-maker that it was: a powerful corporation independent of Earth in a way that Mars, still dependent upon the home planet, was not. Ziggy was done for, played out. All that work had destabilised its trajectory, turning it into space junk, and the station had plenty of that to worry about. Bifrost didn't need Ziggy any more, and it was time to push it away, out of the zone so its unstable path didn't cause trouble down the road.

Two days ago I brought it up in the pilots' meeting.

"I think it's time to let Ziggy go," I had said, leaning back, my arms draped over the grab bars, legs crossed in front of me, riding an invisible magic carpet.

There were groans of the sentimental variety.

"Come on, guys," I had said. "Look, if you want, I'll do it."

It was that easy.

When I logged in to the control system with my flight plan, I used my official logon, but I had copied over the program with the coordinates from Asa's thumb drive. Now, it was time to put the first part of the plan in motion. As the rock came into physical view, I released the two small rockets. A few minutes later they embedded into the asteroid, the tiny lights showing on my screen. The computer pinged gently upon impact. Holding my breath I sent the signal to the rockets, feeding them the duration of thrust and the flight plan.

Another success ping.

But we weren't done. I turned back. Behind me Carter's head popped up. He was fully dressed in his eva suit. I had manipulated the cameras so they were still on – just oriented away from the tiny sliver of the shuttle cabin where Carter was. He gave me a thumbs up and let himself out the airlock.

He was a tiny figure lost in the deep, barely visible against the field of stars. He eva'd without a tether, and for all that Carter was a deeply flawed human being, I shook my head at his courage. He only had suit thrusters, and it wasn't easy to guide a suit with them. He soon disappeared into the vastness of space, absorbed into the distance far beyond what the naked eye could register.

Carter was re-setting the rockets from the official course to our very special program. They would turn Ziggy into a small rocket-propelled spacecraft, accounting for its mass and current trajectory. Instead of a gentle course correction, Ziggy was going to scoot on over to the big asteroid, bump into it hard, pulverising itself in the process, and with a big burst of energy, knock it onto its new track and, eight months later, into the waiting arms of the buyer. If everything went right, that is.

Finally, a proximity ping sounded. He was back.

"B-167, what was that?" the flight controller's voice rang out in the cockpit and I jumped.

"Stand-by, Control," I said. I muted the mic as Carter activated the outside hatch. When pressure equalised, he slipped inside. He positioned himself on the floor between the row of seats. "Ah, Control, there doesn't appear to be anything wrong. All systems optimal. Just a random ping?"

"We'll check it out when you get home," the flight controller said. "Cleared to return when mission complete."

I began the long journey back to the station. "B-167 to shuttle control. Mission accomplished. Say good-bye, Ziggy."

"Good-bye, Ziggy," everyone chorused. I'm not sure why, but I felt a small pang.

You hate this place. This isn't the time to get sentimental.

The trickiest part was yet to come.

Long hours later, the Bifrost station came into view, first its lights blinking against irregular patches of black, then the reflection of light off its arms, and finally the spidery station itself. Cleared to dock, I eased the shuttle back into the station bay and we connected, the anchor catching with a gentle shudder. I ran through the post-flight checklist with the camera on me while behind me, undetected, Carter wriggled free of his suit and stowed it.

The doors finally opened and I stepped out and down the small steps. "Hey, Hawkes," said one of the ground crew – Nguyen, with a tablet and a checklist. "What was up with that ping?"

"I don't know. Maybe there was some dust?"

She tsked. Nguyen had permanent lines across her forehead from worry. She took her job seriously, which made her a pain in the ass right at the moment. "Hey, Control!"

Control turned from the other end of the flight deck. "What?"

"Ground B-167 for a systems check? I want to check out that ping."

I waited, barely breathing. The original plan was for the shuttle to be put in queue for its next make ready, giving Carter enough time to make his escape between shifts. Putting B-167 on the assessment list meant that Nguyen and her people would go in right now, which meant that Carter was screwed.

"Dammit, Nguyen," Control said. "We've already got two shuttles on your checklist. Pretty soon we're going to have to let people jetpack to work."

"Safety first, Control," Nguyen said, not budging.

"I agree with Nguyen," I said, as innocently as possible. "We can't have a broken proximity sensor in an area of space where there's nothing to hit. Maybe it will ping somebody to death."

Nguyen glared at me. "No one asked you, Ziggy killer," she muttered.

Control eye-rolled. "Nguyen, do you have time for this?"

"I don't know, Control. Do you have time to write the report after a mining crew dies in a shuttle explosion?"

He hesitated then snapped, "Fine. Run a diagnostic."

Shit. I watched Nguyen climb into the shuttle cockpit. I waited for the inevitable shouting and questions, but everything was quiet, all the normal hustle and bustle. Whatever they were doing, Carter remained undetected.

"Hawkes?" Control said, still irritated. "You can get out of here now, you know."

I left without a backward glance. I didn't know how Carter was going to get out of this, but I could only make it worse if I stayed to watch.

A few hours later, grabbing a food pack in the canteen, I saw Nguyen and Carter together. *Together* together. Scamp, I thought. I wondered if Rose knew, what with Nguyen being his ex. And then I wondered if Nguyen knew which brother she was with at the moment. And then I wondered if she cared.

Hail Mary

The news of Shane's attack spread throughout the station like wildfire, but the gossip was mostly concern for her well-being. Mostly – every grapevine has rotten grapes. Still, Shane was touched by people coming up to her and asking how she was, and offering remedies for space sickness and vertigo. It was nice to be cared about. She didn't tell anyone that it wasn't space sickness but her old enemy that overwhelmed her, flooding her brain with erratic signals until all she could see was blood and torn flesh. Many therapists had told her about unwanted thoughts and anxiety and stress, and she agreed with everything they said, but in her inner core – when the night was the darkest and there was no sleep to be found – it was the attraction that frightened her even as it sickened her.

Shane and Ray didn't speak about what happened. If he told admin that his rookie partner was crazy and unreliable and needed to go back to Earth, there was no indication – nothing from control, nothing from sickbay, except for an e-mail that said the next time it happened to please come to them and they would take care of her. After several days of flinching whenever there was a message alert from the station server, Shane calmed enough to go back to police work.

And after all that, Ray's pattern had dissipated almost as soon as it appeared. The brothers kept their own company as usual and Hawkes was never seen with any of the others again. Delacort and Martinez were connected, but even they had nothing more than a tangential relationship with the twins or with the pilot. No matter how often Shane re-ran the query, Hawkes was out of the picture.

"So I was wrong," Ray said, when Shane told him about her findings. "You were right. It wasn't important. Don't worry about it."

Shane wasn't an idiot; she knew Ray was eager not to have a repeat of her anxiety attack. But perversely she couldn't let it go, no matter how much she wanted to. "Right after I talk with Carter, he's no longer part of a cluster?"

"Look," Ray said. "Maybe they were planning something, but you put the kibosh on it. That's even better, if you think about it. It's a big administrative headache to arrest people on this thing. It's better for everyone if we made them forget all about whatever they had in mind."

"You don't want to report it to admin?" Shane was still sceptical.

Ray made a face as if he were considering. "No," he said at last. "It'll just complicate things. You did good, Shane. You stopped it. You kept things calm."

He was trying to make her feel better, but she admitted he had a point. Shane went about her business, but she was always aware of the original Bifrost Gang, as she dubbed them in her head. She knew better than to let Ray in on that. Still, one night she woke up in a sweat, hammered by another anxiety attack and bloody thoughts, and she knew that sleep would be futile, even after dosing. Shane unwrapped herself from her sleep sack, and pulled her terminal over. Typing in her password, she decided to run a different kind of query. While she considered, she rubbed her eyes and lifted her thick pony tail off her neck, letting the air cool her skin. Suddenly inspired, she keyed in a set of commands. Did they have any shared connections on Earth? How would Ray's program work with a database of 10 billion names?

The AI flashed a single name, as if the only thing it could come up with was a Hail Mary pass.

Agnes St. Germaine.

"Who?" Shane said out loud. She ran a quick search on the station roster, and came up empty. She went back to the AI screen. No connections radiated off the name. The name was just there. No context. Shane muttered and ran the program again.

This time the AI flashed: *No results found.*

But I just saw – "What the hell?" Shane said. She tried again; same result. The maddening name had disappeared. She ran the name separately through the InterSol criminal database, painstakingly waiting through the time lag for the system to validate her request, and then for it to spit out a response.

No results found.

Shane was getting angry now. "Goddammit," she said, glaring at her screen. "I saw that name. I saw it." She glanced at the small, round clock on her built-in desk; a mid-20th century antique. It was six a.m. She called Ray.

Ray was a good sport. He met her at the canteen before their shift, and they huddled over their breakfast – coffee, reconstituted scrambled eggs, hash browns, and spinach from the grow tank, floating like sleep-tousled genies. While they ate she told him what she had done.

"What would make the AI decide to make up a name? Can it even do that?"

Ray shrugged. "I guess. I mean, the whole idea is that it's a self-learning environment. So it's allowed to be creative. It doesn't think but it does extrapolate."

"And then it decides to stop giving me the name?"

"Yeah, that's weird, but again, it might have decided that it gave you the wrong answer the first time, and figured well, that was a low-value name, so…"

"Ray, that's not a very useful program."

'Look, we don't know if that's what happened. All we know is the AI gave you a name, and then withdrew the name. I mean, did you ask it what it meant?"

Shane stared at her breakfast, steaming in its pouch. If the station was a spider, the AI was a spider's brain. "I don't like asking it things," she muttered.

Ray rubbed his eyes. "Okay, look. Do you want me to ask why it came up with that name?"

"I guess. Sure. Thanks."

"Shane –" He took a breath. "You know, you don't have to stay. Some people aren't cut out for deep space. Maybe, you know, you should think about going Home."

Shane squished her eggs and toast together and didn't answer.

Some people weren't cut out for Earth, either.

Nguyen

"Attention. Attention. Stay in your quarters. Attention. Attention. Stay in your quarters."

The bloody pink light of the station alarm washed over Shane and Ray as they pushed at top speed toward the residential arm. Despite the warning, most of the station population was watching from their doorways, in various stages of ragged middle of the night un-dress, hair floating around fluid-bloated faces.

They encountered the first drifting blood drops as they rounded the corner of the miners' section. Adrift in the corridor was the body of one of the brothers, barely conscious. Shane reached him first, wrestling the body around so she could run a diagnostic. His face was battered, as if the other brother had tied him to a rail and then kept ramming an oxygen canister at his nose. She fished for his I.D. Rose.

"Where's Carter, Rose?" She said. His eyes fluttered, but he made no response.

"Where's medic?" Ray yelled into his mic. "What is taking you guys so long?"

"On our way," came a voice over the radio.

"Rose? Where's your brother?"

Rose made a wheezing noise. Laughter. Shane gave him a closer look. There was no way to detect a scar, with his face in ruin. "Carter?" she guessed. Something shifted in his expression and she knew she was right.

"We're looking for Rose," she told Ray. "This is Carter."

Ray shook his head. "Goddamn fifth-grade bullshit," he said. "Good," he said, as the medics swooped up with a float and the rest of their kit. They swarmed around Carter and the two cops backed away. "Let's go find our boy." His eyes scanned. "Got him. Residential arm in Bravo sector."

"Let's make sure that son of a bitch stays put," Shane said. She keyed her mic. "Station, give us gee plus."

"Order requires authority," came the quiet voice of the station computer. Shane looked at Ray.

"Shane, do we have time for this?" Ray asked. "He can do a lot of damage before he's pinned down."

"By the time he figures it out, we'll have him," she said. "Do it, Ray." *Give me this.*

Ray hesitated, gave in. "Station, authorise override per station security."

"Voice ID confirmed. Override accepted. Order confirmed."

It took them only a scant few minutes to reach security HQ to get their gear. Even in that brief span, Shane imagined she could feel a heaviness begin to descend on her. Was it her imagination or was there a barely perceptible sense of *down*?

She and Ray helped each other into their frames, the exoskeletons that allowed them to move in gee. It would take at least a half hour for the wheel to generate enough momentum to build up the centripetal force necessary to keep Rose locked down wherever he was. By the time it did, the only people who would be able to move would be Shane and Ray.

We're coming for you, Rose.

There was more blood in the res corridor in Sector Bravo, outside of Nguyen's quarters, leaking underneath her door. Without a word Shane and Ray looked at each other, and then activated the door.

"Jesus Christ," Shane breathed. Blood everywhere. No longer floating droplets, as the spin drew the fluids sideways and down. Most of the blood was on Nguyen, unconscious but breathing. Shane knelt beside her, feeling a heaviness that had nothing to do with the increasing gravity or the weight of her frame.

"Medics," Ray said into his mic. His voice caught. "We've got another one."

"Was it Rose?" Shane said.

Nguyen nodded. "I let him in." Her words were barely audible. "Oh my God, I let him in."

"On our way," came the voice on the comm.

"Nguyen, why would he do this?" Shane asked.

"He found out I slept with Carter. He told me – he told me, he said I was sick, to cheat on him with his brother."

"You're not," Shane said awkwardly, and Nguyen laughed at the inadequacy of her attempt at solace. She clutched Shane's frame with bloody fingers.

"Listen – they're cooking up a scheme. Carter told me. Delacort, Martinez, and Hawkes – they've got something going on." She fell to sobbing again, curled around herself, pressing her hands between her legs.

"Where did Rose go?" Shane said. "Nguyen, do you know where he went?"

"He said he was going to kill Hawkes and the rest of them."

Shane felt rage rise in her, pure, clean fury. The Goucher twins, running roughshod over the station. Her station.

"Go get Rose," she told Ray. "But I'm putting an end to this, once and for all."

"What? Shane, what are you doing?"

Shane stood. The comforting pressure of increasing gee steadied her, gave her resolve, like a warm hand on her shoulder. Ray was asking her something, but she ignored him. She started walking, and then, with the help of the exo frame, she began to run.

The news went through the station like wildfire – Rose Goucher had attacked his brother and nearly killed Nguyen. I felt the leaden weight of increasing gee, and my heart compressed with effort, exacerbating my panic. If Rose was on a rampage, I could be next. I struggled out of my sleep sack, casting around for a weapon.

A noise came from the doorway. It was Rose. I think I only had time to widen my eyes when he forced himself through my door, arms splayed. And that was when the wheel achieved gee plus, trapping us like flies in molasses.

Rose strained toward me, his features contorted with effort and rage. I struggled for air, my heart beating hard, working at more than full gee for the first time in years. The klaxon kept on going, the red washing over us. I raised a weak hand, trying to ward off an attack.

The next moment a fizz of electricity sounded and Rose convulsed, going down hard. He hit the floor with a satisfying impact. The cop, Ray, stared at me over his outstretched weapon, the frame of his exo armor bulking him up. Then he knelt and cuffed Rose's hands behind his back. The twin screamed and struggled, but he stayed down.

"Hawkes," the cop ordered. "Get dressed and go to the station. Now."

The station cop doffed his armour and stowed it and then turned to me, gesturing to sit. I obeyed, artificial gravity keeping me in place. The door opened, and Asa came in. We looked at each other and looked away. He was impassive as always, but I could see the strain around his eyes.

"Hey Ray," Asa said. "Can you turn off the gee? My girlfriend's not feeling too good, and this isn't helping. She has trouble breathing."

"Sorry, Ace. It'll take a while," Ray said. He looked at me. "Nguyen said you and the twins were cooking up some scheme. I would appreciate it if you would tell me what that is."

"I have no idea what she's talking about," I said.

He sighed, rubbing his eyes. "Yeah. The thing is, Hawkes, this isn't the first time you've been at the nexus of some shady shit. And Nguyen only confirmed what the A.I. already told us. So why don't you tell me what's going on?" He had the distant look of a man accessing his corneal implant, then re-focused on me.

I didn't say anything. Ray looked at Asa. "Is this about Evangeline?" Asa shrugged. "Ray, let this one go."

"I would love to, Ace. Really. But see, Nguyen is a good kid. Everybody likes her, she organises the Scrabble tournament and the karaoke, and she's good at her job. Yeah, she's into the bad boys, but who isn't? She got hurt. And she says you guys are involved somehow. There's a lot of blood on this station, and if I let this go, I have a bigger problem then you two."

"Arrest the twins. Rose is the one who did this," Asa said.

Ray's voice was as flat as Asa's. "You know that's not an option."

"It's not like it matters, Ray. It's not like you have anyone to report to. Just let it go, man."

"What are you two up to?" Ray persisted. "Does this have to do with Evangeline being sick? How are you all connected?"

Asa's face never changed, but he exhaled slowly, as if it were too much to hold. "We're stealing a rock," he said.

I forced a laugh. "He's crazy, officer. Don't listen to him."

They ignored me.

"Who's the buyer?"

"We don't know."

Ray looked at us for a long time, the ugly fluorescent ghoulishly lights illuminating his face. "You fucking idiots," he said after a moment. "Do you know who you're going up against? Do you think the company is going to let a bunch of goddamn space monkeys steal a fucking rock? You think you can just sit down and steal an entire asteroid out from under the Bifrost Corporation and they aren't going to notice?!" He was screaming now, slamming his fists down onto the table. I flinched with each blow.

In the tumult no one noticed that console alarms had been going off for a while until Asa turned to look at the flashing blue light. Ray's tantrum broke abruptly. "What?" he snapped.

"Unauthorised shuttle launch," came the pleasant voice of the A.I. "Evangeline Martinez has bypassed protocol to take Shuttle B-167 out of dock."

AI

Shane climbed *down* the vertical tube to the control room suspended under the station superstructure, shoulders touching the sides of the tube. The rungs extended below her, the tracklights gleaming off the metal passageway with simulated daylight. In normal zero gee she would have zipped along headfirst, her brain orienting her to think she was going up. In gee plus, she went feet first.

The central nervous system of the station was a huge globe that was suspended beneath the arms. The spider sat in the centre of the web. Shane climbed, not thinking about how she was going to get back, not thinking about how she looked like a tiny fly crawling along a centreline of silk with a giant spider at the centre.

Her mag boots clanged against each rung until she stepped down onto the top of the globe, the airlock at her feet like a watching eye. Even with the help of the frame, she was wheezing by the time she made it. Shane collapsed onto her knees, pulling air into her lungs until finally her heart slowed and her breathing became normal. She slapped at the airlock controls, and the door irised open.

"Hello?" Shane called out, wondering where everyone was. The globe was empty, but there was the hum of machinery and electronics. There was a faint breeze and the smell of organic material, part of the station's power plant. It was incongruous, the smell of shit in this antiseptic place. The globe was lit with UV lighting, but there were no desks or chairs. Just blank walls and floors, in a polished curve of metal, the same color as the floor. The hum came from within the walls; she stood inside the computer system that ran the station. "Hello?" she called again, feeling absurd. Where were the station officials? Where was admin?

A signal came across her contact lens receiver. "Officer Harris," came a pleasant male voice, vibrating slightly in her temple. "Why are you here?"

"Who is this?" Shane said, trying to control the slight shake in her voice. "Where are you?"

"I am the A.I. of Bifrost mining station. I am all around you, everywhere on this station. You might say, I am in your head."

There was the faintest ghost of a laugh, and something flickered behind her eye.

"I need to talk to the people. To admin. The station officials. Where are they?"

"They are not here. Why are you here?"

"I'm here because I need to understand." The A.I. was silent, so Shane pushed on. "Who is protecting the Goucher twins? What is the scheme they've got going?"

"That information is reserved for admin."

Shane wanted to scream. "Answer me! Why can't I arrest Rose?"

"That is up to admin to decide."

"Fine. Let me talk to admin."

"Admin is not here."

"Yeah, I got that. Where is admin?"

"Admin is not here."

Shane rolled her eyes. "Is admin on the toilet?" she said, deeply sarcastic. The A.I. did not answer. Somehow, that angered her more than ever. "Is admin on the fucking station?" she shouted.

"Admin is not on the fucking station."

Shane found she had nothing to say. Her legs collapsed, and she sat down in the center of the globe, in the middle of the floor. *Abandoned. They abandoned us, left us out here. We're all alone.* She folded over, touching her forehead to her knees. Her pulse throbbed, and she made to dose herself, then thought: No. God help her, her heart felt as if it would pound right out of her chest, but she needed to understand. If ever a time there was to be anxious, she thought with asperity, this would be it. She pushed to her feet, shading her eyes against the lights.

"If admin is not on the station, and admin is not here, where is admin?"

The A.I. was silent.

"Are you admin?" Shane remembered arriving, over a year ago now, disembarking from the supply ship that had carried her from Earth to Bifrost in just over eight months. She met Ray, shook his hand, was welcomed on board. She filled out forms. She had not met any station officials or any corporate executives. *I just assumed...*

"I am not admin."

"Are Carter and Rose admin?"

"Carter and Rose are not admin."

"What are they? Why can't they be arrested?"

"They are enforcement."

"Ray and I are enforcement," Shane corrected. "What are Carter and Rose?"

"They are enforcement."

"No," Shane said. "Carter and Rose are violent criminals."

The A.I. was silent.

"When did admin leave?"

The A.I. was silent, then cued up video of a ship leaving the station docking arm. The ship was the *Gagarin-Tereshkova*, a plasma-drive cruise class behemoth that could make the journey from Earth to Bifrost in a blazing six months. The date stamp was 2060, three years before Shane arrived.

Shane sighed, bone weary. Her temples throbbed. The gleaming daylights were painful even on her eyelids. There was so much UV she fancied she could feel the chemical production of Vitamin D on her skin, tingling on her bare arm.

Shane's eyes snapped open. She looked down at her arm, at a tiny artificial spider crawling along her skin. Shane turned her hand, feeling something akin to wonder combined with atavistic, visceral disgust.

"Did you make this?" she asked the A.I.

"Yes," said the A.I.

"What does it do?"

"It creates a direct connection between station administration and my central operating system."

"But admin have all left," Shane said. "Did they – did they connect with you before they left?"

"No. They did not connect."

"Is this why they left?"

"I do not know their reasons for leaving."

"Surmise, then. Guess. Just like you guessed about the name Agnes St. Germaine."

"This is why they left."

Shane nodded. She got that. She really did. Running the station with the A.I. inside your head – that was a deal that the executives of Bifrost Mining Corporation, registered Corporate Citizen Entity had not signed up for. So they left the A.I. to run the station, with nominal oversight by two cops and two brutal miners to keep the peace.

The tiny machine crawled to the edge of her hand and Shane flipped her palm. With a sudden catch, the creature hung suspended by a gleaming line of filament. She gasped. It worked its way back up to her hand. Shane kept turning her hand, allowing the creature to crawl over and over on the same track, from the side of her hand, over her palm, and between her fingers.

"Who is Agnes St. Germaine?" she asked, while she played with the mechanical spider.

"That information is reserved for admin," the A.I. said. "Would you like to be admin, Shane Harris?"

Did she want to be admin? To not just have access to the server, but to have the A.I. in her head? To have the answers to all her questions?

To be the spider at the center of the station?

She licked her lips, trying to figure out how to ask the question. "Do you know about me?"

Do you know how close I am to system failure?

"I know about you, Shane Harris."

Was it her imagination, or was the A.I.'s voice kind?

Shane didn't say anything. She just lifted her hand and let the spider do the rest.

Evangeline

The turning wheel wound down to stillness as the gravity lockdown was nullified. Ray, Asa, and I hustled to the shuttle dock, taking giant, disorienting leaps as null-gee was restored. The shuttle bay was locked, and the crew was buzzing in the control room, working the computers to gain access. Evangeline had not been playing around.

Ray's eyes flickered. "Status?" he said to Control.

Control shook his head, strain around his eyes. "Yeah, she nailed the system good. A localised virus – the control room is separate from the rest of the station for just this reason. We think she got in using a virus on an old thumb drive."

I opened my mouth to say something and found I had nothing to say. Asa's thumb drive with the initial coordinates for the rock – from Evangeline's computer – had carried the virus. Even then Evangeline was planning her big day. And I was the fool who got her in.

"Where's she going?" Ray said, leaning over Control's back and looking at the console.

"We think she's heading toward this rock," Control said. Asa bent over the console, his long fingers flickering over the touchscreen. We gathered around, and there it was in beautiful grayscale, a lovely, large, M Class asteroid with a long serial number beside it, even bigger than the one we sent to the buyer. Of course. Evangeline was the best spotter on the station. But what was she doing with this rock?

What did a dying woman want with her share of five hundred million dollars?

"Twelve hours out," Control said. He played over the touchscreen, and brought up the shuttle, a tiny flickering triangle inching its way toward the target. "Yeah, she's heading there. But where is she going to push it?"

I think they all saw the answer in my stricken expression. "Here," I breathed. Evangeline was going to smash the asteroid into the station.

It was simple enough. Set the rocket bots with a pre-programmed charge. They would steer the asteroid toward the station, while the station continued its path through the asteroid field, until the deadly rendezvous, calculated to be about a month hence. We could divert the station but diverting the station had a cascade of implications. Divert the station, and we would use up ungodly amount of fuel, which meant that we would be at a deficit for normal operations. Then the supply ships would have to expend their fuel accordingly to make a new rendezvous point. Divert the station – and the extensively calculated route through the asteroid field would have to be recalculated, at great expense. The corporation would go bankrupt. Would they try to salvage their investment or rescue the crew?

I had a sudden, vivid image of the spider sailing off beyond Jupiter with one thousand dead miners on board.

Evangeline Martinez was going out with a bang, and she was taking the Corporation – and the rest of us – with her.

I felt the nudge as the docking catch released, and we slid from the shuttle bay. The stars blazed eternal, and Jupiter hung somewhere off my shoulder. I shifted the viewscreen to Bifrost, now below and behind me, and it hung there, bright, illuminated, the great curve of the wheel rising above the bulbous station core and giving it its name. Bifrost, the bridge to the gods.

It took the cutting team about six hours to get through the door into the shuttle bay. I was about half a day behind Evangeline and wouldn't be able to catch her, but I was closer to the rock than she was, now that she had set her rockets to move it our way. While her plan was to unleash the power of her rocket bots to move the asteroid to intercept the station, adding my own bots would boost the asteroid even more. By the time the station travelled along its pre-ordained path, the asteroid would have already moved on, into the black.

The proximity sensor pinged, jerking me out of my reverie.

Control's voice came over the mic. "B-132, was that a ping?"

"Affirmative. Visual shows nothing."

Then another ping and the computer voice. "Danger. Debris in red zone."

"Hawkes?" Control said, chucking protocol.

"Just a minute, Control." I tapped commands into the console, orienting the cameras to look for the debris. The cameras activated the viewscreen.

Evangeline. Her eyes were open and she looked straight at me, before she grew small and then smaller, disappearing into the distance. The void had called, and Evangeline had answered. She'd drift forever now, just another object in the belt. Immortality for a dead woman.

From the silence over the comm, I knew that the control room had seen what I had seen. I did some rough calculations, then oriented the viewscreen where I expected to see her shuttle. There it was, on a return course and coming in fast.

I am not particularly quick. It took me long seconds to understand the implications. When I did, I cued the comm and sent them my findings.

"Control," I said, "We have another problem."

There was a silence, then, a flurry of voices, all against station protocol. I heard Control yell, "Quiet!" and then he said, "B-132, turn around. Make a course for the station. We'll need you to intercept."

I flew under a constant burn, running calculations until I knew to a second how much time I had. Evangeline's shuttle was a steadily pulsing blip on my screen, and mine was rocketing toward it, closing the gap. No matter how many times I ran the figures, it was going to be too close. We might avoid the collision with the asteroid, but we'd be hard pressed to evade a shuttle programmed for the station centre.

As the hours crept along, I listened on the comm as Bifrost personnel evacuated the arm and began the process of uncoupling the substructure. Frozen couplings, badly maintained controls – all of it thwarted the best efforts of the engineers to cut the damn thing loose.

"Come on you guys, come on," I said in my lonely cockpit. Control never answered. I think they all knew that I was exhorting them, not judging.

Finally, the familiar structure hove into view – blinking lights and blank spaces where structure blocked out the stars. And there, coming in fast, was Evangeline's shuttle.

"Guys, I've got eyes on B-167," I said. "Getting in my suit and letting her rip."

"Godspeed, Hawkes," said Control.

"Yeah. Thanks."

I double-checked my course, got into my suit, ran through the safeties, and then entered the airlock.

Suited or not, no one had ever exited a shuttle going at this speed. I ran over in my head what I needed to do. I programmed the suit rockets and gyros to stabilise me after exit, but there was no saying they would be able to work at this velocity. I would probably be torn apart. If I weren't, I would be flung far away from the station and they would never find me, and I would die in space.

"Fuck you, Evangeline Martinez," I said, and hit the button.

When I regained consciousness I was rotating wildly, my helmet filled with blood and bile, the suit cleaners doing their best to suck away the liquid. I couldn't see much so I closed my eyes again, tried not to throw up any more, my eyes tearing from the pain. But I was alive, and with every spin I slowed, until the rockets and stabilisers finally got control, and my spin became gentle. Every breath brought sharp pain to my side. My nose, broken and swollen, pressed against my faceplate.

But the suit held. I had oxygen, pressure, rockets, and stabilisers. I could see the flashing of my suit's automated beacon across my faceplate, the radio wave signal narrowcasting my position to the station, and receiving another signal in response from Bifrost. I was twenty-five kilometres out, and my automated finder aligned itself along the signal, the rockets pushing me toward home.

None of it was good enough; I had a spectacular view of my failure. I floated off the shoulder of the station, a tiny pinpoint of organic material among the stars, as my shuttle slid into Evangeline's, just as it hit the shuttle arm, increasing the intensity of the impact. I closed my eyes but I couldn't turn away as the explosion washed across my faceplate.

Bifrost Mining Station, 2065

Spider

Five more people died in the collision and explosion including Asa and Ray, and the station lost months of productivity, with a conflicting flurry of orders from corporate. Rebuild finally started – grudgingly, Shane thought, as she half-expected Bifrost Corporation to cut its losses and let the station go. Instead, corporate named her Station Head, and told her to fix everything.

Shane watched from Admin Control as the supply ship *Hohmann* slid away from the station, carrying three passengers – Hawkes and the Goucher twins. She had let them go. In a few months they'd rendezvous with InterSol authorities. She was rid of the brother miners at last.

The A.I. was in her head, and the data streaming to her corneal display was a constant murmur of intelligence. The spider nestled just inside the bone over her left ear where it could most easily transmit. Its presence had the added benefit of stabilising her inner ear, providing the governor that she had been missing for so long. After long years of panic and shame, Shane Harris was finally at peace.

Beside her, Ray flickered, a faithful hologram, restored from years of recorded data of his life on board the station. "Did you ever find out who Agnes St. Germaine is?" Ray said, and Shane smiled, because it was exactly something that Ray would say. Everyone on Bifrost had something they were running from, except for Ray. He was always meant to be here.

"Yeah," she said. "Turns out your program knew what it was doing all the time."

Agnes St. Germaine – one of many aliases of the mystery buyer based on Mars, who was even now making the same rendezvous with Hawkes, the Goucher twins, and InterSol.

It was still a delight, finding out how the A.I. worked with Ray's program. It took the code and made it predictive, intuitive; it plotted intersecting trajectories of people who didn't even know they were on a collision course. There were ten billion people in the solar system and the A.I. used all that data to map where they were going to be, spinning filaments of connections between each one, shining lines of data that pulsed with each connect and disconnect. It was beautiful, and it was Shane's.

She was admin. She was home.

Hell: A Rescue Mission

It's said that we're all going to hell in somebody's religion. I have this friend who is legitimately the best person I know. I might have had a bit too much to drink one night when I thought, "She's not going to hell on my watch!"

A fluorescent panel was out on Floor 12 of Memorial Hospital, so the hallway was both dim and lit with a ghastly glow. I was not immune to the metaphor as I walked toward the darkness to Jenna's room. This was the dying floor; at least, that's what we – Jenna and I – called it.

The door to her room stood open. A cheerful quilt covered Jenna's slight frame, her dark hair and yellowing complexion in direct contrast to the white pillow. A monitor beeped a mindless countdown.

I knocked on the doorframe. "Hey," I said, voice soft, just in case she was sleeping. But she turned to look at me, and a smile lifted her lips, chapped and pale.

"Hey, Trudi. How you doing, baby girl?" she managed.

"Just swell, Jenna. You?"

"Oh, you know, dying." She dropped her voice to a conspiratorial whisper. "Don't want to make anyone feel bad, but I don't think these doctors are very good at their jobs."

I snorted. "Want me to complain to management?"

"Don't think it will help any," she said.

"Might as well have a cold one, then." I showed her the six pack of Genesee, and she laughed without sound, the way animals do. I grinned to hide the heartbreak. You used to be able to hear Jenna laugh from the other side of the room. Her laugh was raucous and obnoxious. I'm not gonna lie; it was an annoying laugh.

Right then, I'd have given anything to hear it again.

I sat on the edge of the bed and held her hand, and she squeezed but as if her muscles had all gone to air. I cracked open the can and handed it to her, but she only sipped for form's sake. Her eyes closed, and I drank my beer, and sat with her, holding her cold, bony hand in my life-filled, warm one.

These last few days, I was her only visitor. Six months ago, all our friends came, thronging her room, giving her kisses, telling her she would beat this thing. Fewer and fewer showed up when it became clear she was not going to beat this thing, and now, it was just me. We fell into a habit – I'd bring beer, she'd pretend to drink, and I'd drink three or four, and we would tell jokes, make fun, or I'd watch her go silent. I don't think she slept. I think she just faded in and out, in preparation for the final fade.

Sometimes I couldn't wait to leave and go back to the world of the living. Sometimes I had to force myself to come, resentful that she was making me do this. Sometimes I didn't come at all, the way everyone else had stopped coming, because dying was hard for the person doing it; it was hell on the rest of us, and all the jokes and bravado couldn't make up for that fact.

Today was one of those times; the times when I wished I hadn't come. I was bored, resentful, and couldn't she just get it over with already? I took another sip of beer, hating myself for thinking it, wanting nothing more than to get to the grieving part.

How can I miss you if you won't go?

"I'm going to hell, Trudi," Jenna said.

I almost dropped my beer. "What?"

She lay with her eyes closed, but tears leaked out the corners. Her nose was red and she sniffed.

"Promise you won't leave me," she said.

I put both hands on hers. I knelt by the bed. She opened her eyes to look at me, and the whites were yellow, creepy. I shivered, hid it with an encouraging smile. "I won't leave. I promise. And you aren't going to hell. What are you talking about?"

She sighed, and it looked as if she relaxed. "Okay," she muttered. "Okay. I need to go now."

She slept then, and I watched her in the gathering twilight, drinking my beer, wishing for a cigarette. She slept, and the monitor kept its soothing beat. A nurse came in to check, and we nodded, regular to regular. This was his usual shift – mine too, basically. His name tag said M. Frazier.

"How's she doing?" he asked me.

"Well, she's still dying, if that's any help," I said. I cracked open another can, handed it to him. He waved it away, but with a quirk of his mouth, like he got the joke.

"It's hard," he said. He gave me a look. "How are you doing?"

I sighed. "She's still dying, that's how I'm doing."

He hesitated, then leaned against the wall, arms folded. "What do you want to know?"

"How much time does she have?" *How much time do I have?*

"It's not long. She's sleeping a lot and she's eliminating less. That's a sign."

"Is she in pain?"

"We're managing it as best we can, but yeah, sometimes, the morphine can't keep up."

"Her eyes are yellow," I said.

"Her liver and kidneys are shutting down."

"Every time I visit, she says something like, 'I've got to go.' I don't know if she has to pee, or what?"

He nodded. "It's common for people at the end. They say things like that, or they say they're lost and they need a map. Not to get too woo-woo about it, but it *is* a final journey."

I took a breath. "She says she's going to hell."

He nodded again, and he went over and patted her shoulder, an expression of compassion that made my throat fill up with tears.

"She's scared. Just do what you're doing, just be with her."

He left us alone, and I drained my beer, and then I went home.

Jenna's funeral was in the church she left the minute she finished college on her parents' considerable dime. The casket was closed, a silent presence up on the dais. When we filed past to pay our respects, I had a wild urge to lift up the lid and make sure Jenna was really in there. I could imagine her trying to hold back her belly laugh, but letting it loose when we made eye contact.

I let out a snort, and I had to pretend I was crying.

In the funeral procession I kept thinking how much more fun it would have been if Jenna was in my Honda Civic with me, creeping along with the lights on, laughing about the whole thing, hanging out at the bar afterwards. Then it hit me that she was not ever going to come back. I could never tell her about my nightmare. She wouldn't be able to laugh about her own funeral. We could never talk again.

Those are the rules, Trudi.

Well, fuck the rules, I thought. Just because I'm alive and you're –

"I'm in hell."

I almost hit the car in front of me and slammed on the brakes. I looked reflexively in the rearview mirror and saw the startled driver behind me, but for a second I saw Jenna in the back seat, and I couldn't breathe.

She didn't look too good.

A gentle toot of the horn from behind me, and I fumbled my car into gear and moved forward again, only this time I could feel my heart squeezing itself in a frenzy of adrenaline. My black dress stank with flop sweat, and my hair stuck to my forehead.

What was happening to me?

At the graveside, people were giving me strange looks, probably because I had almost caused a multi-car pileup in a funeral cortege and I looked like the aftermath of a three-day bender. Jenna's weird friend, I could imagine them saying. A bad influence. Jenna and this – Trudi, is it? Jenna never married, you know. So beautiful, could have been a model, so smart.

All Trudi's fault.

And they were right. All of it. Instead of getting her law degree and making the perfect marriage and having the perfect children, Jenna devoted her life to making sure that I, the perennial fuckup, got out of bed, kept a job, broke up with bad men, got off hard drugs, ate reasonably well, and while I would never be a pillar of society or set the world on fire, all I had to do was make Jenna laugh her stupid obnoxious laugh, and in turn, I was her mission in life. Me. Stupid, impulsive, dumb-ass me, was the reason that Jenna Wilkins could not possibly be in hell.

And now she was dead, and I was seriously losing it. Jesus Christ, Trudi, I could imagine her saying. It's been less than a *week*.

I stayed in the back while the final words were said and a few hymns were sung, and then her family threw clots of dirt on the casket, poised above the pit on the lowering device. The sun was going down, and people left, first the family, then friends.

Then I was the only one there, except for the cemetery workers. I was back far enough that they ignored me. When everyone else had gone they began dismantling the props. Down came the canopy and chairs. They rolled up the fake sod and put it back on the truck. And then they began to ratchet the casket into the grave.

The first thing I heard was a groan that sounded both human and unnatural. The workers shouted and scrambled back. With a crack of metal and canvas straps, the casket plummeted into the rectangular pit, landing with a crash. The ground shook, and I almost lost my balance and fell on my ass.

When everything settled, I ran forward to look. The workers peered in too. They were speaking in soft voices, some in Spanish, and a couple of guys crossed themselves. The casket was canted sideways, the lowering mechanism crushed beneath it. I imagined Jenna tossed around inside the box, maybe lying on her side. Maybe her eyes had opened. Would the eyes still be yellow?

"Ma'am," said one of the workers. "I think you should go. We'll take care of your sister."

I didn't correct him. "Thank you," I said. "Thank you."

I walked away, sat in my car, now alone in the parking lot, and went to turn the key. I hesitated, then deliberately looked into my rearview mirror. Nothing to see there, just the back seat, the rear window, and the cemetery in the distance, the flurry of activity around Jenna's grave.

"Jenna," I said. "Are – are you okay?"

There was no answer.

With a shaking hand, I stabbed the key at the ignition, started the car, and drove away.

It was 5:45 pm, almost shift change at the hospital. I waited across the street, leaning against the stone rails of the pedestrian bridge, and smoked. I was still in my funeral clothes – black dress, tights, puffer coat. A few people glanced at me as they scurried by but, you know, a sad person smoking outside a hospital isn't such a strange thing. There were one or two of us, each wrapped in our own grief.

I recognised Nurse Frazier by his height and his bulk, first silhouetted against the bright hospital lights and then a dark shape coming toward the pedestrian bridge. When he got close, tucked into his thick jacket over his scrubs, I called out, "Frazier!"

He stopped, looked at me. It was dark except for a streetlight but I could tell he recognised me after the shock of hearing his name. I said, "I'm Jenna Wilkins' friend. The liver cancer in 1214."

He came over. "No cheap beer? I'd take one tonight."

Instead I handed him the pack of cigarettes. "Do nurses smoke?"

"We do all the vices," he said, and took one.

We both leaned on the stonework, and looked down at the creek, flowing sluggishly the way city creeks do, flush with trash and sewage. Stygian, I thought.

"Jenna Wilkins' friend," he said. "Do you have a name?"

"Trudi. Do nurses have first names?"

"Mike." He took a drag, and recited. "We did everything we could. She was taken care of at the end. She went peacefully." I hoped Mike didn't play poker, because the slight hesitation was a pretty strong tell.

"Well, I don't think she did, Mike."

He looked over at me, and now I could see him recalibrate. Men don't have to assess strangers the way women do, and that goes double for big men. I could see him thinking, *shit*.

"Remember when I told you she said she was going to hell? I think she might be right. There's been a lot of weird shit happening that makes me think something is bad. Real bad." He didn't say anything for a long time. It was hard to see his reaction, but I can tell when someone is thinking. "When she went, did anything different happen?"

He sighed, a mix of resignation and cigarette smoke. "You can't tell anyone I told you this, okay?" At my nod, he went on. "Listen, toward the end, your friend had enough morphine in her system to stop everything. But she fought, man. She was in pain, you couldn't even imagine, and we kept trying to get the pain under control, but it was like she was fighting the morphine and she was fighting the shutdown of all of her organs. She should not have been able to do that, but she did."

A passing delivery van rumbled down the street behind us and we both turned to look – a grocery van, with its bright red fruit painted on the side. When I turned back, Mike's expression was bleak.

"She didn't want to go, and in the end, we made her."

I surprised myself with my little cry. Jenna, fighting for her life, because death was worse. She asked me not to leave her alone, and I did. Now she was in hell, and I should be there, in her place.

Mike fished in his pocket. "This was left behind in her room. I didn't find it until I went to check on the new patient. I didn't know what it meant at the time, but I kept it. Pretty sure it's for you."

It was a scrap of white fabric, torn from a hospital sheet. There was something written on it. I pulled out my phone and shone the screen on it.

T R U D I

The letters were jagged, but they were Jenna's lopsided script. She'd written me plenty of notes, left on my car.

Where were you last night? We gotta talk.

Trudi, don't be mad. Please call.

Trudi, I need you.

There was a faint impression of more letters. I angled the phone. HE

TRUDI, HElp.

"Why would she be in hell?" Mike asked. "She didn't seem like a terrible person."

I said, "Except for the lying and drugs and boyfriend stealing and murder, I guess she was all right."

His involuntary laugh coincided with his realisation that I wasn't kidding.

"Where were you last night?" Jenna shouted at me over the dj. We were dancing, grinding up against each other, hair and makeup and short tight dresses like every other girl in the club. It was so hard to hear it was a private conversation.

"Nowhere," I shouted back.

"You were at Jason's, you asshole," she corrected. She was furious.

"You stalking me now?"

"I just know when you're lying. You're never *nowhere*. You're always with him. I swear to God, Trudi, you're like a –"

I pushed her before she could say *dog to vomit*. She stumbled backward and fell, and her eyes flew wide, her red mouth open, and for a second she flashed everyone her cootch. She scrambled to her feet, yanked down her dress, and stormed off in her high heels. I watched her go, feeling defiance and anger and loss.

Three days later I lit a cigarette and stared up at her building, the key to her condo in one hand, the crumpled note she left on my windshield (*Trudi don't be mad please call*) in my pocket. Of course she wanted me back. Who else could she fix if it wasn't for me? That's why she kept sending me notes, kept reaching out.

I was tired of being her project. I was tired of being the person who she could feel better than.

I let myself in to her apartment, and sat in the living room, helping myself to her stash and the gun, and waited.

Jenna came out first, wrapped in a silk robe, her dark hair falling around her shoulders, and then Jason came after her, naked and pudgy, but still cute. They stopped dead.

"Fuck," Jason said, eloquent as ever.

Jenna didn't say anything. I think she saw my hand on the gun before he did. His eyes got real wide when the situation registered.

"Trudi," Jason said, his hands out to me. "Listen, I'm sorry, babe. I'm real sorry. God. And you're best friends too. I'm such an asshole."

And then he turned and ran back into the bedroom. From the sounds of it, he shoved a chair under the door and started dressing with great haste.

Jenna sighed, and sat down next to me, took the gun and put it in the drawer under the coffee table. She rolled herself a joint.

"Couldn't you have just left him alone?" I said. "I liked him, Jenna." I was weepy.

She kissed me on the top of my head. "I know you did, babe," she said. "But you know I'm just looking out for you."

We could hear more stumbling in the bedroom, the sound of the window being opened. Jenna lived on the second floor, so it was conceivable that Jason could survive the jump.

"Listen," he shouted. "I'm going. And I'm breaking up with both of you."

We could hear sounds of effort, some curses, and a not quite Geronimo shout. And almost instantly the screech of brakes and a thump, and screams. We looked at each other and ran to the picture window, craning our necks to see. People gathered around a Pom's Groceries delivery truck. The shaken driver stood by the open cab, cell phone in hand. What looked like a pile of dirty laundry was crumpled under the front wheel, the red blood like the red fruit on the side of the van.

Jenna's parents got her a lawyer and a ruling: death by misadventure. As almost an afterthought, they made me irrelevant; I was never there. As ever, my presence only complicated things.

I didn't see her for a year after that.

The notes on my windshield dwindled. I moved when my lease was up. I made sure that none of our friends told Jenna where I was. Six months ago, I went out to my car to go to work, and there was a note, as if nothing had changed.

I felt a flutter of anticipation in my belly as I unfolded it with shaking fingers.

Trudi, I need you.

I didn't tell Mike all of that – just the high points. When I finished, we smoked and looked into the turgid creek. When he finally spoke, he was reflective.

"We see a lot on Floor Twelve. Sometimes, even the woo-woo stuff can sound real."

"Like asking for a map," I said, remembering what he told me. He nodded.

"Yeah. Sometimes people even say they know the way. Dying people."

He let that sink in. I looked at him, at his dark face in shadow, only the light glinting off his eyes.

"Are – are you saying that someone knows the way to hell?"

He nodded. "She's in room 1214, too, can you imagine that?"

"Can you take me to her?"

"Why? What're you gonna do? Bust your friend out of hell?"

"If I can." I sounded like an idiot, but the more I thought about it, I was like fuck it. Jenna was sending me all these messages. I could help *her*. Finally. I looked over at Mike. "I know you think I'm crazy, but I also know you told me all of this because you say it's woo-woo, but you believe it too."

"I don't –"

"Yeah, you *want* to, though. Take me in there, Mike. Show me the road to hell."

"Map."

"Map to hell, then." I put my hand to my heart, unable to resist. "I only have the best of intentions."

He gave me an annoyed look. But he brought me back into the hospital.

The patient in Room 1214 was even frailer and more of a husk than Jenna had been. She was a tiny old lady, with scraggly hair and blue fingertips and mottled, papery wrinkled skin. Mike slipped us inside the room and closed the door.

The lights were low and the steady beeping of the monitor was the only sound.

"Can she hear us?" I whispered. At my words she turned her head toward me. Her eyes were the same yellow as Jenna's. I shivered. This wasn't jaundice. This was pure malevolence. "Ma'am," I quavered. "I'm sorry to bother you. But if you had a second –"

She opened her mouth. All I could see was blackness. And then she giggled.

It was a child's giggle. I stepped back, fumbling for the door handle. It turned, and that comforted me for a moment. I could still leave. It was okay. I gathered courage and turned back.

"I want to save my friend. I want to save Jenna."

The giggle turned sickly sweet. The old lady pushed off her covers. She was bony and naked underneath, her remaining breast as flat as an empty pocket.

I pressed on. "Mike said you know the way."

"I am the way."

The sound came from her mouth but the voice was Mike's. He reached out and restrained my arms and legs, starfishing me, one hand under my jaw so I couldn't cry out. The old woman in the bed got up and came over to me, so I could smell every last putrescent bit of her, and she swallowed me whole.

I fell to the ground, gasping. I was trembling so hard I thought my teeth would break. There was a foul wind and it was freezing. Cold day in hell, I thought, and clamped down on a giggle.

I couldn't see at first but I could feel: rocks and dust scraping my knees and palms. I was naked, and the cold wind raked my skin. The darkness waned and finally came a grey dawning. I was able to stand and look around.

I was on a craggy field, littered with rock and dirt, and there was a glow in the distance. Grey storm clouds massed all around me. As if I were watching myself from above, I could see my small naked body on the vast plain. There was no sound but the scraping of my feet on the rocks and the wind wailing around me.

"Jenna!" I shouted. The wind tore the words away. I filled my lungs again, and screamed her name, but it was futile.

I began to trudge, arms wrapped around myself. With every step, the rocks cut my bare feet, leaving thin rivulets of blood in my wake. I aimed toward the glow on the horizon. It wasn't sunlight, but rather a milky colour, like the sun on a distant planet. To keep my mind off the pain, I talked to Jenna, my teeth chattering.

"You idiot," I told her. "What were you thinking? Why did you bring me here? You think I'm going to sympathise with you just because of the cancer? How about all the shit you did?"

How far had I come? It felt like hours. I looked behind me, and saw that I had barely moved ten feet from where I landed, tiny bloodspots staining the rocks. I kept going.

"Poor Jenna, she got cancer. Poor Jenna, needy Jenna, always had to be the centre of attention. Poor little rich girl Jenna, stealing my boyfriends! I should have just left you here! I should have never come after you!"

I picked up a rock and threw it wildly. It landed a few feet in front of me, and I howled with fury, that I couldn't even throw a rock in hell. I'd been walking for hours and my throat was sore from shouting. I turned to look behind me to see how far I'd come, and I was a few feet farther along than the last time I looked.

"Okay," I said. "I get it. It's not a metaphor. I'm not getting anywhere. Fine. I'll stay here, and Jenna can come to me."

"Hey," she said, standing in front of me. She was wearing her silk wrap, and she was kind of dead looking, but otherwise, she was still Jenna. I stood there, naked and shaking, teeth chattering. I was so surprised that I said the first thing that popped into my head.

"How come you get to wear something?"

There was the slightest flicker of amusement in her eyes as she handed over her wrap, exposing her cancer-ravaged body. I tied it around me, self-righteously.

"Are you really being tortured?" It sounded accusatory, but I couldn't help it. I thought she was being tortured. Right now hell wasn't great, but it wasn't torture.

"What do you think, Trudi? It's hell. Yes, is the answer. I'm being tortured right now."

"Okay, well, let's get out of here."

She sort of shrugged and fell in next to me. "Where to?"

"Uh, home?" As soon as I said it, I realised what an idiot I was.

"I don't think I can leave," she said. "I'm dead."

"Well, thank you, Captain Obvious," I said, nettled because I hadn't thought this whole rescue through. The implications of what I'd done hit me. I knew I wasn't going to heaven, but I thought at least I would have a few more decades of denial before I had to face the same fate as Jenna. I suddenly had to sit, the silk wrap no match for the freezing rock.

She sighed, and sat next to me. She squinted up at the pallid sky. She looked at me. "Trudi, why are you here?"

"You asked me to come. You said you were going to hell, and then I got a whole bunch of signs that yeah, that's where you were, so I decided to come and get you."

"I don't know what to say," she said.

"'Thank you?'" I said. She gave me a Jenna look. "Oh fuck you," I said. "At least I tried."

"This what you call trying? Jesus Christ, Trudi. Are you stupid or what?"

I was sick with sudden fury. "If I'm so stupid, why did you stick around?"

"Because I thought I could make you love me!" she shouted. "I tried, Trudi! God knows –" she choked a laugh – "God knows I tried like hell to make you love me. I did everything you ever wanted, and it was never enough. 'Jenna, help me get a job. Jenna, help me get a guy. Jenna, score me some drugs. Jenna, Jenna, Jenna!' Poor little rich girl Jenna, how you despised me and used me at the same time!"

It was all true. "I didn't," I managed. "That's not – that wasn't –"

There was a sound. It sounded like groaning, deep and from the centre of the Earth. It sounded like the worst pain in the world, and I felt it deep inside me. I looked at Jenna, and I could see her fear.

"What is that?" I whispered. She turned her face away from me and she looked so despairing that I shuddered.

"Management," she said. "Go, Trudi, before you can't."

I wanted to but I couldn't. Jenna crumpled to the ground, and I did the only thing I could. I crumpled on top of her, her silk robe covering us both, only our arms and legs exposed, as if we were a single, squashed spider.

I had the lowering impression of something *questing* over us. It lingered, the intensity of its regard a force heavier than gravity, flattening me to Jenna until I thought she would break, she was so brittle. *Please*, I begged. *Please*. I didn't know who I was praying to. I wanted to fling myself upward, screaming. *Get it over with!* Jenna threaded her fingers between mine and held me down, and I focused on the pain, feeling invisible thumbs pressing at my eye sockets, bruising my internal organs, searching in my private places.

It was hours later before we could move again. We separated painfully, as if we were one entity breaking apart. We sat up, looking at each other. I stank of pee, clammy on my bare thighs. Jenna stank too. She looked worse than before.

I was losing her.

We spoke at the same time.

"You have to go," she said.

"Come with me," I said.

"Trudi —"

I grabbed her hand. I concentrated on her face. That was still Jenna-like. Almost. "Listen to me. You have to come with me. We can do this. I know you're dead. I get that, but this whole thing — me being here. If I can do this, Jenna, don't you see? You can come home, and we'll figure it out." I turned and pointed. "See? It's just right there. It's right there."

Not ten feet away was a half-lit fluorescent glow. The hallway to Room 1214. I could see the door ajar, a steady distant beeping coming from the monitor, a beacon drawing me in. I got to my feet and pulled her up. There was something wrong about her face now, but I refused to notice. I was cajoling, drawing her along step by step, and she was coming with me. "Come on, we can do it. You got this, Jenna. We'll beat this thing."

We closed in on the hall, and hope leaped within me. I kept up the chatter. "Five more steps, come on now. Four. You got this, Jenna. We're almost there."

And then we *were* there, standing on linoleum tile smelling of chlorine, the steady *beep beep* of the monitor just beeping on as if nothing were wrong, and I gasped in relief and triumph and turned around to look at her.

I had just enough time to see the hope in her eyes die.

I felt it then, the deepening malice, the focus of it. It had found us again, and now it was *interested*.

"No," I said. I pulled her. "No! Jenna, Come on! COME ON!" I tugged and tugged, and though we had just been on the threshold of Room 1214 now it was impossibly far away. I would have run too, except that I quailed at the thought of trying to cross that barren field as the malevolent presence turned towards me. I thought about reaching safety again, only to have it snatched away from me at the last second, for an eternity. I couldn't bear it. I was too weak. Let me stay, Jenna, I wanted to say. *Please. Please.* Please don't leave me alone.

"Trudi," she said. Her voice sounded different and I looked at her, really looked at her, and the final gift she gave me was the truth. She was dead, she was death, she was corruption and decay. I averted my eyes, but a part of me was defiant. A small part maybe, just a spark, but it was enough for me to reach out and hold her dead body against mine, seeking to warm it. The scent of death made me gag, but I kissed her cheek. It warmed beneath my lips, then my lips iced over and I tasted blood as I pulled away. Her eyes were bright with tears, but even as I registered that her expression transformed sharply into malice.

"*How can I miss you if you won't go?*" she mocked, and I ran, chased by the raucous sound of Jenna's laugh.

Three weeks later I stood at her grave in cold wintry drizzle. Her granite headstone was slick with rain, and the engraved letters and numbers were sharp-edged and meticulous. A couple of small stones were perched on top of the marker. There was no sign of turmoil below the surface. I laid the bouquet at the base of the grave and stepped back. I waited for words to come, but when you've kissed your best friend good-bye in the bowels of hell, there wasn't a lot more that needed to be said.

And then I went back to my car and got in, shoving aside some of the stuffed bags that had fallen from the passenger side into the driver's seat. I checked the maps app on my phone. I knew better than to think I could outrun hell, but I couldn't just stick around and let it come for me. And it was coming for me. Every night the old lady in the hospital visited me in my dreams, promising me what was to come. I saw her around every corner, in every mirror, standing behind me. Sometimes she looked like Jenna, sometimes like Mike, but the message was plain. Hell was coming for me and would have me when it wanted. My only hope was to keep running until I could figure out a plan. Hell, if I lived long enough, maybe I could even become good.

Out of reflexive habit I looked in the rear-view mirror, but all I saw was the back seat, piled high with my stuff. I pulled out of the cemetery parking lot, and looked left and right for oncoming traffic. There was a Pom's grocery van barrelling along, and I waited for it to pass. The flash of red fruit painted on the side was brighter and more hyperreal than I remembered, and for a second I was distracted, wondering if the driver was the same and all. Whatever. I was in a hurry. I had a map and I had to go.

Pigs and Peaches

When I sat down to write this story, I thought I was exploring a post-apocalyptic hellscape, in which people lose what little humanity they have and descend into madness. Nah. It's really to answer the question, "What are zombies really *saying?"*

"So have you girls seen Terri yet?" the old woman called, popping out of the kitchen. Rachel and Ellie froze, Ellie with her hands behind her back like a schoolgirl, to hide the handgun.

"You know," Rachel said. "We haven't yet. We're, uh, looking forward to seeing Terri."

Ellie nodded vigorously.

"She had a boy, did you hear? Nine pounds, two ounces. After you have dinner here, you can go visit her in the hospital."

The old lady popped back out of sight behind the door, and Rachel and Ellie looked at each other, Ellie's face full of exaggerated alarm.

"Shit," Ellie said, laughing.

"Shhh," said Rachel. She wanted to get out of there. It didn't help that Ellie was in one of her moods, deceptively amiable. Her eyes were too bright, her fingers twitching.

"Okay, okay. Don't freak." Ellie set the gun down on the roll-top desk and started leafing through papers, muttering with disgust. Dividing her attention nervously between her and the kitchen, Rachel tugged at the knob on the glass-fronted china hutch. The door stuck. Dim figures lurked behind the glass, porcelain clowns and cloisonne boxes. She tugged harder, her fingers numb and clumsy.

"This sucks," Ellie said. She dropped a pile of papers back on the desk, and the whole stack tilted and cascaded to the floor. Ellie kicked it, sending papers flying across the carpet.

"Ellie," Rachel said, rising exasperation in her voice.

"What?" Ellie said, all innocence. She held out her hands. "It slipped." She made a face at Rachel and went back to ransacking the desk. Without looking at Rachel, she said acidly, "Feel free to help."

Screw you, Rachel thought. She tugged again at the glass door to the cabinet and it flew open with a rattle. A china dog fell over with a loud clatter.

Behind her, Ellie said, "Hey, Rachel, I have news for you. They are not going to put their ration cards in with the little clownsies and puppy dogs."

"Yeah, well, I'm not looking for ration cards." She turned back to the cabinet. Her mother's china hutch had been dark stained walnut like this one, with the treasures of a lifetime tucked away in the dark and dust. Her grandfather's ring. Her mother's pearls. A diamond stick pin. Lost twice, once in tangled plaques caking her mother's brain, and again when the house and its contents were sold after her mother's death.

She reached back into the farthest corners, grimacing as she encountered nothing but dust balls. Ellie was right – she wasn't going to find anything in here.

"Have you girls seen Terri yet?"

Startled, Rachel bumped her head on the shelf before she could get out of the hutch. She turned around, rubbing her head. The old woman had come out again, a cold casserole dish held in kitchen mitts. This time a vee of worry marked her forehead between her grey brows, but her voice trundled on. "Did you hear –?"

"Yeah yeah, a baby boy," Ellie said. "We heard. Come *on*, where do keep the ration cards?"

Tears sparkled on the old woman's cheeks. "So, have you girls seen Terri yet?"

Ellie looked at Rachel and shook her head. "I *hate* Fast A." She drew the handgun and cocked it, pointing it at the old woman.

"Ellie," Rachel said.

"I mean it. We just want the goddamn cards. I don't see that bitch Terri coming around here. Come on. The ration cards. Credit cards. And the car keys while you're at it. Might as well."

"Ellie, you can't shoot her."

"Why not?"

"Because you're not that kind of girl."

Ellie turned to look at her. She actually did kind of look like that sort of girl, Rachel had to admit – wide-eyed, short dark hair askew, low-rise jeans, tank top. Sun-kissed freckles across her nose. Manic eyes.

"Since when?"

"Since always." Between them the old woman whimpered. Rachel sighed. "Look. Why don't you look upstairs, see what you can find. I'll have a few words with her, and see what she can tell me."

Ellie lowered the gun sulkily. "She's not going to tell you anything. Not when she's looping." But she stomped up the stairs anyway.

Rachel looked over at the old woman and went and took the casserole dish from her. It looked like she had stirred together tuna, ketchup, and breadcrumbs. "Come on," Rachel said. "Let's sit at the kitchen table."

The old woman sat hesitantly, flinching at every loud sound from Ellie's upstairs rampage. Her eyes were clouded with cataracts. Rachel set the dish aside. On the table was a stack of ration cards. Rachel slipped them into her pocket, then put one back. Don't be such a wuss, she could almost hear Ellie say, and she sighed and picked it back up again.

While she dithered, the old woman folded her hands in her lap. Her fingers were gnarled and curved, the knuckles swollen. Rachel set down the cards and smoothed the grey hair off the woman's forehead. She kept stroking, and the old lady relaxed, her eyes drooping.

"Shhh. Shhh. It's all right. Tell me your name. What's your name?"

"Ni-nine pounds. Nine –" Her voice trailed off.

Sometimes touch could interrupt the looping, make a person seem almost normal. Sometimes nothing could be done. Rachel kept stroking, on the off chance that she could get something useful.

"Wow. A boy, right? What did she name him?"

The old woman smiled and just like that, it was *hello honey, I'm home.* "Carl Joseph. Carl was so proud. He wouldn't admit it, but he was. Our first grandbaby."

Rachel froze. She had a husband. Was someone else in the house? *Ellie's up there alone.* She probed tentatively, risking losing the woman. "Where's Carl now?"

"He's at the summer house."

She let her breath out. Not here then, if the woman could be trusted. "Really? Do you want to go see him? We could take you there." Maybe if they told the woman they would drive her there, she would give them the keys to the car out front. It was covered with dust and the tyres were low, but they had peeked in and the gas gauge showed half full. A car and ration cards – that would be a haul.

"Summer house," the woman said softly. "Our own secret garden." She closed her eyes and smiled. "Amid all the pretty pigs and feaches."

"Do you want to go there?" Rachel said again, trying to tamp down her impatience.

"Oh, the things we did there," the woman said, rocking a little. "It was our private place." Her smile became wicked. "The things we did there." She leaned forward and whispered in Rachel's ear, her breath so rotten Rachel had to turn away.

"That's sweet," she struggled. "I'm sure you were quite, uh, something in those days."

"The things we did there," the woman said. She lifted her hands with difficulty and pulled back her matted grey hair in a travesty of wantonness. Muted sunlight from the clouded window glinted on diamonds in her ears and at her throat. "The things we did there."

Oh. My. God. For a moment Rachel forgot to breathe. The diamonds were dots of brilliance against the woman's faded skin.

"Shhh," she whispered. She stroked the woman's forehead again. "Just sit nice and quiet now, okay?" She began to unscrew the posts from the woman's ears, her fingers thick and clumsy. "Shhh." The old woman's eyes followed Rachel's hands as she put the earrings in her own ears, each one making a tiny prick of pain. Just to try them, she told herself. I'll give them back.

*

She was clasping the necklace around her neck when a thud from upstairs caught their attention. The old woman looked up, for an instant wholly normal. For a moment there was silence and then Ellie's rising wail.

"*Rachel?*"

Rachel bolted for the stairs. She went down the short hall first one way, saw nothing, and ran down the other end. She stopped in the open door. Ellie stood there, pointing the gun, her hand shaking so much the gun wobbled. Her eyes were huge, her breathing coming in shallow gasps. She turned to look at Rachel and the gun aimed itself at Rachel's heart. Rachel thought she would stop breathing. Instead, she took a step sideways, bumping into the door, and reached out and took the gun.

"Elena?" she said.

Ellie pointed into the room. "I think we found Terri."

The woman sat in a white rocking chair, the rocking chair creaking as she pushed back and forth, back and forth. She held a small soiled bundle in her lap, and her bright birdlike eyes locked onto their presence.

She sees us. Rachel began to back away under the woman's bright gaze, drawing Ellie with her. Ellie made to speak but Rachel gave her a warning shake of her head. The old lady was one thing. She could still be soothed, the virus dormant.

In her daughter it had reached full flower.

Rachel tugged on Ellie's elbow and backed her out of the door, and the woman turned to gaze down on the bundle as if she had forgotten them. Rachel let out her breath.

"Holy shit," Ellie said, voice shaking, too loud in her fear and relief. "Did you see what she was holding?"

The woman's head whipped back up to look at them. Her face went mad.

Rachel pushed Ellie out of the room and slammed the door shut, holding the doorknob with one hand, the gun with the other. From the other side of the door she could hear a moan and a thud. The door shuddered as the woman tried to get out.

"Shit!" Ellie said again.

"Run," Rachel said. "Just run. I'll hold her here."

A noise behind them made them turn around. The old woman had come up the stairs behind Rachel, holding the rail and stumbling.

The hall was narrow – they would not be able to get past her.

The door shook again. Rachel tightened her grip. She raised her voice to the old woman. "Go back. Go back to the kitchen."

"Su – summer," the old woman said. "Hou – hou –" Then she said, "Pigs and feaches."

"What the hell?" Ellie said.

"She's gone. Last stages," Rachel said. She raised her voice. "Go. Back."

Stupid. As if enunciating would help. She steadied the gun. "Cover your ears, El."

"Pigs and feaches!" the old woman insisted. Her voice broke.

My God, Rachel thought. Is she crying? She lowered the gun and looked closer.

"Rachel!" Ellie screamed. The door pulled from her grip and Terri pushed it open, lumbering out before Rachel could slam it shut again. Rachel squeezed the trigger and put three bullets into her. The reports banged sharply in the confined space. Terri slid down the wall, her clawed hand just missing Ellie's ankle as she fell. Ellie jumped.

"Feaches!" screamed the mother.

"Do it," Ellie said. "Dammit, Rachel."

Rachel steadied the gun and fired one more shot.

The old woman toppled over in mid-feach.

They ran.

They clattered down the stairs, bursting through the front door with its faded quarantine poster. The dusty old car waited next to the sidewalk, its tires sagging. Rachel and Ellie jumped down the stone stairs leading from the front door to the street, holding on to each other.

"Okay," Rachel said. "Okay." She forced herself to breathe, to stop repeating herself. "Are you okay?" she asked.

Ellie nodded, breathing hard. She gestured and Rachel handed her the gun. Ellie put the safety on and then put the gun in her belt.

"So, no cards," Rachel said. She heard her voice shake and thought she wouldn't say anything for a while. She sat down on the stairs and Ellie sat with her.

It was a fine autumn day, slightly chill. No one else was on the street. They sat at the top of a hill, the street sloping away from them, a row of narrow townhouses riding the contour of the land, every one of them with a quarantine poster tacked to their front doors. Rachel rubbed her fingers – they had gone numb again. She was glad she had been able to hold the gun and fire it.

"Where did you get those?"

Rachel started. Ellie looked at her, her dangerous brightness muted. Rachel touched the necklace self-consciously. She shrugged and got to her feet, trying to ignore the icy sweat that trickled between her shoulder blades. "I dunno. Listen, I want to check out one more thing." Ellie said nothing. Rachel flushed. "It'll only take a minute." She had to return the diamonds. *Shit. What have I done?*

Ellie waved a hand, looking out over the street. "Whatever."

Rachel left her sitting in the sun, a small figure in the deep stone steps. She didn't want to go back in the house. Instead, she followed a flagstone path to the side of the townhouse. A wooden gate hung ajar. She pushed it open into the shaded back yard. The stone path led into an overgrown garden, weeds and grass springing up between the flagstones. Fig trees, their leaves rounded like puzzle pieces, bent over the path and she had to push the heavy branches aside. The garden opened up, and a twisted grove of peach trees, whip-thin branches scraping the ground, surrounded a stone birdbath.

At the back of the yard stood a small screened house, barely larger than a gazebo. The summer house. *The things we did there.* So this was where the old woman screwed her husband. Despite herself, Rachel grinned. She followed the flagstones straight to the little house. The screen door hung askew, the wooden framing weathered. She strained to see inside and could make out some furniture.

"Did you kill them both?"

Rachel whirled around. Carl?

A skinny old man stood in the peach grove at the bird bath. His clothes were worn, but neat – faded jeans, a work shirt. Boots. His beard was grizzled but trimmed. Still, for good measure she looked down at his hands. He followed her gaze and gave a wry smile.

Shit, she thought. He didn't have Fast A, but that could be worse. More dangerous. He was old, sure, but he was far from frail.

He gave her his own frank appraisal, and she flushed. She remembered the things the old woman had whispered.

In the silence, he nodded at the door to the summer house. "Go on in. Not much to see."

She hesitated, then acquiesced. She pushed open the creaky door and stepped inside.

The floor was a dark wood, stained by time and weather where rain came in the screens. A few bugs scuttled off into dark corners, and it smelled of deep mildew. It was much cooler inside.

An old brass bed took up most of the little house. It had linens on it and was neatly made. He slept here, then; the house was for his wife and daughter.

The door creaked open again and sprang shut.

"How did you keep them from coming out here?" She asked.

"I think she knew not to." He was right behind her. "The more I've seen of it, the more I think they're still in their heads. They just can't get out."

Rachl remembered the old woman's catch in her voice when she stared at her over the gun.

"You just want to believe that," she said. "That they're still in there."

"What do you believe?"

She lifted her shoulders, trying to sound offhand, though her heart beating very hard. She was very conscious of his closeness. "It's Fast A. Once the plaque destroys all the connections, that's it."

138

She imagined the virus racing toward her brain with every beat of her heart, ready to encapsulate her neurons in its own genetic material. Fast A. Super-Alzheimer's.

"So you can just kill them. Convenience or mercy?" Before she could answer, he gestured toward the bed. "Have a seat."

She thought of herself in that bed, with him, doing the things the old woman had done, feeding her own desire. Her heart thundered. She sat down on the bed, and drew off her boots. He hesitated only a second before sitting down next to her, drawing her dark hair through his rough fingers until it hung loose around her face. He pushed down the straps of her thin tank top, dropping a kiss at her breastbone. She lay back and he pressed himself against her and they sank into the old mattress together.

They took their sweet time, and when they finished, lying together in a sweaty tangle with the cool evening air wafting through the summer house, she drifted into sleep.

She woke in the dark, shivering, sweating. She was thankful she was lying down; she felt dizzy.

He muttered something.

"I have to go," she said. "My friend's waiting for me." She didn't really think so; Ellie had probably given up and gone on into town, where there was a safe house for the uninfected.

Rachel sat up slowly, letting the vertigo recede, and collected her scattered clothes. She dressed and he watched her, propped up on one elbow.

"Mercy or convenience?" he said at last.

She stopped and looked at him. "I did shoot her, and I'm sorry for that. But Fast A killed her long before I did."

She sat down to put on her boots, but before she could move away, he reached out and touched her ear, his finger sliding along the earring. She froze.

"Do you know what one of the first symptoms is? Increased sexual appetite. The virus wants to spread, and the best way to do that is to increase proximity to hosts."

"I don't have —"

"When she got infected, she told me she wanted to remember this place. She knew she didn't have much time, so she remembered what she loved the most – here." He gestured. "Our summer house in its grove of fig and peach trees. When I saw you at the gate, I knew she had told you, and I knew she had remembered. She gave you these, didn't she. Her gift – she gave you —"

He was crying. With clumsy fingers, Rachel took out the earrings and pulled hard at the necklace, snapping the thin chain. They fell to the floor with a soft tinkle. She pushed blindly toward the screen door, stumbling a little. It screeched open and banged shut behind her. It was dark in the garden, the flagstone path a pale glimmer, and she had to fumble at the gate latch before it would open.

The front stoop was empty. Rachel began the long walk down to the town.

She was shivering hard by the time she reached the business district. Her throat was sore, her fingers stiff. She stretched and clenched her fists, and the stiffness eased a bit. She had to find Ellie. She had to tell her – she didn't know what she had to tell her. *Hello, I'm in here. Don't shoot.*

She didn't know how much time she had. No, she thought. I can still think. I can still reason. To prove it, she looked up at the street sign, illuminated by a fading electric light from a nearby store. She could barely make out the words – she was at Brookes and Highland Avenue. "All right," she said out loud, her voice shaking. "Fi-five blocks to the safe house."

If they would let her in.

They have to, she thought. They have to. I have to tell Ellie. The old woman was able to remember the two most important things. Rachel knew she could do it too. She concentrated on the words she needed, imagining herself forming new neural connections as the virus wove itself around the old ones.

Someone screamed and Rachel jerked up, but they ran before she could see what they were screaming at. She hurried.

She fell a couple of times – her feet didn't work right. She broke out into a sweat – she could feel it matting her hair. Her fingers finally curled up into useless fists. Damn it, she thought. I need to find Ellie. I have to tell her.

Something hit her, and Rachel fell to her knees, crying out. She put up her fist to her stinging head and pulled it away. It was wet and sticky. She wiped the blood on her shirt and got up shakily. Stop, she wanted to say.

All of a sudden people were everywhere, shouting at her. Another rock hit her. Light flared from flashlights, and she held up her arm, wincing. Where's Ellie? she tried to say. Ellie!

She scanned the crowd, trying to see through the glare, forcing the words to come out. Ellie! "Fi–fi–" No. That wasn't it. She had to find Ellie before it was too late.

"Rachel?" She spun clumsily. Ellie looked at her. "God, Rachel. No. No. Not you."

Ellie, listen. Listen. You have to listen. I'm still in here. "Figs-fig-fi –" Rachel forced herself to stop.

Ellie was crying. She pulled out the gun. "No Rachel. No please, go away."

Listen. I'm still here. And I love you. I keep you sane, remember? You keep me crazy. And this has nothing to do with us. I will go with you, wherever you want. I won't touch you, I won't infect you. Because I can control this. I swear it.

Dammit. It was important and now she couldn't remember what she wanted to tell Ellie.

"Stop saying that!" Ellie aimed the gun. "Please Rachel. Go away."

She sent me to him, and I went. And oh God Ellie, I have so much to tell you. What she said, about pigs and feaches, she meant *figs* and *peaches*. Peaches, Ellie. The summer house in the grove was where they made love, and she sent me to him as a gift. Please, Ellie, listen to me. I love you so much. Fast A is just a part of it.

The sound of the safety clicking off rang like a shot itself in Rachel's ears. She almost wept. Up until this point, Ellie had the safety on. She wasn't going to shoot. She didn't want to shoot. Rachel could still convince her. Rachel stumbled forward, hands outstretched. See? They're fists, I closed them like that so I couldn't touch you or hurt you. I can't hurt you. I'm harmless.

The first shot dropped her and she stumbled and sat down, blinking, staring up at Ellie, who was screaming until her voice almost disappeared. "Go away! Go *away*! Goawaygoawaygoway!"

The pain spread in Rachel's chest. It was hard to breathe. She concentrated with the last of her strength.

Ellie fired again. The bullet exploded through the tendrils of plaque, for one single bright instant throwing Rachel's brain into sudden clarity. She looked straight at Ellie and said, "I'm here, Ellie. I'm here."

Blood on the Snow

An homage to M.R. James. Because who doesn't love a good wolf-were story? That's right: I said wolf-were.

The moon shone down fiercely on the sparkling snow, and shadows from the forest's edge stretched across the field. The Malchik waited just inside the wood and scented the air. Blood. His eyes narrowed at the hot, thick odour, and his mouth flooded with water.

The Malchik bit back the howl that welled up from his throat, the effort bringing tears to his eyes. Will triumphed over instinct, but the reek of blood pulled him out of the safety of the trees and sent him toward the field.

Dead stubble, the remains of autumn's harvest, crackled under his footsteps. The crust of snow was dusted with the fine powder of a late night snowfall. He saw movement, and froze, his mouth hanging open.

Silhouetted against the moonlight, a small beast flopped awkwardly, rising to three feet and then sprawling back into the snow. It was a she-wolf. One paw was twisted in a clawed trap, and she had gnawed at it in hopes of freeing herself. At his approach she lay back in the snow, panting, her pelt a non-colour in the moonlight. Droplets of blood pocked the snow around her.

The Malchik saw the surrender in her eyes. He swallowed hard to get his voice working. "No," he said. "Not this night. I kill not, this night."

A shiver ran through her at his words, a shiver that all wild animals suffer when a human speak, for of all beasts only humans speak through their mouths, instead of properly, through their skin or their touch.

Not-beast, her trembling told him, and he flinched, for it was true. The Malchik took off his cloak and wrapped her in it. With the wolf subdued, he pulled the jaws of the trap away from her paw. She yelped in pain, and he had to bite his lip to keep from howling in return. Carefully he allowed the metal jaws to close on air, then tossed the ugly thing aside. He gathered up the shivering bundle and set off for the woods.

Firelight spilled from the cracks in the door and walls of his little house. It was barely more than a lean-to, made of uneven logs lashed together with old cloth and shaggy bark. It had taken the Malchik many months to construct the rude shelter, and months longer to conquer his fear and master the art of firebuilding. It was just adequate for his needs, keeping him warm and protected against the weather. He even came back some nights when the moon was dark. The Malchik shouldered the door open and laid the little wolf on the packed dirt floor in front of his firepit.

Despite all beasts' fear of flames, she seemed to welcome its warmth that night, just as she suddenly seemed to trust his good intentions. He cleaned her paw gently, bathing it in warm water and bandaging it with a rag that had once been the sleeve of a fine, linen shirt.

She lay in front of the fire, staring into the flames with wise eyes. He brought her water in a stone bowl that had been shaped long ago by the pounding of the river, and some red, raw meat of a luckless rabbit he had run down earlier that day. She lapped the water but only nosed listlessly at the meat.

The Malchik squatted on his haunches, watching her.

The little wolf put her nose on her paws, one black, the other swathed in its linen glove, and closed her eyes.

He too felt himself dreaming in the shanty's heat, and his eyes closed, pulled shut by the moon's fall toward the horizon. With great effort he shook himself awake, for it would not do to stay past moonset; he did not know what would happen to the creature he had taken such pains to rescue. The Malchik yawned and opened his eyes – and could not believe what he saw upon his hearth.

The moon went down and the night turned black.

Vasa Vasiliayevna woke, disoriented. She sat up stiffly. Bright daylight flooded the little lean-to, hurting her eyes. Tidy piles of snow, neatly sifted, gathered at each of the shelter's gaping cracks. It was very cold. Vasa clutched the heavy fur cloak around her body, and only then became aware of the pain in her hand. She looked at the bloody bandage, memory coming back in the shape of hazy images.

Teeth in the snow. Pain! Two-legs not wolf.

She could remember no more. When the moon went down, the barrier between her beast-self and woman-self was a fortress wall. Only in the hours when the full moon rose or set did the fortress become a veil that she could see through to the other side.

Vasa pushed back her tangled red-brown hair with a shaking hand. This was not the first time she had been injured during her transformations; she had always trusted herself to get out of any scrapes.

But this time, evidently, she had not rescued herself.

She wondered if her rescuer thought he had left a she-wolf on his hearth – or if he knew what he had rescued.

When he comes back and sees I am no beast, I am lost, she thought and staggered to her feet. The huge cloak, heavy and unwieldy, enveloped her thin form from head to toe. Her sharp face peered out from the hood. She longed for the comfort of her house in town.

Vasa crept from the lean-to. The snow stung her bare feet, and a sharp wind tousled her hair and snatched at the cloak. She wrapped the garment tighter around herself, wishing she had not slept so long past dawn. I'll have to creep in through the garden, she thought, and slip up the back stairs, past the maid's room. Laria would be busy at her chores, and in any case she had instructions not to bother her mistress until she was summoned. Vasa looked around for watchers, saw none, and began to run awkwardly through the deep snow.

Saw none, but was observed nonetheless; yellow eyes from a stiff tangle of dead brush watched her flight.

She kept to the woods that ran along the wide road, ducking behind the slender birches whenever she heard the measured cadence of carriage horses and the gay bells of their harness. Once a regiment of Cossacks galloped past, their uniforms a flash of red against the landscape. She had to stop several times and sit in the snow, wrapping her poor bare toes in the thick warmth of the cloak before she could go on. By the time Vasa reached her garden her feet were swollen and purple. She could barely climb the back stairs to her bedroom, and she did so weeping with pain, hoping that Laria had kept to her orders and had not gone looking for her.

Giving a sob of relief she closed the door to her chamber. With her last bit of strength and presence of mind, she pushed the tell-tale cloak underneath her ornate bed and crawled into her featherbed. She was shaking with a chill and exertion, and she could barely raise her hand to ring the bell.

Laria's soft knock came moments later.

"Good morning, mistress," she said briskly, setting down the tray. Then the maid looked more closely at her and her jaw dropped. Vasa looked back at her miserably. Her thin nose was red, and she was sobbing. Her hair, a soaking wet mess, clung to her head.

"Laria," she choked. "I feel most unwell."

The maid closed her mouth.

"I should say so, mistress," she said stoutly. She bustled over to Vasa and laid a hand against her cheek. "You've taken a chill and I don't doubt you have a fever, ma'am. Let me get you some English tea and a plaster for your chest."

"And please, Laria, a warm brick for my feet – they are quite cold," Vasa said humbly.

"At once, mistress." The maid hurried away to gather her herbs, the noxious plaster she used for colds, and the footwarmer. Vasa could hear her calling for the undermaid to make up the fire in the mistress's chamber, and she snuggled down in her great warm featherbed, the soft sheets taking away the chill of her wild run through the woods. Warmth overcame her, and she sank into sleep.

Just before she lost consciousness, the question that had been niggling at her came fully to the fore – if she was rescued by a man, as her dim memory told her, why did her wolf-mind recognise him as *wolf?*

Vasa slept.

Snow fell on Vasa's garden, hissing softly in the night, muffling the sharp outlines of the gazebo, the hedges, the small statues, and the trellises until all shapes were muted, softened, blurred. Light from a sparkling chandelier spilled through the drawing room windows.

Through the hissing snow could be heard snatches of music from the piano and bits of merry laughter and conversation. Figures passed briefly in front of the window, all unknowing they were performing for an audience of one, and then disappeared, their part dispensed.

To the Malchik they were as remote as a dream. He waited patiently, his long-legged frame almost indistinguishable from the shadows of the pines at the edge of the garden, watching the window. Snow settled on his grey-black fur and he did not shake it off.

Waiting for her. He whined a little in his throat and his ears flattened against his head. His yellow eyes narrowed.

She-wolf. Beast-human. She was *she. He* was *wolf.* It was all he needed to keep him waiting in her garden with snow heaping up on his back.

Vasa held court from the cream velvet settee, wrapped in a grey robe that accented her reddish hair and pale complexion. One hand was wrapped in a clean linen bandage. She smiled, her small, pointed teeth gleaming in the light. For a moment all her guests were arrayed before her, their backs to the tall drawing room windows, broad shoulders silhouetted anonymously against the cheerful light.

In the garden, a low rumble split the soft hissing of the snow. The Malchik's lips slid away from his teeth, and the hair on the back of his neck rose.

Wolves do not count as we do, but they count nonetheless.

He. He. He. And he.

They were gone. Vasa sighed and got to her feet. It felt good to move about. The doctor had warned her against too much activity after her ordeal, and gravely she had agreed with him, acceding to his face what she would defy behind his back. She arched her back and stretched.

Moonless nights always made her restless. She bore with her suitors out of politeness, and amused herself with dreaming of transforming before their eyes and seeing their astonishment. Though the doctor worried her; the way he looked at her so speculatively made her wonder what, if anything, he knew. The doctor could be her enemy, more so than the peasants who sprinkled wolfsbane at her gate and made the sign of evil behind her back. The doctor was intelligent.

She was closing the drapes when her gaze sharpened, and she stopped and looked out the window, trying to see beyond her own reflection in the glass and the tiny points of candle flame floating in the darkness.

For a moment the veil pierced, and she knew he was out there.

She frowned, her white brow wrinkled, and brought up one slender finger to her lips. With a sudden decision Vasa ran quickly to the study, brushing by Laria without even a nod. The maid watched her disappear down the darkened hallway, shrugged, and went on her way to clean up the drawing room.

Comfortable even in the dark, Vasa pulled out a sheet of writing paper from the desk, dipped her pen, and hastily scrawled out a note to the doctor. She cast a hasty scattering of sand across the paper and rang the bell while waiting for the ink to dry. Laria appeared silently in the doorway, waiting for her mistress to acknowledge her. Vasa finished folding the letter into a small rectangle, sealed it, and blew on the wax to dry.

"Have a stable boy deliver this to the doctor," she said. "If none can be roused, please take it yourself. It is quite important."

"At once, mistress," the little maid said, her face giving away nothing, and she bowed her way out of the study.

It was a test only, to prove her suspicions were wrong, Vasa assured herself. The stable boy was in no danger. It was the dark of the moon, after all. And he, whoever he was, had rescued her, bandaged her hand – she thought of the heavy cloak, hidden in her wardrobe. No danger, she repeated silently as she rubbed her good hand absently against the plush material of her robe.

The men in the garden gathered silently around the torn body of the stable boy. Blood was everywhere. It had melted the snow around the body until grass poked through and glistened frozen and red on the yew trees and the trellis. The statues were spattered with it.

The stable boy still gripped the letter, crushed now and unreadable as the paper ran with blood and ink.

The major bustled up.

"What do you think?" he demanded of the doctor kneeling at the side of the body. The officer wore no hat and his hair gleamed dully in the bright, grey light. Steam puffed from his mouth with every word. He too had been a guest of Vasa's the preceding night.

The handsome young doctor shook his head and got to his feet.

"You can take him away now," he told the servants, and they wrapped up the stable boy in a horse rug and carried him off.

The doctor's eyes were strained and he drew the major near. "What do you think?" the major asked peremptorily.

"There may be – problems," he said, his voice low. "The stable boy was killed, as best as I can tell, around the time we left Mistress Vasa's last night."

The officer stared with horror at the doctor.

"Surely you don't accuse one of us!" he hissed. "Damn it! This is the act of a deranged man."

"One who can open a locked garden gate?" the doctor asked colourlessly. "Or scale a twelve-foot wall? The strength of the lunatic is well-documented but this surely is beyond the pale."

"What do you suggest, then?" the major said.

The doctor put up his hand to his chin.

"One thing is curious," he said, musing on the bloody scene. "The moon was dark last night."

The major stared at him.

"Nonsense," he blustered, but his voice made it clear he did not think it so much nonsense. "You call yourself a man of science, sir! Those are old wives' tales, and nothing more."

The doctor smiled suddenly.

"Yes, yes, Major! And, as I said the moon was dark. Whatever we are dealing with, it is an imperfect lunatic at best."

He turned to go, and the major said suspiciously,

"Where are you going?"

"To see if our hostess heard or saw anything." The doctor paused, observing his rival. "Coming?" he invited. The major grunted and followed.

When the two men were shown into the drawing room, she received them with trembling hands. Her face appeared thinner and more pointed than before, her eyes dark and haunted against her pale skin.

They accepted tea and sat stiffly on the spindly chairs.

"Did you hear anything last night, Vasa Vasiliayevna?" the major asked as gently as his martial manner would allow.

"No – no, nothing," she said, her voice quivering. She buried her face in her hands. "I thought I saw something in the darkness after you all had gone. Ever since I got so dreadfully lost in the woods, I've been frightened, and so I sent the boy with a letter to the doctor, to give me something to help me sleep."

The major looked annoyed that *he* had not been called back; if the doctor felt triumph he gave no sign. He took his patient's hand.

"It's all right," he said gently, his smile reassuring. "I can give you something for tonight. It is my fault I did not think of it sooner."

Vasa looked from one to the other, the fair, heavyset major and the slender doctor with his chestnut hair and pointed beard.

"Who would do such an awful, awful thing?" she whispered.

*

That night the two men dined at the small hotel, taking one of the small dining rooms, and enjoyed its peace and privacy in the company of a fine rack of lamb and a French wine.

"What do you know about her?" the major asked, filling their glasses. The major was fairly new to the region, his regiment having recently been assigned.

"She is rich, beautiful, eccentric – what else is there?"

The major snorted. "I listen to the villagers. The grooms, now – best intelligence in the village, though they're nothing but superstitious rabble. No, I've heard the tales. I want you to tell me what you think."

"I am beginning to think there is no such thing as superstition."

"Surely you don't believe – that. Though she's damned odd, I'll grant you," the major said.

The doctor raised an eyebrow. "I thought you were my rival," he said dryly.

The major laughed. "Beautiful is one thing, rich another, but the eccentricities –" he shook his head. "Besides, how long have you been wooing her? I think she likes to keep us all dancing on a string."

The doctor toasted his perception. "She does. She does not intend to marry any one of us. Boris, Anton, you, or me – we mean nothing to her."

"So what brings you back?"

The doctor swirled the golden wine in his glass, staring into the miniature reflection of the firelight on the curved surface of the crystal. "I go to study. Her and us."

"I'm not sure I like that," the major said shortly. The doctor laughed.

"That's all right. The question is, what have my studies found?"

"All right." The major eyed him keenly. "I'll bite."

"If the moon were full – I think she could have done it."

The words hung between them over the table. The major opened his mouth to damn himself but left the curse unspoken. "You amaze me, Doctor," he said at last. "I had not thought you a superstitious man."

The doctor held up a hand. "Be very clear about one thing, Major. I conjecture only. I will not condemn her for my suspicion."

"A man died –!"

"In the dark of the moon, Major! Whatever she may be guilty of, if she is what I suspect, she is not guilty of this!"

They were standing almost nose to nose over the table but their voices, though vociferous, were low. At the doctor's words, they sat back. Finally the major said,

"The maid would know. Can't hide a thing like that from the servants."

The doctor shook his head. "She's close-mouthed and loyal. Believe me, I've tried."

"Just confirms it, then." The major leaned back in his chair. "But as you say, the moon was dark. Do you think someone else knows and is trying to cast suspicion on her?"

"You know this injury of hers? She took a walk in the woods two weeks ago, she said, and got lost. She fell and put her hand in a fur trapper's snare. Got herself loose and ran home."

"Two weeks ago," said the major, "the moon was full."

The doctor toasted his perception. "If it had been her foot, I could see how she could get herself free. But her hand – impossible."

"Got lost in the woods – but ran straight home," the major added thoughtfully.

The doctor nodded again. "So the only way for her to have got free is if someone helped her."

"Someone who may have thought he was freeing a –"

The door burst open, and Anton stumbled in, despite the desperate efforts of the servant to keep him out. The wine merchant's eyes were wild and his hair was a tangled mess.

"For God's sake, Doctor!" he cried. "Boris is dead! Just like the stable boy – his throat has been torn out!"

"Vasa Vasiliayevna," the major said, his blustery voice reined in to sound patient but fretting under the restraint. "I beg of you, for your own safety, you must leave."

"Major, I have never spent a day away from my own home in my life!"

She was aghast. The doctor hovered behind them, almost invisible beside the imposing, bluff figure of the officer. He stroked his pointed beard, watching keenly as the two argued.

"We know only that this – this madman – has killed twice, both times men connected to you! He may be seeking to rid you of all protectors before he attacks!"

She paced quickly back and forth, her steepled fingers underneath her chin, her amber eyes flitting to and fro. Suddenly she stopped and whirled on him.

"How much protection would I have if I left my home?" she asked. "Your entire regiment, Major? And what then? Would this attacker cut down each one of your men to get to me? Would it not be safer for the villagers to decamp instead? I am, after all, only one."

"They already are," the doctor said dryly, stepping forward. He nodded toward the window. From their vantage point in the study, they could oversee the main road of the town; in twos and threes, guiding donkey carts and pulling stubborn cattle, people were hastening from their homes.

Vasa smiled. "There. You see?"

There came a discreet knock, and Laria, crisp and efficient as always, came in with a tray of tea things, an English custom of which their hostess was fond. The doctor watched as the major eyed her speculatively, but they all were silent as she bustled about, laying out the tea cups and setting up the tray for Vasa. Then she bowed herself out. The major roused himself.

"Well, then," he rumbled. "Should your servants suffer for your stubbornness?"

Vasa smiled and sat gracefully before the tea table. The men followed suit, and she began to pour.

"She is loyal and would never leave me. The others, though – I will free them to follow the rest of the villagers. But you, Major, must order your men to protect the townspeople on the road."

"I will do, mistress." He selected a cream cake and sat back, the tea cup a dainty, fragile thing in his broad hands. The doctor looked more at ease as he leaned forward, his long slender fingers easily holding the tea cup.

"Mistress Vasa," he asked, now that the major was preoccupied, "How is your hand?"

She smiled and raised it up. The bandage was gone, elegantly replaced by a white glove. "Quite well, Doctor, thank you. Your remedies as always are successful."

"You were badly injured," the doctor pressed. The major threw him a quick look. "I trust your maid – Laria, is it? – to follow my orders, but I think I should take a look at your hand once more."

"I am grateful for your concern, Doctor, but I don't think that will be necessary. More tea?"

"No, no thank you." He took a quick sip, set down his cup. "I have much to do to prepare for the evacuation. You will let your servants go, will you not?"

Her lips pressed together and then she smiled, the split second of irritation fleeting.

"I will. All except Laria. Gentlemen –" She stood and once again they followed her obediently.

They conferred briefly on the cold, scraped walk before moving on. Their words sent out puffs of steam.

"Is she watching us?" the major murmured.

"No doubt. No doubt wondering how rivals should become thick as thieves."

"Blast it," muttered the major. He drew his collar up against the cold. "What have we achieved through all this except to arouse her suspicion?"

"Oh, if she is guilty, she already knows we are onto her. If she is innocent – all we have done is express our concern."

"Mmm." The major was silent for a few moments. "Why that, about her hand?"

"If she had shown it to me, we could have gone home right then," the doctor began. "There would still have been the mystery of Boris's and the stable boy's deaths, but she would not have been involved."

"I am a soldier, not a clever man," the major said. "Explain your reasoning."

"She wears a bandage not to protect an injured hand – but to conceal one that has already healed."

The winter twilight yielded sullenly to dark. It was bitterly cold, too cold even to snow. The village, mostly emptied of its inhabitants, stood silent. Usually lamplight or candlelight gleamed from behind the shuttered windows or smoke rose from the chimneys; now all was lifeless and frozen, with two exceptions; the doctor's house, and, across the street, Vasa's.

The doctor and the major peered out at the darkening street from behind the heavy drapes in the doctor's study.

"What did Anton say when you told him to flee?" the major asked without taking his eyes off the view. A heavy pistol drooped from his right hand.

"He said I was a fool to stay, grabbed his money box, and jumped on his horse."

"He might be right about that," the major said. He glanced back. "We are fools."

"Perhaps. The real fear I have is that we are actually safe."

The major laughed.

"I had not thought you a daredevil, sir!"

The doctor's next words chilled his amusement.

"That is not what I meant. I mean, what if this killer – beast, madman, or some confluence of the two – has followed the villagers? Your regiment, for all its strength, will not be able to deter this creature from its quarry. And in the meantime here we stand, with silver bullets in our pistols and looking like fools hiding behind curtains."

The major paled, but he added stoutly,

"If you had truly thought that, we would be on the road with the others."

The doctor's thin shoulders lifted carelessly.

"I think I have chosen correctly. But I have to look at all the possibilities to make sure I have not missed something."

"So who do you think we are looking for? The girl? Anton himself, perhaps? Or has the head groom marked us for death?"

"It won't be a man, whatever it is. Or a woman."

The major began to bluster.

"Now you are splitting hairs, Doctor!" he said angrily, gesturing with the pistol. The doctor looked at the wildly waving weapon and withdrew a few prudent paces. "Of course it is a beast, a terrible, unnatural beast! But it will walk on two legs, and converse as we do, and before I send a bullet into its heart I would like to make sure I have killed the right creature!"

"We are looking for a wolf."

The major's mouth hung open. He snapped it shut, and swallowed.

"There is no moon," he managed thickly.

"No, and that's curious, isn't it? We have all along been thinking this is a werewolf, of course, for such is this creature's modus operandi. He stalks a female, follows her home, and methodically begins to slaughter her suitors. The stable boy must have stumbled on him in the garden on his errand. But as you said, Major, *the moon is dark*. Werewolves do not kill when the there is no moon. They walk about like you or I. No different from you or I."

The doctor paused in his lecture to glance at the major's pistol, now still. He drew aside the drape to cast a quick glance at Vasa's house. Satisfied there was no change in its silent aspect, he resumed.

"I have often speculated that if we humans, through whatever means, can be caused to utterly transform from rational creatures to slavering beasts, then what of its corollary? Are there beasts that become humans in much the same way as our unfortunate brothers become creatures of the night?"

The major's brain appeared to have stopped working.

"Were-human?" he asked finally, his tongue thick and confused.

The doctor smiled.

"Well, etymologically speaking, I think it might be better termed *wolf-were*."

"Then – we are looking for a wolf."

The doctor's smile widened to a pleased grin, and he clapped his hands lightly over his pupil's successful lesson.

"Indeed, Major, so we are!"

"And here he comes," the major announced, after another reflexive peek behind the drape. The doctor was nonplused for only a second, then he grabbed the other side of the drape, positioned his body sideways, and looked out.

Darkness had almost completely fallen, and so it was difficult at first to pick out the long-legged animal mincing through the snow. The major's eyes were keen and he was able point out the wolf to the doctor. Both of them dropped their voices as if the wolf could hear them two storeys above.

Its stiff-legged gait carried it to Vasa's house. As if guided by some vestige of rational thought, the wolf walked straight down the empty street confident it was alone. It must have seen the villagers decamp, the doctor thought, and understood what that meant. Just as a werewolf takes on attributes of the beast it becomes, this *wolf-were* had adopted the thought patterns of a man. *Would it try to speak if I got its attention?* he wondered. He started to open the casement latch to hail the animal.

"Are you crazy, man!" the major hissed. He grabbed the doctor's hands and they struggled for control of the window. The drapes swung wildly, and the wolf looked up at the movement in the dark house. In another instant it wheeled and dashed off.

"You fool! You scared it away!"

"I, the fool?! What were you trying to do?!" the major was almost screaming.

"I was trying to communicate with it! Don't you realise what this means? A wolf – that is almost human! That can *become* human! It is a scientific discovery that could change the world!"

"May I remind you, Doctor, that your scientific discovery has killed at least two men that we know of and is trying to kill at least two more – including us?"

A muffled thump caught their attention. Impatient, no longer attempting to conceal himself, the major flung back the drapes so violently they were ripped off their rods and slid to the floor. A cloaked figure ran down the stairs from Vasa's house and dashed after the wolf.

"She follows," the major said grimly.

"If she's what it's after, she will be safe."

The major muttered something, and the doctor waited. The burly man caught his eye and said defiantly, "I said, I'm not sure I care! What kind of woman would go running out after a creature like that?"

"One of its own kind."

The major snorted. "You said yourself it was a wolf-were. But she is a werewolf. A match of unequals, I should say."

In answer the doctor kicked his ruined curtains into the corner and headed for the door. Over his shoulder he said, "You are probably right, Major. But I think we should be there just the same – if not to pick up whatever pieces are left, then at least to prove honest witnesses to a most unusual affair."

Still muttering, the major shoved his pistol into his belt and followed his host.

"Sorry about the drapes," he told him as they gathered up their cloaks and heavily knobbed walking sticks.

"Never mind. They're only drapes. This is science."

"Or love," the major said with a straight face and a certain grim irony.

"Major, you amaze me."

"Carry on, sir, carry on," the officer said, but by his voice it was clear he was pleased.

The Malchik slowed to a trot, then a stiff-legged walk. His hackles rose as he paced back and forth across the end of the road, yellow eyes peering through the darkness at the houses. A light, stinging snowfall pelted his coat. He ignored it, letting a low growl rumbled up from his throat.

"Please," Vasa said, gasping from her run. She clutched her cloak to her throat with one hand and held out the other, much as a person beseeches a pet with some tidbit. She squatted in the snow.

"Come here. Come here, malchik. Come here, boy."

Malchik. The only name he knew. The wolf paced back and forth, alternately whining and growling, the name drawing him toward her.

"Come on. Come on. Please."

Her face and form were a blur of darkness against the night. The wolf was like a piece of shadow against the snow.

"You see," she whispered. "I think I know what you are. You're like me. Except you turn into a wolf at the dark of the moon. I change at the full. But – if you're in there and you can hear me – if you come with me, we can be together. Only a few hours, only one night a month. But – we can be together." She sobbed once. "I still have your cloak."

The wolf's pacing stilled and he became a great, black shape, his eyes indistinguishable from the rest of his body. She could see by the shape of his dim silhouette that he was looking somewhere else, at something beyond her. The wolf growled anew.

Vasa got to her feet and swung around.

"Go away!" she shouted. "Whoever you are, this does not concern you!"

Her cultured tones left no echo. The only reply was the hissing of the snow. She looked back at the wolf.

He was gone. Dumbfounded, Vasa stared into the dark and then screamed.

"Now where are they going?" the major asked. They ducked out from behind the miller's gate to watch the woman run off once more.

"Do they teach you to track in your military training?" the doctor asked in turn, instead of replying.

"They teach us to hire the natives to do it for us," the major said. "Can you?"

The doctor shook his head.

"It will be like the blind leading the blind," he said. "Come on. Keep your pistol handy. We'd better stay together. Who knows where they're going."

Though they lost sight of the wolf immediately, they managed to keep track of Vasa; the woman was having as much trouble in the dark woods as they, and she had the added difficulty of manoeuvring in the snow in a cloak, satin gown, and evening slippers. The two men followed at a discreet distance, pausing when they got too close.

She led them to a lean-to that rested against a tumble of rocks by the river. Vasa, sobbing, pushed her way to the door of the little hut and peered in. It was empty. The fireplace looked as if it had not been lit for many days. More drifts had accumulated at the cracks, and the stone bowl sat empty on the hearth.

She sank down on the floor, too exhausted even to cry.

"Where are you?" she whispered. "Please come back. Please."

The major made a face and went to go in; the doctor pulled him back.

"Chivalry, Major?" he asked with deep irony.

"She's still a woman," the major said indignantly. "Well, at least now. Besides, what's the matter with chivalry?"

"Nothing – except this time it could get us both killed."

With a sardonic look, the major said, "Chivalry can always get you killed, sir. That's the point of it."

The doctor gave a laugh that was dry as dust.

"I'll keep guard outside."

Vasa looked up as he stooped through the door.

"Good evening, Major," she said, a travesty of her gracious hostess self. "How delightful to see you."

"Vasa Vasiliayevna, why don't we go home? This isn't safe for you."

She laughed, much as the doctor had.

"Thank you for your kind thought, sir, but I believe I'm safer here than you are."

"Where is it?" he asked abruptly. She sniffled and shrugged, laughing again with no humour.

"I wish I knew. I wish I knew why I cared so much. Why I need so much." The major moved restlessly, hunched over in the shelter. "Does that trouble you, Major? That I have a need to be here?"

"I don't know what you are," he said flatly. "Beast, were, woman –"

He stopped, his attention caught by the sound of snarling and a shriek of terror and pain. The major's muscles turned to water and the pistol drooped in his nerveless fingers. Unaware, Vasa stormed on.

"It was not the beast that followed him here tonight, but the woman!" she said sharply. "He is a man like you or the doctor! He is just a *were* at the dark of the moon, not during full!"

"He is a wolf," the doctor said, falling through the door. His face was very pale and he carried himself stiffly. Only when he fell to his knees did they see the blood draining from his side. "He changes at the full moon as you do, Mistress – but into a man, for he already is a beast."

160

He slumped to the ground. With shaking hands the major forced himself to aim the pistol at the door.

"No!" Vasa screamed and grabbed his arm. They struggled awkwardly in the confined space, and he bellowed when she bit him on the hand.

The Malchik bolted through the door and launched himself straight at the major. The gun went off, the report sharp and crisp in the night air. Vasa's gasp gurgled away into nothing, and she sank down in a pile of satin and wool, a spreading stain on her bodice. For a moment an overlay of wolf spread about her and then was gone.

The major died quickly, his throat torn out.

The wolf nosed the woman carefully, whining, then stretched out against her crumpled form, as if hoping to share her body heat or give her some of his own. He lay like that for a very long time.

The tall grey man appeared at the gate outside the finest mansion in town, looking as if he wished to push it open and go in, and he paced, or sidled rather, in a graceful way.

"Hey, you! What do you want there, malchik?"

It was a servant from the house, looking sharply at him.

"Who lives here?" the Malchik asked abruptly.

The servant raised an eyebrow.

"'Who lives here?' he asks. Don't you even know at whose gate you loiter? Why, this is the wine merchant's house, Sir Anton to you. Look, if you want work, go to the tradesman entrance by the kitchens. Don't hang about here at the gate."

The servant turned to go, but then looked back at the man. He hadn't moved.

"Here now, what did I tell you –?"

"This house was hers?" the Malchik said.

"What?"

"This house. It belonged to her before?"

Fearfully the servant made the sign against evil.

"Here, you. I have to go. I can't spend time jawing with strangers. Go round to the stables. They'll find work for you."

With that, the servant scuttled off on his errand, looking back once and increasing his speed thereafter.

Stables were no good – horses hated him. He went around to the side gate, fumbling a little with the latch.

A small, silent woman watched him keenly from the stoop where she swept away the springtime mud. He recognised her from his long vigil in the garden.

"Full moon tonight," she said after a time.

He could think of nothing to say.

"I reckon you're a little slow in there," she said after a moment. "I've wondered about you, ever since the mistress died. How it must be, to change into a man for only one day at a time. What was it like, that first time? Did you have to learn to talk, to stand upright?"

She began to sweep again with long, slow strokes.

"Now a person becomes a wolf, that isn't hard. The wolf is always in there in everyone. But you –" she looked at him straight in the eye. "To change into people. That's hard. That's hard. I reckon that there're some full-time people who are more wolf than people anyway."

"I learned. I was hoping – she could teach me the rest."

Laria laughed.

"The mistress? She needed some lessons herself." She nodded at the garden. "She's the one who sent the stable boy out there. To draw you in."

"I never killed a human before," he said, careful to use their word for their kind, instead of not-beast.

"That's her influence then. See?"

"Not just her," he said, struggling for the words. "I tried to stop it, but I brought it back into my true self, anyway." He shook his head. "I never wanted to kill like that. I thought it was because I wasn't really a human."

"No," Laria said. She cocked her head at him, her bright eyes as beady as a chickadee's. "No, it's because you really were."

She went back to sweeping long even strokes, wiping the mud clean from the stoop. Then she went inside and closed the door behind her. It took him a moment to realise that she was not coming back, and the Malchik turned and walked away, breaking into a rolling lope as soon as the gate closed behind him. He didn't stop running until he reached the woods.

Caro Comes Home

I live in a neighbourhood of post-WWII houses that were built in one of the first housing booms in Texas. These houses are small and resilient and have sheltered families for more than 75 years. What stories they could tell. Granted, maybe not this one.

Caro met Ray at a small village pub on the approach to D-Day. He sat with his fellow Yanks at a corner table. She sat at the end of the bar, nursing her sherry. His mates were all bold talk and bluster, their accents and loud voices shocking in the quiet pub, getting them looks from the locals. Ray wasn't loud, but he could make his voice heard. She liked his drawl and pale eyes, and his measured way of looking around him. When he left his table to come over to her, she smiled before turning around to meet him.

"Ray Hayes," he said, reaching out a hand. His uniform emphasised his broad shoulders and lanky form. Taking her time, she tilted her head to the side and only then accepted his hand. Was that a flinch? She kept contact as he recovered.

"Good to meet you, Ray Hayes," she said.

"You have a name, darlin'? I'd like to know who I'm going to propose to." He grinned, and behind them the US boys hooted and hollered.

"In that case – Caro. Caro Hayes."

His smile was warm and broad, much as hers was. "I like the sound of that, Mrs. Hayes. Do you dance?"

"I'd love to," she said, and she slid off her stool and they swayed to imaginary music in a twilight corner of the small pub.

Later that night, in her small attic room over the greengrocers, Caro's eyes were open and unseeing. She could feel Ray's heart beating in his chest, hear the rush of fluids throughout his body, smell the rich sweetness of his organs. He stirred and she moved, and when he opened his drowsy eyes and smiled at her, she smiled back.

He sat up, leaned against the headboard, and fumbled for a cigarette, lighting it with a Zippo lighter, drew on it, and exhaled a cloud of smoke. Caro watched, fascinated. He caught her gaze and winked at her, but he drew on the cigarette again, and his smile faded.

"I don't mind telling you, baby. I'm scared as hell."

"Shh, darling," she said, not understanding. "There's nothing to be afraid of." She reached out and took the cigarette and stubbed it out in the ashtray on the bedside table. She straddled him, leaning down to kiss him. "Don't be afraid," she whispered again.

He kissed her back with a hunger rivalling hers. "Wait for me, Caro Hayes," he said. "Promise me."

"I promise, Ray Hayes," she said. She shushed him, and his eyes closed.

If anyone were to look up at the small attic window, and if there were enough light to see by, they would see the still form of a U.S. soldier in the embrace of a monster, tenderly lapping at his face.

Ray wrote her letters. He survived D-Day and Bastogne and the end of the war, and telegraphed that he was coming back for her. She wore her travel suit and sat on her suitcase waiting for him, eyes unseeing, body unoccupied, for two weeks. When he rapped at the door, she stirred, smiled wide.

"Come in," she called, her voice lazy.

He opened the door and stepped inside. He was thinner, sharp-skinned and bony. His uniform hung off his frame, and the easy smile hid something darker now, something that haunted him far more than she did.

"Hey, baby," she said.

He didn't respond at first, then said, "Didn't think you'd wait. Huh."

She got up off the suitcase and wrapped her arms around him, kissing him. He resisted at first, but she persisted, and he relaxed in her arms, heart beating hard, shoulders slumped, as he cried hot tears down her neck.

They put fifty dollars down on the American dream, on a house in a new development that had been cotton fields just a few years before. Their neighbours were ex-GIs and their pretty wives, starting families and new lives, some going to the university and some going straight to work. Ray left each day. Caro sat in her kitchen, silent, unseeing, unmoving, until he returned, and she would stir at last, her smile lazy and wide. He'd smile back to see her.

"Is that you, Ray?" she would say.

"You bet. What did you do all day, darlin'?"

"Just waited for you, Ray," she'd say back, and he'd sink into her embrace.

After supper, when the heat lifted, everyone went outside. Ray and the other husbands worked on their new cars or gossiped across the fence line, wives sat on their front porches, rocking and fanning themselves. Over those first months the wives increased, their bodies thickening and rounding, and their offspring started to emerge.

Ray looked upon the pregnant wives with a regret Caro could sense. As with many human emotions it had no impact on her, except that afterwards he was sometimes distant from her, though never for long; she saw to that. It was same with the gossip; she smiled and nodded to the wives, and their whispers were like smoke. Nothing mattered; she had Ray. Ray was hers.

When the new couple moved in at the end of the street, the gossip about Caro ended. Mari was lush and rounded, with reddest lips and bluest eyes. Her hair had an unearthly shine, iridescent in the Texas sun. Mari's husband Lee Jeff was in a wheelchair. He was spindly and pale, almost more insect-like than Mari. He spoke little and his eyes were filmed.

Mari and Caro. Lee Jeff and Ray. The two couples didn't speak, but they didn't have to. They looked at one another, and they recognised. If Caro could scold, if she even knew what that meant, she would have. Mari was too hungry, too eager. She should have left something but instead, Lee Jeff was almost consumed. Caro didn't want to take all of Ray. She *husbanded* him. Sure enough, as Lee Jeff waned, Mari looked on Ray with hunger, and Ray responded. And Caro felt her monstrous nature begin to itch at her human skin.

Day was the most dangerous time. Caro sat in a stupor, cocooned in her human form, waiting for shadows to lengthen and Ray to come home. In the summer, with the sun lingering and the heat suffusing the house, she was harder to rouse, more stupid for a long time before she came back to herself. Only after she fed did she regain her strength. The afternoon that Ray didn't come home, it was full night before Caro opened her eyes.

The kitchen was dark except for the backyard light, insects zinging themselves into mad oblivion. She felt light-headed and giddy with hunger, and it took long moments before she understood that Ray was not there. Caro stood. Her skin split. What was birthed was shiny and wet and new, sharp-jointed legs trailing. When she went through the screen door, she left behind a slick trail.

Caro burst into the bungalow at the end of the street. Lee Jeff sat in a corner in his wheelchair, and Mari crouched over Ray in a feeding fugue, her proboscis stuck down his throat. Ray's eyes were slitted in the darkness, only the tiniest bit of shine under his long lashes.

When Caro ripped her rival's head off, the proboscis came up in a gout of blood and bile. Ray half raised up and gasped and coughed. He vomited up more blood, and then went limp.

Mari lay in two pieces on the bedroom floor, and Lee Jeff watched without moving as Caro carried Ray in her forelegs and brought him back to their house, the humid night air softening her carapace. The neighbourhood slept save for possums and raccoons and rats scuttling out of her path. Caro set Ray down on the living room floor and poked at him with one claw. Ray moaned and stirred, his breath rattling. She settled next to him, one claw on his hand, and then, responding to some compulsion, changed back to her human form. She didn't know why. She stayed that way through the long hours of the night as Ray struggled to live.

Caro stirred with the morning sun. She sat up and looked at Ray. He was still, his face covered with blood and vomit and Mari's digestive fluids. A spark of life remained. She felt a sensation she could not identify. It was weariness, yes, but something else. It felt correct that she continue to sit with Ray until the spark faded to completeness. She felt an unusual need that had nothing to do with hunger.

At length, she rose and went to their bedroom. Caro dressed with careful attention, putting on her brassiere and panties and hose, then her travelling suit from England. She brushed her hair and applied her makeup, and slipped on her pumps, and when she looked in the mirror the only sense she had of her true self was a tinge of green at the back of her eyes. Behind her, in the mirror, she caught sight of the black Zippo on the bedside table, next to half a pack of cigarettes. Caro picked up both, inhaling the scent of tobacco and lighter fluid that reminded her of Ray, and slipped them into her purse.

Caro went to the closet and stood on tiptoe to find her suitcase at the back of the shelf. She got it down and pulled away the silk lining for the small grey stonelike egg that clung to the material. It came away with a tug, cool to her fingers. Caro went back to Ray, and with tender hands, she lifted his head.

"Shhh, baby," she said. "Shhh." And she forced open his jaw, and put the egg underneath his tongue. She laid his head back down on the floor. Satisfied, suitcase in hand, Caro stepped over the body of her husband and left the house behind.

Seventy years passed. As was the nature of her kind, she wandered and was pursued, her name whispered where they knew of her and where she was feared, sowing uncertainty in other places where her kind had been forgotten. Remembered or forgotten, it didn't matter – wherever she was, she fed, and when she was sated, she'd grow still and dream. And in those dreams she walked with Ray, his warm hand in her cool one, in all the cities of the world. Rome, Vilnius, Tel Aviv – she was a dark shadow against white walls, and always the Texan walked with her.

"Where are we, sugar?" He'd say, with his wide-eyed boyish gaze, and she'd tell him. And he'd smile, the lazy broad smile that had captivated her when first she met him in the pub, and he'd say, "Baby, you always know how to show a man a good time."

And then in Oporto it happened. She roused, sluggish and swollen, an instinct driving her to migrate back to Texas. The egg was ready to disgorge their child.

Caro gathered her small suitcase and let herself out of the taxi. She stood for a moment in the blazing Texas sun, looking at the house she hadn't seen in seventy years. Still hers – she never sold it.

The building sagged. The windows looked like blank screams. The cement front porch was cracked in half, and the blue siding she remembered had faded to grey. Caro walked up to the front door and pushed it open. The living room was empty except for a ladderback chair and some old newspapers all over the paint-scarred hardwood floors, as if someone had meant to paint and left in a hurry. The walls were dingy yellow, the ceiling was popcorn, and there were dangling wires from where a light fixture had been removed.

There was a stain on the floor, an oily sheen, where she had laid Ray to rest. Caro sat down on her suitcase and set herself to wait.

Night fell, and the oppressive heat of a Texas summer lifted. She stared blankly into the night, sensing the possums, rodents, and the bats, her eyes flickering with their own light, a green like algae on top of a pond.

She roused when she smelled his scent – tobacco and lighter fluid and something else, acrid and artificial. Caro smiled, slow and wide.

"Is that you, baby?" she said.

He didn't speak. Caro turned to look. Ray was a shape in the dark, standing in the kitchen doorway. He was hulking and broad, his body swollen, his bloated form a grotesque caricature of his former self. The tattered remains of a funeral suit draped over him, and he smelled of the graveyard, both the casket and the dirt. For seventy years he had nourished their offspring, until he was driven here, as she had been, by instinct and need. Caro had a sense of satisfaction that was stronger and sharper than even the satisfaction of hunger sated, of feeding completed. She had given Ray what he wanted – offspring.

She had only a moment to recognise that she was in danger when he rushed at her, the ladderback chair held high overhead. Caro was already moving, and she slid up to the ceiling, hovering near the light, arms and legs splayed. Her back split open, and four more legs unfolded themselves, ripping through her demure pink-checked button down and pale green capri pants. The chair hit her suitcase where she had been sitting. The suitcase fell open, spewing out her carefully folded clothes.

Caro attacked. She scuttled down toward Ray and he fell underneath her. He kept his hands up, one hand holding her off, pressing against her thorax, the other still holding the chair leg, the broken end jagged and sharp. He slashed at her with it.

She experienced confusion. This was not what she expected. She had left him with an offspring, which is what he wanted. She waited until the offspring was ready to eclose from the egg. And now here she was, in time for the birth of their offspring.

She looked at him through bulbous green eyes and she saw his fear. Slowly, Caro lowered her fangs to his throat, and grazed the skin, letting him know what she could do. Then she backed away, one deliberate leg after the other. Ray propped himself against the wall. He groped for the piece of broken wood, and she knew if he tried to attack again she would have to kill him, so she did the only thing she could do. She changed back into her human form.

He stopped. She knew better than to say anything. She was vulnerable and acutely aware that she was nearer to death than she had ever been in her long life. She breathed and waited, breathed and waited, and after long seconds he set the stake down on the floor, and slumped as if his strength had given out. He patted the floor next to him, and she came and sat down. He put an arm around her. She let her head rest on his shoulder. After a long moment, he spoke.

"I feel sick, Caro," he said. He never called her Caro. He always called her darling or baby.

"I'm here now, Ray," she said. "It's coming. Can you feel it? Our baby." She didn't understand the words. The other wives had said them, though. Our baby.

He groaned. His throat convulsed and he vomited bile. "Oh, Caro. Why did you do this to me?"

She didn't understand these words. She was used to his slow, soft words. *Missed you, baby. Love you, baby. Promise me, baby.* She didn't understand these new words.

"I'm here, baby. I'm with you," she said, trying to bring him back to what she knew. "I promised I'd wait for you. I –"

"I'm not an idiot," he said. "I knew what you were. After what I went through, what I saw, I wanted it. I wanted what you did to me. And when I saw Lee Jeff, I thought, lucky man, because he was almost gone, and it would be over for me too, someday." He sighed, and shifted his body. "But instead, you turned me into a monster, just like you."

"I'm here now, Ray. We can be tog –"

"It's over, Caro. I'm over."

She tried to understand the words and failed. Caro thought, I will say what I want, even though I don't understand what I want.

"I need you, baby. I want us to be forever."

"Well," he said, and his voice sounded like it did sometimes when he laughed. "Imagine that. You love me, baby." She nodded, even though again, she didn't understand, except that it was a word he said often, and it meant something to him.

"I love you, baby," she agreed. "I promised I'd wait."

His throat convulsed again, and she could see the bulge behind his lips. When he spoke next his words were unclear, but she understood them.

"Promise me, Caro. When it's born, kill it."

Promise me. Promise.

"I promise, Ray," she said. And again she thought, I will say what I want, even though I don't understand what I want. "Promise me, one last night, Ray."

He couldn't answer, because the offspring oozed from between his lips. It was expelled out of his body and slid down his torso, landing on the floor with a wet splat.

It was a monstrous thing, and it wanted nutrition, and if she was not quick it would consume Ray.

Caro took the stake from his limp fingers and stood and plunged it into the midsection of the offspring, pinning it to the floorboards.

The neighbours might have wondered about the old house coming to life, if any happened to look. In the old-fashioned lamplight Ray and Caro danced the night away, slow dancing to no music. If anyone did notice, they'd see a husband and wife grown old together, but in the next turn they'd see a young couple straight out of a 40s newsreel, a handsome soldier and a pretty girl.

And a passerby might see something monstrous, an entwined embrace, and hurry on before looking closer, plagued by uneasy nightmares for the next few days.

Before dawn, Caro laid Ray down on the floor of the old house, and reached into his mouth to retrieve the empty egg sac she had placed there so many years before. "Shh, darling," she said. "Shh." She sat with him while he disintegrated, next to their offspring shrivelling into a husk.

In the grey light of early morning, Caro lay out a collection of found scraps on the wood floor – bits of newspaper, the broken rung from the ladderback chair, a few tufts of stuffing from her suitcase. She clicked the Zippo lighter, and touched the flame to the kindling. A line of flame ran along the edge of the scraps, black soot in its wake.

Caro picked up her suitcase and closed the door to the old house. She walked down the steps toward the street. Behind her, smoke puffed out the windows, and then yellow flames flickered, tinged with green. She kept walking as the house went up in flames, and turned the corner without looking back.

Red Ned Mederos and the Sea Girl of Port Saint Frey

Behind every great family is a great crime, said Balzac (and Mario Puzo).
Behind the Mederos family, there's also wild magic.

The merchant brigantine *Elphantine* struggled against the waves and the tides, dashed about by the remnants of a gale that originated halfway across the world. The ship was so close to shore that if the crew were not careful they would be dashed upon the rocks and the rich cargo would be lost. The master had done all he could, and the men reefed the sails and the helmsman steered into the gale. Now it was up to Him of the Sea Above, and the master was not in the habit of prayer. Still, he raised a defiant cry to the heavens: "Damn you, God! Damn you and curse you for your treachery!"

"Look!" cried the boy from the crow's nest, a spindly lad on top of a spindly mast, almost invisible in the gale. The master wiped the seawater from his face and peered at a pinpoint of light, blinking steadily through the storm. A beacon of hope, the light strengthened, pulling them in.

The master smiled. It was not a nice smile. The master raised his voice.

"Mr. Jockerby, two points sou-sou-west!"

"Aye sir, sou-sou-west!"

The Elphantine turned ponderously, wallowing for an anxious moment against a swelling wave, dipping so much that the mainmast hung at a steep angle over the sea, the boy clinging like a rag to the crow's nest. The master squinted through the squall, knowing if he miscalculated, all would be lost. The investors would be displeased, and he would lose all hope of shares in the profits, if he didn't die outright.

The Elphantine righted and made her turn, and the master brought her in, the beacon of light guiding them off the ship's starboard side.

The rain and wind lashed Ned Mederos as he stood on the cliffs overlooking the sea and watched his quarry turn away toward safety and the harbour. He doused his lantern. He was a tall, pale man, his watery blue eyes and reddish beard accentuated with a cruel mouth and impatient expression.

"Well," said his companion, the rotund and genial Theo Balinchard. "That's another one."

Ned Mederos raised his eyes to the heavens. "Oh is it, Theo? Is it really? Do you think you could not chatter so much?"

"I'm just saying, Ned. The game has run its course. The merchants all know to steer to port when they see the light. Word at Aether's is that the town is raising money for a lighthouse on Dolphin Head."

Theo always had the news. That's why Ned kept him around. But damned if it wasn't hard to hear it at the absolutely worst time. Ned said, "You didn't think to tell me before we stood out here in a hurricane waiting to bring the ship in?"

"I thought you had a plan," Theo said, guileless as always. Ned began trudging down the goat path toward town. He would build his house up here one day. He had scouted it out in daytime, the perfect site for a mansion that would say to all, House Mederos. He did not care for the merchants of Port Saint Frey and their lighthouse to keep him from his ambitions.

Theo kept on with his nattering, and finally Ned stopped. He couldn't take much more of it.

"Go on," he told the short man. "Find out all you can at Aether's."

"What? What about you?" Theo hunched in his coat. Ned despised him for his care. No matter how he treated Theo, Theo always acted as if – well, as if he liked Ned. *He just knows which side his bread is buttered on*, Ned thought. *He knows he'd get nowhere without me.*

"Go on. Get dry and get some rum in ye."

Theo didn't have to be told three times. He hurried down the path as fast as his rotund body could move, and Ned was alone on the hill.

The rain had stopped though the wind still cruelly whipped Ned through his coat. A pale moon lit up a distant cloud with a white glow. Where the clouds parted, a single star shone – Saturnus. Ned remembered his father teaching him the stars and planets. He had been a wee lad when his father died of drink. His mother had remarried soon thereafter, and Ned took himself onto the streets.

No point in thinking of the past. Ned set his sights on the future. He stood on the high cliff, looking out to sea. The clouds drifted away, and more stars appeared. The white path of the moon illuminated the dark sea, and Ned was caught for a moment by the grim and dangerous beauty.

It came to him that he was hearing a sweet air and had the impression that the wordless tune had been going on beneath his awareness for some time. Ned looked for the source of the music, and saw a form in the trail of moonlight.

Her face was in shadow, her hair streaming behind her. He could see her head, shoulders, and breasts above the water, and she bobbed in the surf.

Ned plunged down the hillside, grabbing onto stunted pine trees and digging his hobnailed boots into the rocks and dirt to slow his descent. He hung the dark lantern on a tree branch – stopped and thought a minute, and lit the lantern again as a precaution. The little light would be his beacon of safety, and he knew that for the irony it was.

When he made it to the shore, he stopped, panting. He stood in a natural cove, high tide spilling almost up to the edge of the cliff, leaving a bare crescent of pale sand in the moonlight. Off to one side was a cleft in the rocks, and Ned noted it with interest, filing the thought away while he focused on the girl in the water. She had stopped singing.

He could see her better now, though her face was still in shadow. Her hand was wet and stringy, and there was seaweed wrapped around her head and shoulders like a shroud.

"Hello, love," he said, his voice thick. Ned Mederos was no stranger to lusts and appetites, but he also knew better than to follow his lust into the water, no matter how much it drove him. "Come here, my darling, and let me see you."

For answer, she swam backward into deeper water. He almost followed. Almost. Instead, he took off his great coat and tossed it onto the rocks behind him. Hopping on one foot, he drew off first one boot and then the other. Ned stood in his trousers and shirt and suspenders, bare feet cold and pale on the wet sand.

"Oh, no need to be like that, sweetheart. Ned here is a good 'un. I won't hurt you, not one bit."

She made a sound – it was low, amused? He couldn't tell. It sent a thrill of fear down his spine at the same time it electrified him further. He fished into his pocket, and pulled out the pocket watch that belonged to his dad. The watch was silver and brass, and it was the only thing he owned that he had never pawned. He held it up on the chain, and he could see the way she came alert that he had her.

"That's right," he said, his voice rough, a smile in it. "You like that? You want that? Come to me, darling, and you can have it all you want. I'll give you anything."

The glow of the moon intensified, and the sea-girl stood up. Yes, stood. For Ned had thought that he was dealing with a mermaid, but she was a girl with legs and all. The moon shone silver on her legs, and he could see mottling like scales, but she was a girl all right. Ned grinned again, and he came a few steps into the sea.

Ned woke in full daylight, cold air and bright sun shining down on him. He opened his eyes and looked up, confused. He lay on wet sand, the sea lapping at his bare feet and bare legs. With a curse, he scrambled up out of the water, shivering with cold. He still had his shirt, but no trousers. His legs were white and goose-pimpled under thin reddish hair. He staggered a little and looked out to sea, shading his eyes against the sun. It was one of those days, filled with glory, a blue sea, white clouds, and a blue sky, the ocean fooling all but the canniest with its calm and peaceful demeanour.

The sea girl was nowhere to be found, and neither was his pocket watch.

His trousers had disappeared as well, but there were his boots where he left them, tossed upon the rocks at the foot of the cliff. They were soaked through, but he shook out a hermit crab from one and poured water out of both, and forced them onto his bony white feet. His great coat was wet through but he shrugged into it to hide his embarrassment. He looked out to sea one more time, before clambering back up the cliff.

His lantern still flickered where he left it, the pale flame brave against the sunlight. He blew it out and looked back again at the now distant sea.

"Just you wait, missy," he said. "I'll have you. And you'll regret the day you ever met Red Ned."

When Ned walked up to the docks in the morning sun, hoping to cadge a rum and a cigar, he had a dawning awareness that people were laughing at him. His first thought was that his coat had opened but a hasty glance down showed him he was decent. He gave the crowd a glare, but the muffled laughter started up again behind his back.

Ned grew large with rage. If they knew what was good for 'em, they wouldn't laugh, no they would not. He walked up the docks, head high, and plotted revenge.

At the door to Aether's, Theo caught up with him. "Ned, man! Let's go down to the shore." Theo took him by the arm, a bit of audacity that made Ned snarl. Theo recoiled but stood firm. "Ned," he stammered.

"Ned Mederos," came an unfamiliar voice. "I've been waiting for you, you son of a bitch."

Ned turned. At the other end of the dock stood a strange man in a merchant master's coat. He had a black beard and thick hands, and his coat was an oiled canvas slicker that would stay dry in the fiercest blow. When he saw he had Ned's attention, he grinned and held up a pair of trousers.

Ned howled with rage. Theo tried to hold him back, but the little man slid as Ned pulled forward like a snorting drayhorse. The merchant master reached into his pocket and pulled forth a pistol, drew back the hammer and aimed it at Ned. Ned stopped short.

"This is for trying to sink my ship!" The man snarled. "Ye scurvy devil! Trying your tricks with your tricksy lantern! Trickery! Trickery!"

"What are ye blathering on about!" Ned yelled back. "You're alive, ain'tcha? Your ship's safely docked, ain't she? Tweren't for me, you'd have been dashed on the rocks!" The merchant master stopped short at Ned's logic. Ned pushed. "Ye should be thanking me, ye damned git!"

He knew he went too far as soon as he said it. The *Elphantine* master planted his feet. "Yer a damned rogue, Red Ned Mederos, and it's high time someone put a stop to your crimes!"

"Ned –" Theo said, low in his ear. Ned ignored him, thrusting his arm back to shake him off. The giggles rose up again, but Ned ignored that too.

"You want to come at me, man? Come on, then! I'll give ye the thrashing ye deserve!"

The merchant master smirked.

"Ned –"

Ned felt a breeze where no breeze ought to be felt. He took a second to look down.

"I pride myself on not fighting an unarmed man," the Elphantine master said with a grin. The crowd roared at his wit and he raised his arms, encouraging them on. Then he uncocked his pistol and thrust it back into his coat, and with great ceremony threw Ned's trousers into the drink. They swelled and filled with air and wafted on top of the water before sinking into the harbour.

"Come on, boys!" the merchant master called. His sailors fell in behind them and they all sauntered down the docks toward the sailor's hells.

Ned watched him go. Theo let go of Ned and knelt at the dock's edge, fishing for the trousers with a stave, grunting with effort. "Got 'em!" he crowed. He held up the trousers, cascading with water. Theo dumped them on the dock, looking expectantly at Ned like a retriever with a duck. Ned roused. He picked up the trousers, wrung them out, and got into them, boots and all. They hung wet, cold, and heavy on his hips, and his member shrank in alarm, but he felt a better man for having all his clothes just the same.

"I'm going to get that son of a bitch," Ned told Theo.

Later that day, Ned stood on the rocks at the end of the small cove. It was sunset, and the sun laid down a golden track to his left, around the corner of the jutting outcropping. That way lay the harbour, and the current flowed in that direction. That's how his trousers ended up on the docks. He looked the other way, toward the east. His one big mistake was setting up his lantern too far to the west. He'd have to go farther round the headland to Dead Man's Drop. Break the ship there and the current would bring the cargo right to the cove.

There was just a matter of storing his prizes from prying eyes. Ned looked at the cleft in the outcropping that jutted into the waves. He sloshed over to it in water up to his knees and ducked through the cleft. Immediately he was plunged into darkness. Water lapped at stone, and the air was cold and smelled of brine and dead fish. Ned waited for his eyes to adjust and his surroundings to come into view. What he saw made him smile.

The cleft was a cave as he had hoped. There was a sandy shelf high enough to stay dry even in high tide. He could stack the cargo, lashing casks together until he could deliver them to buyers. At the back of the cave, just visible in the dim light, he could see where an opening led into the cliff. Ned waded over to it.

A half-hour later, he birthed himself from the cave halfway up the cliff, covered in muck and pushing rocks and debris out of the way. Panting, cursing, livid and scratched up, Ned stood, sucking a cut on his knuckle and looking around. Oh yes, he thought. This will do nicely.

Two months later, on the night of the new moon, a flickering light shone through the darkness. The merchant master of the *Elphantine* looked through his spyglass at the signal light, and grinned. Ned Mederos. The bastard would never learn, would he.

"Two points sou-sou west, Mr Jockerby," he told his helmsman.

Jockerby hesitated, as if to say something, but then swung the spokes. The *Elphantine* turned west, her sails billowing with a freshening wind, driving her toward the shore.

The casks came up first, and Ned Mederos and Theo raked them in, pulling them onto the sandy cove and towing them to the cave. They worked hard, reaping the heavy cargo. The foundering ship wallowed on the rocks, and the lifeboats headed farther round the coast to the harbour, the hapless sailors rowing with the current. In the dim starlight, Ned could just see a standing figure in the prow of one of the boats. The *Elphantine*'s master, no doubt sore about being bested by Red Ned Mederos.

When the cargo was stowed in the cave, Ned and Theo rested. Ned took a prybar and opened up one of the casks, pulled up the protective canvas cover, and peered at the silks and cotton material. It would fetch a pretty penny on the Mile, where all the dressmakers had their shops. He put the lid back on, and opened another – ah, here was rare treasure indeed – gold and silver wire and stones for lapidary. He could find a buyer for all of these. He opened a velvet sachet, and inside was a heavy silver necklace, a pearl and sapphire pendant hanging from it. He put that in his pocket.

The revenuers out of Port Saint Frey would ask for provenance and look askance on Ned Mederos's new-found wealth, but there were plenty of men who would do business with a wink and a nod. Port Saint Frey was all business now, and Ned wanted but a chance to make his mark on it.

The moon was new so only the stars shone down on the ocean, the sky a swirl of stars and blackness. Ned was restless. He had a feeling. He turned to Theo, handing him some of the gold wire and gemstones.

"Go to Aether's, on the double now, Theo. Tell Aether himself that Ned's in business, and we can make a deal."

Theo grinned. "You're a good smart man, Ned Mederos. We'll make our place for sure, you'll see. House Mederos and House Balinchard too."

Ned watched him go, and then sloshed back out to the sea. The cargo was safe for now. He'd got it stowed and secured, and not a man would take it from him. Ned would see to that.

He stood in surf up to his knees, the quiet rolling of the sea like breathing. He waited, gently shaking the necklace, and at last he heard the wordless tune.

She was there, head and shoulders in the water, her face in shadow. There was no moon to light her by, but the gleam of starlight was answered in the gleam of her eyes and her teeth, more pointed and brighter by far than a human woman's teeth.

Ned smiled. "Hello, darling. My little thief." He held up the silver and sapphire pendant. She stiffened and came closer, and now he could see that she had his pocket watch in her fist. It would be rusted and the works frozen after its dunk in the seawater, but no matter. The watchmaker on Barrell Street would repair it for him.

He held up his shining pretty, and she held up his pocket watch. They came toward one another, and he could see her mottled, scaled flesh, her long seal-brown hair, and her deep black eyes. Her eyes were spaced too far apart, and her mouth was too wide, but he shivered as he remembered their last carnal encounter.

When she reached out for the necklace, he caught her hand, and when she went to throw the pocket watch into the sea, he caught that hand too.

"Now now," he said. "None o' that."

She watched him, unafraid, and he knew she could tear him apart with those sharp canines if she so desired. Ned Mederos spoke fast.

"You can have all the beads and pretty ye want, darling, and ye can go back to the sea anytime ye want. All I ask is ye give me my watch and share my bed, and when Ned Mederos builds his house –" He turned and pointed at the darkness at the top of the cliff, and her black eyes followed – "ye visit me there. But ye don't have to stay, for I know ye can't be caged or kept. And if we have children, they can't live in the sea, so I'll keep them for ye, darling, for I know ye prefer treasures of another kind."

He waited, holding his breath. And then she nodded, and she gave him a wicked, pointed tooth smile, like that of a shark, and handed him his pocket watch. Ned strung the necklace over her head and around her mottled neck, her skin cold, the faint fishy odour arising from her. It was like blood, like the sea.

As they embraced in the ocean, Ned murmured against her cold skin, "We're two of a kind, sweetheart. You and me. House Mederos." The sea girl pressed her teeth against his neck and nipped him. He figured that was agreement.

"Darling," he told her, "You have no idea of the pretty, pretty things I will bring you."

The Lunch Thief

Get enough office workers together, and they will tell war stories of bad bosses, annoying coworkers, and the mightiest scourge of all – the lunch thief.

"This really isn't what we do," the consultant from Rheinhart & Ritter tried. The CEO bulled on, running over his words.

"You have to help. This is beyond anything we've ever dealt with."

"Mr. Maher –"

"Call me Simon. Look, I've heard a lot of things about your outfit, and believe me, this is right up your alley." He tapped a finger on the embossed script of the consultant's business card. "'Discreet, creative solutions for the modern office.' If word gets out that Maher Industries is being undermined this way –"

The consultant took a deep breath. "Mr. Maher, someone is stealing lunches from the break room refrigerator. That's hardly –"

"That's the problem. We can't stop him."

"Surely you've tried cameras."

"Of course. And we've captured the thief on video."

"You have? Why haven't you fired him?"

"We can't. We don't know who he is."

The consultant blinked. "Someone is breaking in from the outside?"

"He has a badge, but no one recognises him, and all the badges are accounted for."

The consultant sighed. "Maybe you'd better show me what you have."

The consultant watched the video in the small conference room, without distractions. It was refreshing to be alone, with only the subaudible presence of the consulting firm to keep him company.

Against the backdrop of that ever-present communication, he watched the company's morning routine unspool on tape. People dropped off their lunches, got their coffee, exchanged greetings, all in

183

stark black and white. The break room emptied out and, except for one or two people passing through for a mid-morning coffee, it stayed empty. The moments ticked on; the consultant viewed patiently, never moving. Finally, at about 11:35 am, someone entered the break room, opened the fridge, and selected a lunch. He turned and smiled directly at the consultant. Then he left, out of the camera's view.

The woman whose lunch had been stolen searched through the remaining lunches with increasing fury, finally slamming the fridge shut in a crescendo of violence.

Even through the videotape the energy from her rage shocked the consultant from the soles of his shoes along his spine. He pressed pause on the remote. If the people at the company felt anything remotely like that, he thought, no wonder the CEO was worried.

"Did you see it?" he said. The hum intensified. He nodded at the response. "And did you feel that?"

Again he nodded. "It could be a Bad Amy. I don't want to rule out that possibility, but it is not usually that sort of creature's modus operandi. I did not perceive individually focused malice, for instance."

The consultant smiled. "Yes, it's interesting. I don't know where my investigation will take me, but I intend to enjoy it."

Simon Maher rose and offered his hand as the consultant came into his office the next morning. "I'm glad you decided to take the job," the man said. "It's been a little embarrassing, this lunch thief problem."

The consultant gripped his hand. "I'll need free rein of your site," he said. "A badge of my own. And I'll have to talk to people."

The CEO nodded. "That's fine. Whatever you need. You just let Helen know."

Helen was Simon Maher's administrative assistant, as briskly competent as promised. In short order the consultant had a visitor's badge and she led him to the lunch room. "We're all so glad you're here," she said, her heels tapping away on the linoleum floor. She wore fashionable slacks, pointed pumps, a lavender twinset, and prim jewellery. Highlights streaked her chin-length hair. She opened the door to the break room and nodded at the red light shining near the ceiling. "The video camera. Though it hasn't done much good."

The consultant glanced at it, then looked around the room. A refrigerator hummed in one corner, a microwave next to it. The long counter was taken up by a machine, its various displays blinking. The consultant frowned at the machine, puzzled. Helen glanced at him, identifying his confusion.

"Here, let me help," she said, selecting a foam cup from the stack. "You take this packet and put it in the slot, punch in brew, strength, kind of coffee, whether you need room for cream and then put your cup here. Press a button, and there you go! Coffee." She beamed. The consultant beamed back.

"Thanks. It's very modern." The coffee machine blinked and hummed, and coffee trickled out into his foam cup.

"Well, it's a little silly, to have a 'coffee system' –" She made air quotes with well-manicured hands. "I usually get my coffee on the way to work, but sometimes when I'm running late it's all I have time for."

The consultant took a sip. The brew was insipid, vile. She laughed at his expression and he found himself revising his first opinion of her.

"And there's the catch – it's terrible stuff," she said frankly.

He glanced at her over the cup and then poured the coffee down the sink. "Do people complain?"

She reddened, touched her necklace. "Well, I don't know. I guess that would be kind of ungrateful, to slander the coffee. It's free, you know. And it's not all that bad." Her voice faltered.

They both looked at the sink with the last of the coffee draining in it. Her phone rang, and she started. "Let me know if I can help with anything else," she said hastily as she left. "Hope you find this guy. He's worse than the coffee, that's for sure."

The consultant nodded, and waited. A couple more people breezed in. He frowned at the coffee machine again.

"Need a hand with the coffee?" one said, his eyes flicking over the consultant's visitor badge.

"Yeah, I'm not sure where to begin," the consultant said.

He poured out at least seven cups of coffee as the morning wore on. Finally, the break room emptied out. The bright industrial lighting fell over the sink, the coffee system, and the fridge. The only sound came from the humming of the machinery and the ticking of the clock.

Outside the room, the consultant could hear the intercom, people's voices, cell phones. A printer and a fax machine. Deliveries.

At 11:45 the first of the early lunchers came in. It was Helen. She looked at him, startled. He realised he hadn't moved. She smiled breezily.

"Still here? Well, hopefully you kept him away at least for today." She opened the freezer door and stood there for a long moment. Then she slammed the door closed. "Son of a bitch," she said, the professional persona slipping off her as if it were part of her outfit.

The consultant felt the same jolt of energy; this time, proximity made it painful. She had no reaction, he thought. It should have knocked her over.

The firm responded without words and he acknowledged it. Aware or not, she had to have felt it, and the aftereffects would be devastating.

An entire company feeling this… they were being tortured, and didn't know it.

She looked at him, frustration and anger pouring into her voice. "What happened? Didn't you see him?!"

The consultant shook his head and she exploded. "What the hell kind of consultant are you? He stole my lunch!" She threw up her hands and stalked off. The consultant frowned, and headed off to view the video.

"I was in there the entire morning," the consultant said. "You can see me."

Simon Maher didn't have the consultant's patience, so he fast forwarded through most of the tape. He gasped when he saw the lunch thief walk in, grab the frozen entree from the freezer, glance at the consultant with a grin of malice, and then walk out.

"How could you miss him?" Maher said. "He was right there."

"I know." The consultant smiled and then gave Maher an apologetic look. "Sorry. It's not often we get a challenge like this."

"I'm glad you're enjoying this," Maher muttered.

"So does he just steal women's lunches?"

"No. Equal opportunity thief. He'll take veggie meals, meat leftovers, anything. Totally random. He only ever takes one lunch. He always smiles for the camera."

"Has anyone tried sabotage?"

Maher wrinkled his nose. "We have some creative people here. Laxatives were popular for a while. He has never eaten a sabotaged lunch as far as I know."

"Anything more – final?" The consultant's voice was bland.

When Maher spoke next his words were careful. "The company is not aware of any kind of unlawful entrapment efforts by employees. We do not condone any action that could bring harm to anyone and will prosecute to the fullest extent possible any attempt at revenge."

"And unofficially?"

"There is no 'unofficially,'" Maher snapped. "And everyone knows that. He's just a lunch thief – we'd be crucified in the press." He sighed. "What next?"

"I'd like to see your employee roster cross-referenced with photos."

"It's not one of the employees." Maher hesitated again. "And privacy laws…"

"I just want to check faces."

Maher capitulated. "Helen will get you what you need."

After hours at Maher Industries was a quiet place. One security guard sat at the front desk and another prowled the dim halls. The consultant sat in the small conference room that had been assigned to him and reviewed the tapes. He had the electronic personnel files up on the computer. At first glance there was nothing to distinguish the lunch thief from the employees. It didn't take the consultant long to realise, though, that whereas he could close his eyes and visualise any employee after one glance at a photo, he could not remember what the lunch thief looked like. He studied the tape and got a hazy impression of dark hair, male, white. Then he looked away and the image dropped from his mind.

"Are you getting this?" he said to the room, just as the door opened and the security guard poked his head in.

"Sorry," the man said. "I have to check all the offices."

"Not a problem," the consultant said.

The security guard took in the monitor, with the lunch thief frozen in action, and the computer screen with employee dossiers. "So you're the one trying to find the guy. Man, he really sounds like a piece of work. Where I used to be stationed, at the fab out there north of town, some guy used to steal lunches and go eat them in the bathroom. You'd go in there and someone would be in one of the stalls, chewing away. That place went out of business, though. Hey, maybe it's the same guy." He grinned.

The consultant nodded at the monitor. "You ever see this guy? Maybe working late or something?"

The security guard looked, frowned, and shook his head. "Nobody I know." He touched his flashlight to his visor and backed out of the room.

The consultant looked at the monitor. The lunch thief stood there, plastic container in hand, a smile on his face. The consultant looked away and couldn't remember if the thief had brown hair or black, if he wore khakis or jeans, a button down or a polo. He sighed.

Then he wondered about what kind of thief would steal a lunch only to eat it in a men's room stall.

Maher Industries had four restrooms, two each for men and women. The consultant stood in the doorway of the closest restroom, just looking in the dimness of the off-hours lighting. The cleaning crew had come for the night, and the urinals and stalls gleamed with strong disinfectant. A faucet dripped at the end of the row of sinks. He walked through, pushing open doors. Nothing.

He did the same with all the restrooms, including the women's, which had a heavy floral scent. He pushed on the last door, only noticing at the last minute two pointy-toed pumps under the door.

"It's taken," said a familiar voice. The consultant opened his mouth, realised that was a bad idea, and walked out.

The next day, he met Helen in the break room at her usual time. She raised an eyebrow at him taking up position in the same spot, and shot a tiny glance at his shoes.

"Still need help?" she said, turning her shoulder as she pretended to choose a coffee packet.

"No, I have it now," he said. "Here." He handed her a mug of coffee, still steaming. The coffee smelled strong and bitter with chocolate notes. "It's a peace offering," he said. "And an apology. I didn't mean to frighten you last night."

Her eyes flicked from the coffee to him. She took the mug, but warily, eyeing him over the rim. Good, he thought. He didn't want to talk to office personas. He needed to speak to people who were stripped down to their core.

"A peace offering or a bribe?" she said, her bright voice challenging. A few people came in and she and the consultant stepped out of the way, their bodies moving together.

"Why a bribe?" he said.

"So I won't say anything about you, last night, in the restroom." The break room had been rebounding with talk that skipped along the surface of the room but at her words, everyone turned to them. The consultant felt almost the same jolt he experienced when a theft was uncovered. Helen's cheeks got pink and her voice went bright again. "I'm sorry. That was rude of me. I know you're here to find this guy. I was startled, and you know." She gave a little wave.

It's armour, he thought. Like the twinset and the pumps. Another bout of curious glances and then the conversation rose up around them again.

"It's all right," he said, and nodded at the cup in her hand. "You should drink that before it gets cold." He gave a cordial nod and went off to the small meeting room.

The consultant replayed their encounter on tape. There was the usual swirl of activity around the coffee machines and he and the woman off in the corner, quiet over the coffee mug. The mug had a bit of a halo around it but the consultant dismissed that – only he could see it and he was used to it. He watched himself leave, the woman watching him go. She wore an odd expression – puzzlement, a bit of enjoyment at their encounter, a sort of half-arousal that made him smile wistfully. The arousal was buried far deeper than even she was aware, stuffed down beneath the armour of business casual. After a moment she took a sip of the gift coffee. Her face lit up with a grin and in the meeting room the consultant grinned back.

This time the lunch thief never showed

Simon Maher wanted to count it a job well done with a handshake and payment due, but the consultant shook his head.

"I'm not even close yet," he said. "And according to the security tapes, he didn't steal a lunch every day anyway."

"No," Maher admitted. "He would lull us into thinking that he stopped and people started bringing lunches again and leaving them in the refrigerator. Then it would start up again."

"Has Helen been here long?"

"Six months. You can't possibly think that she has anything – anyway, we're looking for a man."

Not really, the consultant thought. "No," he explained. "I meant only that I needed someone who had been here for a long enough time that they could review the tapes and correlate the date stamps with anything unusual that happened that day."

Maher shook his head. "That would take weeks. And anyway, I can tell you that the days the lunches get stolen are just like any other day around here."

"It's not the days the lunches get stolen," the consultant corrected. "It's the days they don't."

Maher was reluctant but he finally agreed, proposing they turn to Helen's assistant, Suzanne. She agreed to review her calendars, but she looked dubious. "Exactly what am I looking for?" she said.

"Anything that jogs your memory," the consultant said. "They say you know everything about this place, better than anyone. I need that kind of institutional knowledge."

She smiled to cover up a deep-seated disgruntlement that the consultant had come to recognise at Maher Industries – the entire company was a stew of resentment. Nevertheless, three days later she emailed him her notes, a play-by-play of the daily life of the company. The consultant reviewed them late at night in the quiet presence of the consulting firm.

The first pattern was no pattern: the lunch thief stole lunches or did not steal lunches and Suzanne's meticulous notes made no connection. So the consultant stopped trying to fit the two together and looked only at her notes. He could feel her resentment through the computer monitor, a subaudible grudge through which she filtered everything. Armour, he thought. Armour against what? He thought about Helen, her airy breeziness hiding explosive anger.

No, not anger, he thought. Fear.

What were they so afraid of?

He scrolled through the notes. Meetings, shipments, e-mails, accounts receivable, quarterly earnings. Vendors delivered, the company signed new customers, engineers designed new products, marketing launched them. Coffee was delivered.

The consultant stopped. He had asked Suzanne for the noteworthy, and instead she dutifully transcribed the unremarkable. But noting the coffee order? He almost laughed, until the room's silence pressed itself upon him.

The endless communication from Rheinhart & Ritter had ceased.

The consultant felt a sick pressure that he identified as fear. He turned and flicked on the security monitor.

The lunch thief grinned maliciously back at him. It took the consultant a moment to recognise that he was not in the break room. The monitor lost the signal and when it came back the lunch thief was gone, and all he could see was the empty restroom.

Empty except for a pair of pointed pumps just visible under the door of the last stall.

He pushed the door just as Helen pulled it open, almost flinging it into her. They collided, grabbing each other.

"What are you doing?!"

The lunch thief was gone, but a lingering sense of oppression remained. Rheinhart & Ritter remained blocked.

"Let's go. We're in trouble."

On the heels of his words the bathroom mirror shattered as if someone had taken a baseball bat to it. They ducked as glass showered down on them. The consultant grabbed her wrist and pushed her through the swinging door ahead of him.

Something shrieked behind them and they ran, her shoes clicking on the floor.

"What's going on?" she panted. He ignored her, his hand hard around her wrist, pressing on the silver bangles.

"When was the coffee system put in?"

"Three, four months, I don't know. Listen, what is this about?" She pulled back. "You need to let me go."

"Who ordered it?"

"I don't know! I'm not in Facilities, I don't keep up with this stuff."

They had come around the corner to the break room and pushed through the door. The break room was quiet in the dim light and looked empty, but he thought of the lunch thief's face on the monitor and knew they weren't alone. He started to pull the coffee system with its packets and brew sections away from the wall. "Give me a hand."

She stood still. "What the hell are you doing?"

"Killing your lunch thief."

The big three-prong plug resisted his attempts to pull it from the socket. The sick pressure increased. The coffee system groaned and swayed, but refused to come off the counter. He turned back to the woman. "Listen, I need…"

Her face had become the face of the lunch thief. She started for him. They fought, falling to the floor. The consultant banged his head and saw a flash of white. Several canisters of non-dairy creamer rolled off the counter on top of him.

Helen was trim but not strong, and after the first surprise he managed to overpower her. Her face came back and the lunch thief was gone. She looked at him, pale and frightened. A groaning noise made them both look up in time to see the refrigerator coming down on top of them. The consultant rolled left, Helen right, and the fridge crashed between them, its thick cord pulling out of the wall. A flash of sparks came from the microwave in the corner. The appliance hurled itself at them, turntable plate flying out and rolling out the door with a clatter. The microwave smashed to the floor.

The air buzzed with malice.

They got to their feet. Helen's twin set was grimy, and she had lost a pump that now lay under the fridge. She pulled off the other one and tossed it aside. "It was the coffee?" she said uncertainly. "Because the coffee was so bad?"

"It used to be a communal pot. It used to be that the company was a company, everyone pulling together." He started pulling at the coffee system again. This time she helped.

The plug burst from the wall with a flash of electricity, and the woman gave a little shriek. They pulled the unit off the counter and poised it over the edge, plastic tubing trailing behind it like veins.

"Will dropping it be enough?" she said.

"I don't know." He knew he should send her away, but the image of the lunch thief on the monitor, in the restroom where there had been no cameras, made him loath to let her out of his sight. "Be ready for anything. It's going to be mad."

She gave a grim smile. He had seen that smile before – rarely in this century though. "It will be a pleasure," she said, grunting with effort as she pushed along with him. "To not have to drink this lousy coffee ever AGAIN!"

On the last word the coffee system went over the edge and landed with a crash that rivalled the fridge. The unit crumpled, and water and coffee packets fell everywhere. The tubing writhed.

He could hear an impotent, distant screaming. She might have as well because despite her defiance she looked wide-eyed with fear. The coffee system began to pulse at their feet.

That was enough – they bolted for the door.

They watched the rest from the security guard's monitors. The coffee system took a long time to die. It twisted and thumped and bubbled. The lunch thief appeared and looked as if it were trying to get into the fridge, which had fallen face down. It gave a heartbreaking cry. Helen put her hand to her mouth.

"Did we ever find out who it was?" she said.

"What it was. Betrayal. Despair. A community breaking up. All the things a company is not."

"It was us." She said it flatly.

He nodded.

She sighed. "We're in manufacturing. The rumours are that we're supposed to outsource to India. And when it happens – after that we aren't worth anything except what Simon can get for parts."

He thought about what the security guard had told him, about another lunch thief who stole lunches and ate them in the restroom. It was more common than people thought. Civilisation was a thin veneer, and even the best business casual could not hold the jungle at bay.

"Start with the communal pot," he said, and she looked at him, a vee of confusion between her eyebrows. "You are all in it together," he said. "It can't hurt."

It wasn't like him to be foolishly optimistic but sometimes a cup of coffee was the only logical response when faced with dissolution. Coffee and a little something sweet, a shared communion. They turned back to the monitor and watched the rest of the coffee system break down on the screen.

The next morning employees lined up outside Simon Maher's office, where Suzanne presided over the old coffee pot. The mood was light but sad, as if everyone knew it was a temporary reprieve. People had pitched in for coffee, cream, sugar, and donuts. As the maintenance crew cleared away the mess in the break room, Maher stood next to the consultant and grinned.

The consultant knew how he felt – the company's old comfortable connection was back. Then he forgot about the firm. Helen came toward them, carrying two cups of coffee. She had on a red suit with a vee neck that should have been worn with a silk blouse but in this case only a bit of lace bra peeked out. Her skirt stopped well above the knee, and her heels were easily four inches. Maher radiated shock and confusion.

"You both look like you could use coffee," she said, and handed them cups. The consultant's was in the mug he had given her. Simon still looked boggled.

"Helen! What –"

"Celebrating," she said firmly. "I didn't come to this company just to be here at the end." She looked at the consultant, her colour a bit high. "I prodded accounts payable and they have a cheque ready for you. If you would come this way."

He followed her to her office, a smaller one next to Simon's. She leaned over her computer and clicked. The printer whirred and spat out the cheque. She clipped it to the invoice and handed it to him. Their fingers touched lightly. He felt a hint of wistfulness. He had to go soon and would never see her again. That wasn't unusual, but he had been interested in seeing what sort of person she was without armour. Away from the office. He thought about the flash of temper he had seen in the break room his first day, and her smile when she helped him destroy the coffee system.

Again he was struck by the silence in the room, but this time there was no danger. The firm had just let him alone for the moment, turned its back discreetly. The consultant curved his hand over hers.

"Coffee?" he said.

Into the Dark

This is one of the first stories I wrote that dug deep into what it means to be a mother, and how sometimes the oldest myths still resonate.

Eleanor Blaylock could see Matt on the pitcher's mound as soon as she got to the Little League fields. Settling in next to the backstop, her dress heels sinking messily into the damp turf, she watched her 11-year-old son concentrate fiercely on his next pitch.

Matt raised the ball to his thin chest, his shoulders so narrow that his uniform draped awkwardly to his waist, his shoulder blades jutting out like budding wings. He peered intently at the batter, his lank white hair falling into his eyes, wide as an infant's in a face that stayed forever unfinished, roughed in but never filled out. A slight hush fell over the stands, and the players shifted nervously.

The pitch was high, and she let out her breath as the players rearranged themselves, stepping back and scuffing the dirt. Someone began a little half-hearted chatter from the dugout but it hastily died away. Matt glanced her way, the look in his eyes remote, and gathered himself once more. Eleanor felt sorry for the batter having to face him, and guilty for thinking it.

"Hey, give me a hand here," said a voice at her elbow. She turned to see her husband, hands full with two Cokes and a bag of popcorn. Eleanor took one of the Cokes, wondering if he expected a welcoming kiss.

"I didn't think you were going to be able to make it," she said. "Was your meeting cancelled?"

Phil made a noncommittal sound, and she realised the meeting had been an excuse in case he decided against coming. Fifteen years of marriage, and they were negotiating a breakup, sometimes tearing at the connections, sometimes tugging at them.

They watched the game in silence, a careful distance between them. The inning ended and the teams switched places, Matt tossing his mitt as he trotted toward the dugout. His awkward gait smoothed out in the deepening twilight and he moved with a secretive grace, the shadows filling in the unfinished features of his face.

When they brought Matt home from the hospital, months after he was born because he was so sick, she rocked him for hours in the dim, unlit house, letting the twilight soothe him after the harsh brightness of the hospital. The memory only creased her anxiety.

"Jeez, what inning is this?" Phil said, as if he still had the right to know what she was thinking. "Fifth? It'll be dark soon."

"The field lights will come on in a bit," she said, fighting to keep her voice calm.

A breeze ruffled Eleanor's hair and she lifted it away from her face. As she did, a different presence caught her attention. Frowning, she turned. Down at the end of the field, where the baseline extended into the grass, a figure watched them intently. He brought a nagging familiarity, though the harder she stared back at him the more elusive he seemed.

The air had become thick with twilight. As the rest of the player faded into the darkness. Matt drifted into view, solid among shadows. The watcher solidified too. A waiting silence fell over the field.

With blinding suddenness, the field lights switched on, setting off a rising whine. The parents and the boys winced and shielded their eyes, crying out, but laughter rose up too, intermingling with relief.

Eleanor cried out too, as Matt disappeared in the flash of artificial daylight. It took him a moment to come back into view, a moment after the bright spangles faded from her eyes, a moment of *not there*, before he was suddenly *there*, holding his mitt across his face. One day he won't come back, she thought. The black spots blocking her vision would clear but Matt would be gone for good. She looked for the stranger but he was gone.

She didn't remember much of the rest of the game, applauding politely when it was over, and parents and kids streamed out toward the parking lot. Outside the playing fields, fireflies peppered the darkness. Matt walked between Eleanor and Phil, bouncing lightly on his feet, enthusiasm lighting his face, his wide-set round eyes bright with the pleasure in the comfortable darkness.

"Did you see the last pitch? It was a curve ball, Dad! A curve! I threw a curve!"

Phil's face relaxed into a smile, so unguarded and sweet that Eleanor had to turn away.

"Yeah, I saw it," he said gruffly, and made to drape an arm around his son. Matt wriggled free before he even made contact, and with Phil making a futile grab at his shirt he took off running, looping around in a circle, energised by the falling night. His laughter and light voice floated back over the fields. Parents flinched but the boys turned toward Matt, forgetting their fear and distrust. He called again, a wordless summons like a silver trumpet, and Eleanor gasped as a pack of children streamed after him and disappeared into the night.

"Phil!" she cried. Other parents panicked too, deep-voiced fathers bellowing for their sons. For a brief moment the kids were illuminated by the field lights and then disappeared again.

"Goddammit," Phil said, staring into the dark. "He's got to stop doing this."

"Bring him back," she said, fear catching in her throat. *Just bring him back.*

At home at last, in the brightness of their kitchen, Matt's exuberance dulled. Eleanor turned all of the lights on and took a good look at her son. Gone was the light-footed miscreant who ran like a deer. Matt slumped on the counter stool, still in his uniform, his eyes heavy and his face slack. A new burn shone on his arm, already puckering into a scar. The note from the school said it was from contact with a door handle. She tried to ignore it.

"Want a snack?" she said cheerfully. He nodded with great effort, taking the bowl of sweetened milk and slurping at it. She bustled around the kitchen while he drank until he set the bowl down. "Ready for bed?"

"Yeah." He dragged himself off the stool. "Can I have the lights off tonight?"

Panic stabbed her in the heart.

"We talked about this, sweetheart," she said. "You rest better with the lights on." She didn't say sleep. She didn't know if he did sleep. He didn't argue. "Good night, then. Don't forget to brush your teeth."

He trudged off up the stairs, and a moment later she heard the water running in the bathroom.

She gave him five minutes and then went up after him. He was in bed, eyes shut against the light and one arm across his face. She picked up his discarded uniform, soiled with grass stains and mud, where he had left it on the floor, and rolled it up in a ball. She leaned against the door, her head cocked as she watched him. He didn't look at her, but he knew she was there. He spoke very quietly, but the hopelessness was evident.

"Can you at least turn off one light, Mom?"

She ached to do it. She clutched the balled-up uniform, remembering his flight at the ball field.

"Will you promise not to go out?" she asked. He didn't answer, just rolled over on his side, still protecting his eyes. That was answer enough, she realised. "Good night then," she said, and left him to himself.

She could hear the television clicking through the channels as she went around the house, turning off lights, leaving only one small night light on in the kitchen, as she finished up the dishes. Phil had left out the iron skillet; Eleanor tightened her lips over her annoyance and wiped it clean, rehanging it on the hook over the stove. Finished, she gathered the recycling to put it out for pickup. A burst of canned laughter followed her as she picked her way down the walk to the curb. It was cool, a light breeze fluttering her hair. A few stars floated in the misty night sky. Eleanor dropped her burden at the curb and turned to look at the house. Matt's window was a rectangular yellow square against the dark house.

As she stood there in the cool evening, something brushed by her, a firefly she thought at first, and she had the dim impression of gold and green, of chill morning air and dam earth, heading for the window. She started, flapping her hand at her hair. For an instant she thought she saw a shadow of something at Matt's window, but whatever it might have been was soon gone, and the window was blank with light once more.

She never used to think of morning as twilight until Matt came along. Now she woke early, before dawn, when the light was just beginning to fade in above the horizon. She lay there in the comfortable darkness, listening to Phil rumbling in his sleep beside her. Hard to think that he would be leaving soon. They were just trying to find the right way to tell Matt.

She heaved herself out of bed and shrugged into her robe, padding out to Matt's room to turn off the lights and get him up. It was hard leaving the peaceful semidarkness and she winced against the flaring light of his bedroom when she opened the door. She closed her eyes and felt for the switch, shutting off the ceiling light.

"Hey, kiddo," she said. "Time to get up. School day today."

He moved sluggishly, burrowing into his pillow, his angular and narrow body trying to curl into the small bit of darkness. She moved around the room, turning off lights one after another, chattering to him.

"Come on now, Matt, try to get up. Do you want a breakfast bar or cereal?"

He murmured something; she deciphered it as "just milk."

"I found a cereal bar that's not iron-fortified. You should try it."

He sat up in the dim room and blinked at her. His long, lank pale hair hung in dishevelled locks around his head, as if someone had twisted it wildly into the night.

"I'm not really hungry," he said.

"Well, get dressed. You'll get your appetite when you've been awake a while."

She watched him drag himself off to the bathroom and went downstairs to start breakfast.

Matt drank his milk from around the cereal, leaving it a mushy brown paste in his bowl, and pushed it away.

"Can I go out and play until it's time for school?"

She looked out the window, automatically checking the level of light. The sun was fully up, sparkling on the early morning day.

"Okay. We'll be leaving in fifteen minutes. Got your backpack ready?"

He nodded, and bolted from the table. A few minutes later she heard the first *thump!* against the garage. From the upstairs she could hear the buzzing of the alarm clock. Just as she was clearing the table, Phil came down, heavy-footed, heavy-eyed. He looked around, glared when he saw where the skillet was and pulled it down, tsking loudly. He set it on the stove with more force than was necessary.

She bit her tongue, said nothing, by the glanced up at her anyway. *"What?"*

I think we should get rid of the iron skillet, she thought. Instead she just shrugged and left him to get breakfast for himself. Choose your battles, their therapist had said. She happened to be tired of the war. It didn't matter anyway. If Phil didn't take the skillet when he left, she would throw it away.

When she got herself ready for work, she headed out, laden with her briefcase, Matt's pack, and lunch. He was pitching at the garage, his hair peeking out from his Rangers ball cap. The ball thudded against the wall and he crouched and caught it as it came back at him, running in. She could hear him whispering to himself, announcing some stream-of-consciousness game – sure enough he whirled as if to cut off a runner at first, the move fluid, adult. He stopped when he saw her and for a moment, they stared at one another as if at strangers.

"Come on, Matt, time to go," she called finally, and he came as if pulled, reluctantly. Matt slid into the car, neatly twisting to avoid the door, still whispering his play-by-play. She bent and strapped him in, making sure the buckle steered clear of his bare skin. Their drive was silent, the rising sun quieting Matt with each passing minute. When she dropped him off at school, she watched him join the streaming crowd of children, disappearing in the usual way.

She saw the stranger again two nights later, during Matt's practice. The early spring warmth had retreated against the cold; a misty wind blew and Eleanor and a few other diehard moms huddled on the bleachers. The boys practiced on a damp surface, fielding grounders from the coaches. Matt crouched and ran with concentration, his long legs spider-like, and he was unerring, scooping up ball after ball. His hang hung damply down under his cap, and his lips and cheeks were flushed with the palest rose.

Movement at the end of the bleachers caught her eye and she turned. He was looking at her straight on, and she wondered how long he had been watching her. Much like the other night, the rest of the world dropped away as she took in his white hair, blue eyes that were too wideset, and the delicate features that looked fox-like in the misty grey air. *I know him.* The thought nagged at her.

"What do you want?" she said abruptly.

"The boy."

She had not expected that.

"My son?"

"He is not your son."

She stared at him, dumbly uncomprehending.

"He was never meant to live among you. He was meant to fade away. But your machines kept him here, and now he suffers for it."

"I don't know what the hell you are talking about," she said, regaining her voice.

"You know – you just refuse to see. This world is too bright for him. You can see how he fades in the light. Better to let him go into the twilight with us than to fade away forever."

"You expect me to believe that?" she managed at last. He shrugged.

"It doesn't matter whether you believe me or not. He is still not your son."

Not your son. Against her will she thought back to the night of Matt's birth, when they were all three in the birthing room, and she cuddled him in her arms. He slept and she dozed, safe in the cradle-like hospital bed, and she thought it was a dream that someone came in, took her baby, and put a different baby in her arms. She had thought she had forgotten the memory. Now she looked at his fox-like features and knew where she had seen him before.

"Why?" It came out as a croaking whisper.

He stepped back from the bleachers, looking up at her through the light mist.

"For the brightness," he said. "We can't resist the brightness an infant brings into the world."

She hugged her elbows to her sides, looking out over the field at Matt. "You took my son," she said. "And in return you gave me this –" she stopped before she could say the rest out loud.

"You were supposed to let the changeling die," he said. As if that explained everything.

"And you expect me to just – give him back to you?" she said, her voice shaking.

"You see how he suffers in your world. He would go if you let him."

"He does not suffer!"

The fox-man put his hand on the metal support of the bleacher. It was only for an instant, then he snatched it away. When he held it up to her Eleanor could see the burn across his palm, already festering.

"Leave the lights off tonight and you will see."

He walked off then, as ordinary as anyone in his long coat, hunched against the rain, but there was an overlay about him, of fox and bear, and small ferns that grow in shady places, and even something scaly, as a fish. Eleanor watched him until her eyes burned, and she had to blink.

"Wait!" she cried. A few mothers turned to look at her, but she barely noticed. He stopped, an ordinary man once more, and turned back to her. She struggled to keep her voice under control.

"If he's not Matt – where's my son?"

"Turn off the lights," he said, "And I will show you."

Just like that, he disappeared between the raindrops and was gone.

"I can't believe you fell for this guy and his mystic mumbo-jumbo. Fading, my ass," Phil said, pacing their living room.

"You weren't there, you don't understand," she said. They argued in whispers, their voices low but vituperative, trying to keep their fight from Matt, upstairs in the bright light.

"Forget it, El. This guy is a child molester, and I'm going to call the police."

It was an empty threat. He wouldn't call. They both knew what would happen if the police saw Matt's scars and burns. It was bad enough dealing with new teachers each year, new nurses at the clinic.

"How did he know about the light?"

"Jesus, Eleanor, all he has to do is come by the house, see the lights on in Matt's room every night." A thought struck him. "You didn't tell him where we lived, did you?"

She breathed out, running her fingers through her hair. She had been doing it all night and the fine strands were rumpled and tangled. She couldn't bear to look at Phil, not with what she had say. So she spoke to the far wall, where the TV stat in hulking, big-screen silence.

"I think he's right about Matt." She shot him a glance. "About him not being ours."

As emotionlessly as possible, she recounted her memory of the night of Matt's birth.

"And then the next day, Matt started having apnea," she finished. "I couldn't say anything then – it would have sounded..." she trailed off. She had been ashamed of speaking up, as if she were trying to say she didn't want her own baby. She took another quick look at her husband. Phil was silent at first, his face a mask. When he finally spoke his voice was heavy with anger.

"And you're just telling me this now? Eleven years later? Jesus, Eleanor –" he shook his head. "Even if we had a case against the hospital, even if it weren't *crap*, what the hell can anyone do about it now?"

She winced even as anger darted through her. Forgetting herself, she raised her voice.

"Crap? What the hell do you know about it? At least I had an excuse. *I was the one who just had a C-section!* I didn't see you wake up and try to stop whoever came in and took our son!"

"Oh, for –" he laughed, but his voice caught. His eyes glistened. "That's what this is about, right? My fault. My fault that Matt is messed up. That's what this guy is all about, if there is a guy. Just another reason to blame me for Matt."

His voice broke completely and he stopped, swallowing hard. When he could talk again, his voice was thick.

"Yeah, well, I'm sick of being blamed for this. To hell with it. Live with your fantasies, Eleanor. I'm not having any part of it."

He threw down the remote and left her standing in the living room. A moment later she heard the front door open and slam shut. She picked up the remote and set it gently on the couch, trying to ignore the sick feeling in the pit of her stomach.

Before she went to bed later that night, she looked in on Matt. He lay in his stupor, his long arms and legs twisted in the blankets, lank hair knotted and tousled. His skin was sallow and dry in the bright lights, nothing like the glow it took on in the pale evening, when the dusk could hide the rough scar tissue that disfigured his skin. His hands were knotted and his arms were brown and lumpy with scars, remnants of metal burns. She thought about the other boy, the one she had held for only a few short hours the night of his birth. It was strange to think about, having another son. A normal son.

Eleanor's hand moved to the light switch but she didn't turn it off. After a long moment she left the room, closing the door behind her.

*

Phil moved out the next day. Matt said nothing when his father gave him a hug and told him he would see him the next morning, and then headed off to a motel, suitcase in hand. That night, Eleanor and Matt sat at the dinner table and pushed the food around their plates. Though dinner was usually silent anyway with the three of them, Eleanor imagined that the humming of the refrigerator and the ticking of the kitchen clock sounded louder that evening.

"May I be excused?" Matt asked at last, and she nodded, letting him go. He pushed back his chair and brought his plate to the sink. He glanced back at her and caught her eye, and quite deliberately bumped up against the handle of the cast-iron skillet.

The shock brought him to his knees, his plate crashing to the floor. Eleanor jumped up, her chair overturning, and ran to him.

"Matt!" she cried as he rolled on the floor, curled up in pain amid the broken china and spilled food. He made strange bleating noises, which she hated, and she was rougher than she meant to be, shaking him. "Matt, stop it! Stay still and it will go away after a minute."

He continued to roll back and forth and she struggled to hold him, crying as she saw his arm, already pus-filled and weeping from the iron burn.

"Don't touch it! Don't touch it!" he screamed, pulling away from her, and she lost her hold on him, sitting back suddenly and knocking her head against the fridge. He scooted backward and scrambled to his knees and one hand out of the kitchen. It was ugly and painful watching him gallop that way as if he had momentarily forgotten how to stand on two feet. She sat on the floor of the kitchen in the middle of the mess, and watched him run off somewhere into the house.

When her tears stopped and her heartbeat slowed, she got up and wiped her trousers clean of the food and went in search of him. She was surprised to find him in his bedroom – it had never been a sanctuary. But he lay in bed, clutching his arm and staring out the window. He was crying, another surprise. She didn't think he could shed tears.

"Oh, Matt," she said. "Why?"

"So you'll let me go," he said, and this time the glance he gave her was triumphant even in pain. "You have to see it now. I made you see it. I don't belong here. Why won't you just let me go?"

She sat down next to him and smoothed his white hair off his forehead.

"I can't let you go. You're my son."

He shook his head.

"Mom, I don't belong here. Look at me!" He held up his arm, and she turned away, ashamed of herself. "No, *look!*" At the adult command, she looked at him, meting his gaze. "Something is pulling parts of me away and I can't get it back. "Even baseball–" he faltered. "It doesn't work any more."

He fell silent and she wanted to laugh and cry at the same time. Had it been baseball that kept him here? She thought of him accepting the prisoning light, even as it hurt and bound him, until the only time he could be free was in the purple twilight at the end of a game.

Matt reached out and touched her arm, his fingers dry and dusty. Gon was the strange maturity. He looked at her with an 11-year-old's fright in his eyes. "I think I'm dying, Mom."

You're just feeling this way because of your burn and our separation, she wanted to say, but she was suddenly tired of discounting Matt's life. She had had enough practice at it. Leave the lights on with a cheerful smile and a kiss good night, as if that made it better. Pretend her world was the normal one, as if all children could only drink milk and honey, and they were all burned terribly in the summer sunlight, as if contact with iron caused their skin to break open and ooze pus.

Her gaze wandered around his room, touching on the baseball gear thrown in the corner, the books on his desk, the trophies with their cheap gold pain piled on the shelf. A normal boy's room, waiting for a normal boy.

It would be easy to say she left the lights off for Matt's sake, not for the sake of a dream child who existed on in her deepest memories. Eleanor looked down at Matt and touched his head.

"Hey," she said quietly. "I'm going to clean up in the kitchen. Try to get some rest, okay?" She got to her feet. Matt rolled over, keeping off his injured arm, and turned his back to her. It was early evening, still bright out, sunlight streaming through his windows. *I don't have to decide yet.*

She worked slowly, picking up the pieces of the broken plate and mopping up the mess. She carefully hung up the skillet and washed the few dishes by hand, the warm soapy water soothing her nerves.

Outside the kitchen window the sunlight faded, the evening deepening toward grey, then twilight. Eleanor wiped down the counter, the table, and the stove, taking her time. It was full dark out when she finished, and she sat down at the table, looking around at the spotless kitchen. It was quiet and peaceful, the only lights the small ones over the stove. She wished Matt could see it before he left, and realised that she had made her decision.

She didn't know if she should go up and watch him leave. She didn't know if she wanted to. She sat in the darkened kitchen, listening to the humming of the fridge, feeling a sleepiness come over her that made her head nod and her eyes droop.

Something made her snap awake. Eleanor gasped, heart thumping, and got up shakily. The house was full dark; the stove clock read 10:00, red numbers glowing.

"Matt?" she said softly, barely above a whisper. She listened with acute hearing, but the only sounds were the noises of a slumbering how. Eleanor willed herself to walk up the stairs, with every step wishing she could stop and go back to the kitchen, to wait for Phil to come home and berate her for leaving the house in darkness.

She pushed open the door to Matt's room. It took a moment for her eyes to adjust to the faint starlight coming through the open window, the curtains blowing in the sluggish breeze. A still form lay on the bed, and her heart leaped painfully. He was still there. Somewhere in the back of her mind the image of a normal boy was lost forever, not even to be mourned.

She came in and touched Matt's head, resting her hand there lightly. "I'm glad you didn't go," she said in a low voice. She was about to say more when it registered he hadn't moved. Frowning, Eleanor knelt beside the bed, peering at him in the darkness. She shook him. "Matt? *Matt!*"

The house seemed too small for her shriek, and she started her feet and fumbled for the light switch, crying out again as the form on the bed exploded in the light.

Perhaps it was just the afterimage shocked onto her eyelids, but she saw that it had not been Matt. It had been a boy with light-brown hair like hers, a small, compact body, a face like Phil's, his complexion pale and freckled. What Matt might have been but was not, she thought, and now gone forever.

Still wincing from the light, she lowered her arm and squinted at the bed. The boy had disappeared. Instead, Matt lay there, a skinny stick of a boy, with no more life left in him than a collection of twigs and leaves. It was not just that he had died, she saw; he had never lived.

She sat next to him and touched his straw-like hair, feeling that if she tried to pick him up he would fall apart in her arms, pieces trailing off down the stairs like twigs from a scarecrow. Her face screwed up, she hugged his mitt instead, crying soundlessly, rocking back and forth. Oh Matt. Matt.

"I don't understand," she managed at last. "I kept my part of the bargain. I thought if Matt went away – the other could come back."

"What's done cannot be undone." The stranger from the ball fields waited at the window, insubstantial in the bedroom light. "Your machines and medicines fought hard to keep the changeling, and each time they revived him, they tore more life from the human boy. He could not withstand the struggle and gave in. His body died long ago."

The room was quiet for a long time. Eleanor thought of the long days fighting for Matt's life, pumping his lungs, squeezing his heart, the monitors cycling endless jagged green lines. Had *they* sat by, she wondered, while the life was sucked from her son? Had they tried to save him, in their twilight world?

If she had known, would she have pulled the plug on Matt's battle?

"Where is Matt now?" she asked, her voice thick with tears.

"He is with us. Though he is not human, he keeps enough of the human boy's spirit that perhaps he will bring us the brightness we crave."

She thought of him running in the purpling darkness, free of the light for good.

"Will he be lonely? Frightened?" *Can I see him, just to give him a hug, to comfort him? Will I ever see him again?*

The stranger stared at her, and she wondered if he knew what the words meant. But Matt would know, and she cringed to think of him no longer in pain, but forever alone among these strangers. Just as he had been all his life, she thought.

"Wait," she said, as the stranger turned to leave. She held out the mitt and the ball. His face registered surprise, and she smiled thinly. "He likes to play catch."

He took them cautiously, and was gone.

*

Death from complications due to xeroderma pigmentosum, said the coroner's report, and Eleanor supposed it was the closest they could come to a diagnosis. She doubted that 'changeling' was in the medical texts. The funeral was private, as neither she nor Phil were close to their families, and Matt had no close friends.

That evening she sat by herself on the bleachers at the Little League fields, watching the fireflies. She saw someone out of the corner of her eye and her heart leaped, but the tall man in the twilight was Phil. He looked up at her, hands in the pockets of his overcoat.

"I just want to know one thing," he said. "Did you leave the lights off?"

She nodded. "He'd suffered enough, you know."

"And you made that decision unilaterally?"

"No, Phil. He did."

She waited uneasily for his burst of anger, and when it came it was low-voiced and vociferous.

"I will never forgive you for this."

He turned and walked off, disappearing into the dusk. Eleanor watched him go, fireflies in his wake, and said to the quiet night, "Neither will I."

Ice

As with many of my stories, this one started with an image – a snow that never stopped falling, and a modern city caught inside a fairy tale, glittering and beautiful, icy and dangerous.

One night in a distant city, the snow began to fall and never stopped. It dropped on the wide avenues, filled street corners with sculpted drifts, and filigreed railings, grates, and trash. The dark subway entrances were closed. In the grand concourse of the train station, snow spilled in from the street, cascading over the marble stairs and glittering in the dim light of the ceiling's heaven. The only way in and out of the city was on foot, and the great bridge, which saw a terrible exodus that one day years ago, ushered people across its snowy span. Only a few made the journey; most took one glimpse at the surging grey waters under the icy bridge and turned back.

Delacour leaned back against the locker room wall and briefly closed his eyes. He fought the sleepiness. It helped that his arm was being manoeuvred into a sling – a check into the boards had dislocated his shoulder. It was an old injury. The pain seared and he made a sound. The trainer glanced up at him and tugged ruthlessly.

"Almost done," he said. Delacour nodded, thinking that the pain was better than the strange stupor that had come over him lately. The endless snow made him want to sleep for hours. He thought he played as well as he always did, but that morning he had to be rousted out of bed by the team manager banging on his hotel room door.

"All right," the trainer said, helping him up. "Get that looked at later," he added. Delacour heard it from a long way away, the pain having receded enough to let the weariness wash completely over him.

He showered and dressed with difficulty, and by the time he finished almost all of his teammates were out the door. They were going to a bar in midtown, they said, and he promised to come. Out of habit he checked messages. Cynthia had called. She had watched the game at home – she said she was worried about his injury. Call me, she said. Delacour stared down at the phone for a long moment, then closed it and put it in his pocket. He wrestled his arm into his coat and set off for the bar.

He had to walk several blocks, and the cold began to wake him up. Snow bit at his face and puffed over his shoes, gathering in frozen clumps along the bottoms of his jeans. Delacour pulled up the collar of his heavy jacket and hunched against the cold. He winced as his shoulder woke with fresh pain.

Bells jingled behind him and Delacour turned at the sweet, loud sound to see a horse-drawn sleigh coming down the street. He watched, snow frosting his dark hair, and the sleigh swept past him in the narrow space, the horses' heads bowed in twin black arches. Steam blew from their reddened nostrils. Delacour caught only a glimpse of the passengers – three women and two men, bundled in furs and cloth coats. One woman turned to look at him as they slid past, sleek sable rising around her face from her hood, putting her eyes in shadow.

Walking into the long narrow bar, Delacour was greeted by his teammates at the far end with cheers in English and French. At the other end by the door, sitting at two small tables, were the five passengers who had passed Delacour in their sleigh. All of them looked up at his approach.

He nodded curtly to the woman with the hooded eyes – she had slipped off her cape and let it spill over the back of her chair. She wore a yellow dress with a high Chinese collar. Her lips were very pale, her eyes and hair dark. She was not beautiful – her nose was a blade-like structure in her narrow face. It should have made her seem masculine. It did not. Delacour slid onto a bar stool pushed out for him by one of his teammates, glad to be able to put his back to her.

Over in one corner Albrecht was holding court, his teammates roaring with laughter at something he said. He turned around at Delacour's entrance but pointedly turned back.

"Hey, man, you're good?" said Yuri the goalie in his accented English, sliding over a beer and nodding at Delacour's shoulder. Delacour shrugged experimentally. His shoulder twinged; the look on his face was enough for both of them.

"I'll be ready tomorrow." He didn't know who he was trying to fool. He didn't want to play any more. He thought about his home, his bed. His wife. He wanted to sleep.

The attention had shifted to Delacour from Albrecht, so the rookie swivelled around. He shook out a cigarette from a pack on the bar.

"If you ask me," he said to everyone in the little bar, "I'm ready to get banged up for a day off." He bent to light the cigarette, his lips tight. Smoke billowed around his head and he snapped the lighter shut. From the end of the bar, the bartender fished out a dusty ashtray and slid it down to Albrecht.

"That's not what I did," Delacour said, and immediately wished he hadn't said anything.

Albrecht laughed. He was ten years younger than Delacour, only nineteen. This was his first year in the pros. He skated without a care, which is not to say carelessly, and he was nicknamed Invisible, for the way he could suddenly seem to disappear and then reappear in front of the opposition's goal with the puck. Three weeks ago he had jumped over a fallen defenseman, skates flashing in the air, puck hanging in front of his stick as if attached by a wire – the photo could be seen in almost every sports magazine in the world.

Movement caught his eye and Delacour turned. The woman from the sleigh came towards him, her dress whispering against her slender form. He had the uneasy feeling he knew the texture of the yellow dress, the silk against her skin, the fur she left spilled carelessly across her chair. He felt the weight of his teammates' attention – even Albrecht had stopped talking. She held out her hand to Delacour, and he took it, her fingers swallowed up in his until he let go.

"I must apologise," she told Delacour. "Had we known you were coming here, we would not have let you trudge in the snow." Her accent was eastern European, like Yuri's.

Albrecht was suddenly beside him, clapping Delacour on his bad shoulder, ignoring his wince of pain, the flash of anger that was as quickly dampened.

"Delacour here doesn't mind the snow. He's a country boy." Albrecht held out his cigarettes. She regarded him steadily, unsurprised by his sudden approach, and drew a cigarette from the pack. He lit it for her, cupping his hand around hers to hold the cigarette steady. She looked up at him through the thin veil of smoke, her dark eyes shrouded.

One of the men from her group came up behind her, claiming her with a possessive hand on her shoulder. He wore evening clothes, a silk scarf draped elegantly over his suit, and his hair was slightly damp from the weather. He was as tall as Delacour but slender, his shoulders narrow. Only his hands gave him away – they could not be disguised with expensive clothes. His hands were gnarled, the knuckles enlarged and the skin rough and red. Delacour's eyes were drawn to those hands. The man saw the direction of his gaze and for a moment their eyes met, and then the man looked at the woman.

"She felt very badly for you," he said. "I told her, no no, he is busy, see he walks quickly, he can take care of himself tonight."

She blew a long trail of smoke in the direction of the bar, and without turning to look at the man, she said, "It would have been no trouble, Hilaire, to have stopped and asked."

The man's face tightened. "Should you be smoking, my love? Your heart…"

She smiled a secret smile, looking down at her cigarette.

"Just this once, darling," she said. "Once can't hurt, can it? And it keeps me warm." She turned and smiled brilliantly at Albrecht, who smiled back.

"Tsk," the man said, but he threw up his hands in mock surrender. "You know I can deny you nothing." He included Delacour in his conspiratorial grin, the one that said, *Women!* to other men. Delacour just nodded, but the man was not deterred. "So, you are from the country? Where? What brings you to the city?"

"Hockey," said Delacour, limiting himself to the last question. He straightened and half-gestured around himself at the team. The man brightened.

"Hockey," he said. He dropped his shoulder and mimed throwing a punch, landing it lightly against Delacour's bad shoulder. "Like that, eh?"

Delacour was getting tired of people hitting him. "No," he snapped.

"Darling," said the woman. She stubbed out her cigarette and laid a hand on the man's arm, her hand pale against his black overcoat. Delacour was reminded of the way Cynthia placed her hand on his arm at parties when he drank too much, talked too much. She turned to

Delacour. "He means no harm," she said, giving a deprecating smile. "He forgets that not all people are like him. Sometimes I think it was wrong to leave our little village for the wider world."

"Now, my dear," the man said, "our new friends will think we are simple country folk."

He removed her hand from his arm with barely disguised violence, gripping it so hard her fingers were folded in upon themselves. She did not cry out but colour stood out on her pale cheeks and her eyes glistened.

Delacour stood and grabbed the man's wrist. Startled, the man let go. Then he smiled nastily.

"You are a gallant man," he said. He jerked his hand away. "Take my advice – save it for a woman who deserves it."

He stalked back to his companions. Albrecht, Delacour, and the woman were left to look at one another.

"You okay?" Albrecht said finally. He wore a look of faint shock, casting nervous glances between her and Delacour, as if he wondered what he had stepped into. She smiled a little, tears sparkling on her cheeks. Her hands shook as she rubbed her hurt fingers. Albrecht lit another cigarette and handed it to her, and she drew on it thankfully.

"Thank you," she said. "I apologise – he tries so hard, but I think that only makes it worse." She sighed. "I think we were never meant to be." She looked at Albrecht, waiting.

Albrecht shifted uncomfortably. "Well, hey. You should probably sleep on it, you know. Things always look better in the morning."

A rush of emotions crossed her face in the split second before she looked away. Surprise. Disappointment. Malice. The latter sharpened her next words.

"I see. Trite but true, no doubt." She stubbed out her cigarette and slid off the stool. "Perhaps we will come to one of your matches," she said. She nodded at her companions, now standing and getting into their long coats. "You must come to the ballet. Our engagement has been extended because of the snow." She turned to Delacour. "It is our apology, for leaving you to walk in the snow."

"Giselle!" the man called out. He held up her fur. She looked at him and then back at the others.

"He's such a peasant," she said, and walked back to her table.

The man draped the fur around her shoulders and kept his hands on her shoulders. He spoke something to the others in their party, and then they swept out the door without looking back.

"Delacour!"

Delacour leaped up, disoriented, in his darkened hotel room, grey light coming in between the thick curtains. He stared around himself, breathing hard. He had been dreaming, but all he could remember were images of fur and ice and the woman in the bar.

A sharp rapping came at his door. He fumbled shakily out of bed and staggered over to the door, unlocking it and peering into the hall. He had to blink several times to focus.

"Delacour," the manager said, his face ashen under the sallow hall lights. It looked like half the team was behind him. "It's Albrecht."

The rookie had had a heart attack in his sleep. The police and emergency response team had come on foot over the frozen, snow-packed streets, but he had been gone for far too long – now the coroner's office had him, and the city's machinery ground into action.

The team stayed at the hotel bar that day, talking over their shock. Delacour hardly listened, worrying at the memory of his dream. The more he thought about it, the more he thought that Albrecht had been in it too. The thought enraged him – could he not be free of the boy *anywhere?* He stood up, halting the conversation. The team stared at him, their faces round with surprise.

"I need some sleep," he said, and he could feel their eyes on him as he made his way back to his room.

By the time he was at his door, fumbling with his key card, he felt as if he could sleep for the rest of the day. When the light blinked he pushed open his door, spotting a small envelope half-way under his door. He frowned and bent to pick up the envelope, which bore the logo of the hotel.

Inside were two tickets to the ballet.

The front desk sent word that a sleigh would be waiting to take him to the theatre, and did he need a suit for the performance? He did. The team had not expected to stay so long and he had not brought one, he told the pretty concierge at the marble counter. She smiled and made a discreet phone call, and later a tailor from one of the prestigious men's clothiers came to his room with a selection, carefully wrapped in plastic garment bags. Delacour chose a black suit, stroking the fine wool for a moment before letting the tailor hang it up. He had never owned a suit so fine – the tux he was married in carried with it the shape of all the men who had ever said their vows in it.

Cynthia would be surprised that he had gone to see a ballet. He felt suddenly pulled to call her and tell her about it. Delacour even turned to pick up the phone, its message light blinking patiently as it had been for days, and stopped with his hand outstretched. No. He would have to tell her about Albrecht too. He imagined her hanging up the phone to go sit back down to dinner with the kids, crying over Albrecht.

He would tell her later, after the ballet, to soften the blow. Delacour tucked the tickets into his jacket pocket and rubbed his fingers against the slick cardboard. When he got home he could take her to the ballet in Montreal.

The driver of the horse-drawn sleigh said nothing more than "Good evening, sir," and "Enjoy your evening, sir," when they pulled up at the entrance to the theatre in a driving sideways snowstorm. A bright electric light streamed out through the snow onto the shallow stairs and the street. The fountain gleamed in a half-circle, frozen in mid-spray. Skyscrapers loomed overhead; here and there a few windows were illuminated, and with the snow so thick it was as if they were suspended in mid-air.

The coachman rolled out a little step from the side of the sleigh and Delacour stepped down. No one looked at him as he headed toward the entrance, one ticket clutched in his gloved hand, the other in his pocket. He had not asked anyone to come with him – he did not think any of his teammates would want to come, and he knew they would not want to grieve for Albrecht by going to a ballet. He did not know why he went.

He checked his coat and showed his ticket to an usher who handed him a programme and led him to his seat. The theatre was nearly empty. He sat four rows back from the stage – he would have felt more comfortable in the upper balconies. In the orchestra pit, the musicians tuned up, the strings and woodwinds and horns sounding strange, disjointed tweaks and pips and long droning sounds that changed pitch mid-note. He leafed through his programme, feeling like an imposter.

A dowager with scalloped white hair, jewels dripping from her ears and her gnarled fingers, sat right next to him. They were the only people in their section. She looked him over, raising one brow.

"Is your wife late?" she demanded, gesturing at the empty seat on his other side.

"No," he said. "She cannot be here tonight."

Too late he realised he spoke in French. The formidable woman softened, and she patted his hand. She replied in the same language. "You can tell her all about it when you see her again," she said. She turned to her own programme, and Delacour felt unaccountably cheered up.

The lights dimmed.

The curtain rose on a rustic peasant scene: the ballerinas in pretty bright skirts, the men wearing tights, billowy shirts, and sashes. Delacour sank into his seat, letting the music and the movement wash over him. It was pleasant – he did not have to concentrate. The programme recapped the story anyway, so he could watch and disengage.

Albrecht would have *hated* this, he thought, as the imposter Loys danced with the peasant Giselle. Don't take it so serious, the boy would have said. He would have laughed at Hilarion, who strutted his jealousy. Don't wear your heart on your sleeve. That made Delacour think of Cynthia, touching his sleeve to signal something. His shoulder twinged and he rubbed it restlessly.

I should call, he thought. She might need to talk to me. He would have to wait until the intermission, though. He moved surreptitiously to feel for his cell when he bumped the old lady next to him. She scowled and adjusted herself. Chastened, Delacour renewed his attention to the stage.

Giselle's boyfriend Hilarion came to the front of the stage. He carried a sword, but none of the other dancers watched him. They had just finished crowning Giselle Queen of the Harvest, but she was looking at Loys. The tableau froze behind Hilarion and the music faded away.

Hilarion sat down on the edge of the stage, one knee bent and the other hanging over the edge, and looked straight at Delacour.

"Well, you see my problem," he said, holding up the sword for Delacour to see. He gestured carelessly at the tableau behind him. "I know who he is."

Delacour turned around to see who the ballet dancer was talking to. The scattered patrons were transfixed by the stage.

"The question is, what do I say? Do I tell her, he's not who he says he is, and break her heart? Or do I let her fall in love with him, and let him break her heart?"

Delacour's mouth hung open. Finally daring to speak he said, "I don't think you're supposed to be talking."

Hilarion made a face. "They can't hear. The snow, the ice – we're all frozen inside here."

Delacour darted another look around. No one noticed them. Emboldened, he said, "Shouldn't she know the truth?"

Hilarion sighed. "She has a heart condition. It will kill her."

Delacour nodded. "Oh."

"I wish I hadn't found out," Hilarion said.

Delacour thought he could relate to that. Telling Cynthia Albrecht was dead – would it be worse if it broke her heart, or if it didn't? "Yeah," he said heavily.

Hilarion turned to look behind him. "Look at him," he said. "He doesn't even care about her. She's just a stupid peasant girl to play with." He gave something like a laugh but the sound was ugly. "She *is* stupid. I'm well rid of her. I should tell her. Break her stupid little heart, just like she broke mine."

He leaped to his feet, a lithe unfolding of long muscular legs.

"Don't!" Delacour said quickly. The old lady elbowed him.

"Shhh!" she said. Confused, he looked from her to the stage, and she put a finger to her lips, shushing him angrily and then folding her arms across her chest. Delacour reddened and settled back into his seat. If any more ballet dancers spoke to him from the stage, he was determined to keep his mouth shut.

Giselle collapsed in a cloud of white when she saw the sword and heard Hilarion's revelation. Loys, unmasked, became Count Albrecht. He was pulled backward by his entourage, surprise and shock turning to anguish. But – but it was all supposed to be in fun, he said, dragged farther and farther away from Giselle until he was at the furthest edge of the stage. It wasn't supposed to be serious!

The dancers froze in another tableau, Loys-Albrecht at the far end of the stage, Hilarion in mute stubborn anger off to one side, the peasants surrounding the fallen body of their Queen. Amid their unmoving forms, Giselle rose to her feet, her pale face and hands reflected in her white dress. Her hair and eyes were very dark. She fixed her gaze on Delacour.

"Oh," she said faintly. She hugged her elbows like a very young girl. "What happened?" She looked around.

Delacour felt a muscle jump in his cheek. His shoulder throbbed. "You're dead," he said flatly.

Tears shimmered in her eyes.

"I didn't mean to," she said. "It just happened." She ran back among the frozen dancers, touching first one, then the other. When she came to Hilarion she covered her face with her hands. "I can't bear it," she said. "It wasn't supposed to be like this."

"Yeah," Delacour said. "He loved you."

She laughed into her hands. When she raised her head her face was smeared with tears, but her expression was no longer that of a frightened child. Her lips thinned, her chin narrowed. "Yes," she said. "He loved me, and he made it a crime that I did not love him." She swept her hand around at the stage. "Harvest Queen. That's me. Every year, Harvest Fucking Queen. " She laughed again, looking around at the peasantry. "Some queen." She looked straight at Delacour. "You're on his side, because you think – all of you think – that just because you give us your love, we have to accept it." She pretended to open an imaginary present with mock surprise. "Oh! For me? The gift of your love. How sweet!" She threw it over her shoulder.

"So why Albrecht?" he said. He nodded his chin at the distant figure of Loys, impossibly far away on the stage – a prince in disguise, pretending to be a lowly peasant so he could seduce Giselle. Albrecht, pretending to be nothing but a rookie.

Giselle folded her arms across her chest and cocked her head.

"Because when he looked at me," she said. "He saw *me*. And not the Harvest Queen." Movement caught Delacour's eye. Out of the wings came the silent ballet blanc. The women surrounded Giselle and she looked back at Delacour as they gathered her up.

"Just because you love her doesn't mean she *owes* you."

There was no message waiting for him on his cell when he checked at intermission.

In the heart of the city, with the silhouette of darkened skyscrapers rising all around, the park gleamed like a milky opal under the white light of the moon. Unbroken swathes of snow sloped gently among the trees and swept down to the frozen pond. The roads shone white, the paths where carriages, sleighs, and skis had travelled packed down tight. Delacour sat at the edge of the pond, his breath puffing out in front of him in the scant light from the moon and the yellow street lights. He banged the back of his skate against the ground, jamming his heel into the boot, and laced it up tightly. Then he did the other one and stood, a big man on narrow blades of steel. Delacour hit the ice with one long stride and skated out into the centre, filling his lungs with cold air, pushing hard and effortlessly.

A snow halo clouded the moon, but the stars were clear. The city lights were few, just enough to trace the outlines of the towers that rose against the night sky. Delacour skated harder. The wind whistled by his ears. His head was bare and the cold wind tousled his hair, but he was warm enough.

The cold felt good. With every stroke his sleepiness drained away and his head cleared. He felt as if he could skate all night without tiring.

Someone else was on the ice, a still, shrouded figure. Delacour slid to a halt, sending ice into the air. It was Giselle. She wore white furs now, not sable. Even in the cold her cheeks and lips were pale.

"I just want to know," she said. "Do you still love her, after what she did?" Delacour looked around. The ballet blanc waited in a half-circle around him, waif-like girls dressed in white clouds of fur. Their faces were all pale, their eyes in shadow. They looked like wolves.

Their queen wore a crown of ice and her face glittered with triumph. He made a sound of recognition – she was the old woman who sat next to him.

He slid back a little from the intensity of their gaze. "That's none of your business," he said. He pushed off, and they closed around him. Delacour stopped abruptly, his skates sending up a small spray of ice. "What do you want?" he demanded, braced to flee. Slowly they began to walk around him, and he had to turn to keep facing Giselle.

"To finish the dance," the old queen said from behind him, and he whipped around. She lifted her narrow shoulders draped with lush sable. It was a young gesture, and it said, what else is there? There was only the ballet eternal – a lie revealed, a love betrayed, one heart broken.

One young man danced to his death.

Delacour looked straight at Giselle. "Last night – you killed Albrecht."

Like the old queen, Giselle shrugged as she walked. "And tonight, Hilaire." She eyed him obliquely, her eyes almond-shaped in her narrow face. "Judge me as you will, Delacour, but never forget – no matter the performance, *I always die.*"

He had nothing to say.

Giselle stepped close to him, and in spite of himself he breathed in her scent, the scent of snow and fur.

"I don't want any part of your damn play," he said, but his voice faltered.

"Why do you get a choice?" she said.

She held out one small hand and put it against his chest and he took it, feeling the cold against his own warm, rough hands. His skates felt heavy, rooting him to the ice. Barely breathing, Delacour pulled her close, wanting to feel that cold against his lips, against him. He bent his head to kiss her pale mouth, shuddering, for the cold was more than just the clean cold of snow. Her kiss was sweet and it shot straight through Delacour. He cupped the back of her head, forgetting everything. Forgetting, for the first time in months, Albrecht and Cynthia, as they must have kissed during their brief affair.

Blood thundered in his head. He felt his knees buckle and finally, only then, did Delacour struggle.

"No!" With all of his strength he pushed Giselle off him. She was more wolf now, her teeth and nose pointed, her eyes amber, her thin lips red. Delacour staggered. She smiled at him with reddened lips but it was more like a snarl. "Stay away," he said, and pushed back again, only to bump up against the rest of the women. One reached out and touched his chin with a long finger. Delacour closed his eyes at her burning cold touch and tried to move away, but he was so weak he fell to his knees. In the web of cracks in the clear black ice he could see a hazy shadow of himself, silhouetted by the moon.

Someone knelt beside him: Giselle. She crouched in her cloud of white dress and furs, and lifted up his head by his forelock. "Don't take it so seriously," she whispered. "It's what we do." She kissed his forehead and his heart beat slower.

No, he said, but he did not say it out loud – instead with his remaining strength he grabbed her hand and twisted it hard. She gave a startled cry and jumped back, wide-eyed, for the moment almost human again. Delacour slumped to all fours but lifted his head and snarled at her. At his defiance the wolf girls fell back.

He had to stand. He concentrated on that. It took long moments, as if time had slowed along with his heart. He concentrated on moving one skate, and he got that foot under him. His arms trembled with the attempt to push himself to his feet, and his injured shoulder screamed with pain. He welcomed it. It meant he was alive, gave him energy. He tried again and again to get his skates under him, until finally, shakily, he stood and faced the wolf girls, his arms wide.

They hesitated, milling. He looked at Giselle.

"Maybe your life would have turned out better," he said, "if you had better taste in men."

With shrill screams they rushed him. Delacour let himself slam into the ice under their charge and it split beneath his body with a tremendous crack.

He went under splashing and shuddering, knocking into thick slabs of ice as he flailed and gasped and sucked in icy water. The water closed over his head and for a moment he looked through the greenish-black water roiling with his struggles at the watery crescent moon. All around him he caught glimpses of white fur and dark hair thrashing in the water. Then the moon began to retreat and he sank alone, drawn to the bottom by his skates.

He thought: Cynthia.

Delacour breathed out ice water and pushed upward with tremendous effort. He reached for the surface, grappling for the edge of the ice, bumping into the jagged broken edges that remained overhead. His fingers slipped in the icy air and then he gripped the ice.

When he broke the surface he gasped at the pain of the cold air. Ice coated his hair and his body – what water that was still fluid streamed off of him. He gasped and shuddered, trying to get air into his pained lungs. He shook his head and stretched his arms as far as they would go, digging into the rough ice for handholds.

He got himself out of the water that way, scraping for inches with his bloody fingers.

Dawn came in pale streaks against the night sky. It rose over Delacour as he walked out of the park covered in ice. He still wore his skates: the laces were frozen solid and his battered fingers plucked uselessly at them until he gave up the attempt. So he walked in them up the long drive in the park toward the main avenue fronted by the museums, stopping when he reached the street.

In the early morning light he could hear the sound of water running and he looked around in blank surprise. Asphalt glistened under streaming water, the only snow remaining in dirty patches by the gutters. Snowmelt dripped from the eaves of the stone buildings and ran down their front, staining the grey with dark streaks. The chill air held a hint of warmth, as if the rising sun had strength to it for the first time in days, and it lay across his shoulders like a blessing. Behind him the park was still swathed in snow but it was receding fast, pocked with fallen icicles and broken twigs. Somewhere in the woods a bird poured out its heart in greeting to the sun. There was another rising noise, a distant murmur. It took him a moment to identify it for what it was.

Traffic.

A yellow taxi rolled out of the steadily brightening morning and pulled up next to him. Delacour opened the door and got in, settling back into the warmth, letting it seep into his bones.

As the taxi pulled away from the curb he thought he would try Cynthia when he got back to the hotel.

A Prayer for
Captain La Hire

I have what might be called an obsession with Joan of Arc. I have a bookshelf full of research materials. But this story came from a weird little monograph called The Book of Werewolves, written in the mid-19th century by Sabine Baring-Gould.

The gates of Vaucouleurs stayed opened those days, a welcome sign of peace. La Hire touched his tired horse with his heel, and the horse jogged forward amidst the swirl of carts and livestock. Market day, he saw, and turned his horse away from the square to the courtyard. It was quieter there. A few men at arms were practicing swordsmanship, the others lounging idly. At first La Hire went unnoticed. Then one hapless soldier saw him and stopped dead in mid-lunge, mouth hanging open. He was almost skewered, his partner stumbling to catch himself at the last minute and cursing the other's clumsiness. Everyone turned to look, and silence descended. A page, cleaning armour, dropped a helmet and bolted for the castle.

"La Hire. La Hire." The whispers rose to the bright summer sky. "It's La Hire."

The men surged forward, laughing, shouting, their eyes bright. "La HIRE!" They swarmed around him, a cheering mob, reaching out to touch his cloak or his sword, their eager hands almost pulling him from his horse. La Hire reined back, bellowing curses.

"Back, damn you all! Back, do you hear?"

"That's enough!" Jean de Metz, with the little page panting at his side, came down the steps into the courtyard. He tilted his head sharply and the men backed away.

"Let him be. Get down, La Hire, they won't hurt you. It's not often we get heroes in Vaucouleurs. Besides me, of course." He grinned.

La Hire dismounted, wincing at the pain in his stiff back. He handed his reins to the page.

"De Metz, you ruffian. I heard you were captain here. It's good to see you."

"Good to see you too, old man. Come on in."

He could feel de Metz watching him over his cup, and La Hire laughed at his intent expression. "So what do you see?"

"I see the bravest man in France."

La Hire shook his head. "No more. I *am* an old man, de Metz. I was old ten years ago. Now I am old and fat."

De Metz raised his cup. "May we all grow old and fat."

La Hire waved his. "Hear hear." He took a swallow. "Where is de Poulengy?"

De Metz shrugged. "He's off to visit Domremy."

La Hire set down his tankard and swung his feet off the table. He stared. "The family is still there?"

"No – the father is dead, and the mother is living off a pension in Orleans. Why not? They should be grateful, after all. No, de Poulengy just goes to stare at the house. Then he gets drunk and comes home. He'll be back later today or tomorrow."

"Do you ever go?" La Hire asked.

De Metz's black eyes slid away from his gaze. "No, I – well, what would be the use of it?" He shrugged again and took a drink. "What brings you to Vaucouleurs, old friend?"

La Hire held out his cup and de Metz filled it.

"Now that the Burgundians have come back to the fold and the goddons have fled to England, I've had to take on other commissions. Gilles de Rais sent me a message, asking for my help. He didn't say what for."

De Metz stared. "De Rais? Name of God, La Hire, do you know what you're getting into?"

"Oh, not you too, de Metz. Don't tell me you believe all those stories of werewolves in Brittany?"

"No, no, of course not." The Vaucouleurs captain shifted uneasily, just barely keeping from crossing himself. "But there are other tales with de Rais's name attached to them, stories of witchcraft and murder

– you've heard them too, don't deny it. And what does de Rais want with La Hire? Ten years ago you were at each other's throats."

La Hire grinned wolfishly. "Oh, he was jealous all right! I had the Maid's ear at Orleans, and not he. Thought he was going to pull his beard right out, he was so frustrated."

"She listened to his counsel too," de Metz reminded him.

La Hire snorted. "Yes, afterwards, at Paris! Any fool could have told you we could not take Paris. Tell you the truth, Jean, our little Maid was quite the soldier, but she was also a bit of a snob. If it had a title, she listened to it. Me now, just a mercenary, well, I couldn't get the time of day from her after Orleans."

"Try telling that to Dunois, or even Charles," de Metz said. He looked down at his cup, rolling it between his fingers. "Jeanne D'Arc didn't really listen to anybody, La Hire. She had her saints, and that was counsel enough. De Rais had no more influence over her than anyone did."

La Hire grunted. "Those days are long gone. And any animosity between de Rais and me can be smoothed over with coin."

"So you're going?"

La Hire eyed him over his cup. "I hoped you and de Poulengy would come along."

De Metz leaned back, his expression curious. "Us? Why?"

La Hire chose his words with care. "You know I have little faith in God, Jean, and barely more in myself. But I think – and don't laugh at crazy old La Hire – that I've been given a sign to go to Brittany and do what needs to be done for de Rais."

De Metz's mouth hung open for a moment. "A sign. You. From God?"

"No. From the Maid."

He presented de Metz with a small, bent ring, battered and tarnished. With a shaking hand de Metz took it and held it up to the light. La Hire watched him read the worn inscription, his lips forming the words: *Jesus +Maria.*

"This is her ring. How did you get her ring?"

La Hire lifted his broad shoulders. "De Rais sent it with his letter."

In the name of Jesus Christ our Lord and by this token of the faith of Jeanne the Maid… the letter had begun. La Hire had not been prepared for the memories the little ring raised – or the uneasiness. The Maid was dead, and nothing could bring her back. If anyone betrayed her it was Charles the King, not La Hire the mercenary.

But he thought he should go help de Rais, anyway.

Footsteps on the stair caught their attention, and they could hear a voice bellowing an offkey tune. The song stopped abruptly and the door thudded, as if someone bumped into it, and then slammed open, banging into the wall. De Poulengy stood there, arms wide, a bright grin on his lean face, his greying chestnut hair standing out wildly.

"La Hire!" he cried out, beaming. "Old friend! They told me you were here."

And with that Bertrand de Poulengy slid to the floor, out cold.

La Hire said little as they journeyed south from Vaucouleurs. He rode grimly, in constant pain in his hips and his knees. Drinking helped, but he couldn't ride drunk across France. He concentrated on fighting the pain. De Metz, catching his mood, kept his own counsel. Only de Poulengy seemed cheerful, once his hangover wore off. He didn't try to make conversation, sensing the sombre mood of his companions, but he rode with a light expression, as if a smile waited just beneath his skin. Only once did he exclaim,

"By God, it feels good to ride again!" but he said it more to himself than the others.

The roads took them through the farmlands of Lorraine, tinted with the light green of early summer crops. The bells of sheep and cattle could be heard jingling across the fields, and here and there in the distance they could catch the grey-green waters of the lazy Meuse.

Only a few years before, those fields had been charred black, the villages ravaged by fire and war. What the Maid had wrought was, quite simply, the miracle of France's rebirth. La Hire's hand twitched to make the sign of the cross, but he held it back and instead cursed under his breath so violently that his horse started and pulled at the bit.

It was a relief to his aching joints when twilight fell and they could stop for the night, choosing a campsite along the outskirts of the Bois Chenu. The trees pressed in on them and the evening air was cold after the strong summer sun. La Hire rolled his broad shoulders under his shirt and cracked his neck, swearing at the cold stealing into his joints. De Metz looked up from starting the fire.

"Sounds bad," he commented. La Hire only grunted sourly and de Poulengy guffawed.

"Losing your touch, La Hire?" he said cheerfully. "You used to peel paint with that tongue."

"Go bugger the devil!" La Hire snapped, and de Poulengy laughed again. De Metz shook his head and went back to his fire building.

"So," de Poulengy said when they had eaten and were sitting comfortably around the fire. "Do you really believe de Rais is behind these rumours of witchcraft and werewolves in Brittany?"

"I never liked him," de Metz said loyally, glancing at La Hire. "But he was a brave knight, and he was always at Jeanne's side. Still, these rumours, spreading even into France –"

"Jeanne would have known if he was evil," de Poulengy said, crossing himself. He leaned forward earnestly. "God would have told her."

"What do you think, La Hire?" de Metz asked.

La Hire stared into the fire, dozing a little. Or not exactly dozing, but seeing behind his eyelids another fire, and inside the leaping flames a darkened form. With an effort, he dragged his attention back to the others.

"What? No. De Rais was a son of a bitch, but I don't think he is a werewolf."

They laughed, but de Poulengy persisted.

"What about the other tales, of murder and kidnapping? Something bad is happening in Brittany. And if even half the stories are true, we might find ourselves wishing for the *goddons* to come back."

"Might be fun to fight *goddons* again," La Hire said lightly. De Metz snorted.

"Speak for yourself. I'll take a Breton werewolf any day over an English goddon."

"What's the difference?" La Hire shot back and de Metz laughed.

When they sobered a little, de Poulengy said reflectively, "I know what La Hire means, though. By God, raising the siege of Orleans, then taking back the towns on the way to Rheims – we were invincible!"

The other two nodded assent. La Hire thought back to those days of triumph, following the Maid and her white banner. How her self-righteousness chafed him and the others – yet everything came out just the way she said it would.

I have been sent by God to do these things: raise the siege of Orleans; crown the dauphin at Rheims; and drive the English from France.

She had even predicted her capture; he wondered if she knew the rest of her fate, or if her saints had kept their counsel out of pity.

"Would that Jeanne were with us now," de Poulengy said finally. He ducked his head, muttering something about the smoke. The other two exchanged uncomfortable glances and waited for him to compose himself. Instead, he caught their expressions and burst out, "I know you think I'm a sentimental fool, both of you, but I'm only a fool for saying what I think." His voice went thick. "She was a good girl and a great soldier, and she was badly used, badly used by France and Charles and the rest of us. Sometimes I think she would have been better off if we *had* had our way with her and left her in that ditch, eh Jean? At least then she would not have come to such a wicked end."

De Metz straightened quickly. "Ho, now, Bertrand. Take it easy."

La Hire stared at both of them. "What is he talking about?"

"Nothing, nothing, we were young," de Metz said hastily. De Poulengy laughed.

"Yes it was nothing, because she shamed us out of it. When we took her to Chinon to see Charles, the plan was to take advantage of this poor, mad, innocent peasant girl. How did you put it, Jean? Put her to the test? Instead, she lay between us for ten days, La Hire, and we did nothing except cover her with our cloaks and *we never touched her.* Because she was Jeanne the Maid and was destined to save France from the English, and be burned at the stake for all her pains!"

His voice rose to a shout.

"We didn't do it," de Metz said softly. "It's all right, Bertrand."

Again there was silence, punctuated only by the snapping of the fire. La Hire thought about what would have happened if they had tupped the Maid on the road to the King. France would not have survived. He shook his head at the thought and de Metz rolled his eyes in scorn.

"Don't act so righteous, La Hire. Would she have been any safer in your hands?"

"You'll get no blame from me, de Metz. I'm just amazed you didn't try it anyway."

"We couldn't," de Poulengy said flatly. At La Hire's raised eyebrows, he went on, "Listen, we were young and cocky, like anyone, and – we couldn't. Oh, we *wanted* to, and I have never ridden in such painful discomfort in my life. But I couldn't even speak to her of it."

La Hire stared at him and suddenly guffawed.

"My God! I just realised *that's* what that expression was on everyone's faces! Especially d'Aulon's, that time he caught a glimpse of her in the baths. I used to wonder why she always wore her armour, even slept in it. I thought it was because she was so damned proud – What?" he asked at their expressions.

"He did?" they chorused.

"What? Oh, d'Aulon. Yes, you should have seen him. He was shaking as if he had seen one of her saints. He said her breasts were beautiful."

Once again there was silence as they digested this. De Metz shook his head.

"Too many revelations for one night, La Hire. I think I'm going to sleep with that image to lull my dreams."

Following his lead they rolled out their bedrolls, settling into the lumpy ground as best they could. But de Poulengy wasn't finished. From the darkness on the other side of the dying fire, he asked reflectively,

"La Hire, why didn't the three of us just storm the prison in Rouen and rescue her?"

La Hire rolled over on his back, staring up at the distant stars.

"She was Jeanne the Maid, Bertrand," he said gruffly. "We all thought she'd win. Now shut up and go to sleep. We have a long ride ahead."

It was a cold August evening when they reached Chateau Machecoul. The twilight pressed in, mist stealing across the road in low, feathery patches. The castle loomed ahead of them, a dark hulk between the trees. La Hire exchanged glances with the others as they stopped at the gate and looked up at the heavily guarded walls of the castle. At their approach the portcullis was cranked up, and they rode in, their horses tossing their heads uneasily. La Hire choked, and he saw de Metz and de Poulengy bring up their gloved hands to cover their faces. The smell of offal wafted over them, a sweet, rotten stench that hung heavy in the air, mingled with another odour he couldn't place.

That is no midden heap, La Hire thought. But it was tantalisingly familiar.

Out of the twilight a servant came forward, attended by another holding an ornate candelabra to light his way. The servant bowed, a nervous little grin twitching at his lips.

"I am Henriet, my lords, at your service. As guests of the Marechal, you are welcome here. You will come with me, please."

They dismounted warily, exchanging glances, and at a sharp word from Henriet grooms ran forward to take their horses.

With a snap of his fingers and another nervous twitch at his mouth, Henriet gestured them into the castle. Even in the great hall the stench lingered, though it mingled with the smell of beeswax from the phalanx of candles that gleamed from the walls. Between candelabra hung heavy tapestries, their golden threads shining.

Henriet and the servant led them through the hall and up a narrow staircase, a tight and gloomy space after the expanse of the hall. Shadows moved around them jerkily. La Hire held his breath, straining to hear furtive sounds over their footfalls, cursing de Poulengy's heavy steps. Rats, he thought, or other vermin – he could hear rustling sounds like tiny footsteps and every once in a while a broken sob that raised the hair on his neck. Candlelight glanced off a miniature door, waist high and barred like a small cage. It seemed to him an eye peered back at them, catching the light and then disappearing into shadow. But he could hear scratching, straining noises and a breathless, unhappy cry. The others had pulled ahead, and La Hire lengthened his stride to catch up.

"When can we see Sire de Rais?" he called out, a little breathlessly.

Henriet turned, licking his lips indecisively. "The Marechal is at Mass and does not like to be disturbed at his devotions," he said at last. "He asks that you attend him after the evening meal." He unlocked a door and showed them in to a chamber. A cheerful fire took the edge off the seeping chill, but the same stench that clung to the courtyard permeated the air. "You may wait here and rest yourselves after your journey. Food and drink will be brought up." Henriet looked at them as sternly as he could, though his quick nervousness betrayed him. "The Marechal is a very private man, sires, and Chateau Machecoul is very large. It is easy for visitors to get lost in its halls and passageways. Please stay in this room so as not to inconvenience yourselves."

He bowed himself out. The three men looked at one another, and de Metz raised an eyebrow. He walked over and tried the door. It was unlocked; he closed it carefully, but with a look of relief.

"I hadn't realised how different things are in Brittany," he said flippantly. "What have you got us into, La Hire?"

Wincing, La Hire eased himself down onto the bed, rubbing his knee. Hunger and pain inflamed his temper and his words were short.

"You know as much as I do, de Metz. What else do you want from me? De Rais will tell us more, when he's ready." Irritably La Hire raised his voice. "Hey! Someone bring us the food and drink you promised! Damn!" The last was aimed at his leg, which was throbbing miserably.

The dinner hour passed and the chamber began to feel more like a prison. They paced and bickered, tempers flaring under pressure of their uncertain position. When at last they heard servants at the door, the three knights turned toward it eagerly.

"Finally!" de Metz muttered as the servants bustled in, bearing trays of meat and wine. The fragrance of the meat made La Hire's mouth water; he felt himself grin. The aroma of roasted meat pulled them all eagerly toward the table, when, coupled with the pervasive stench of Machecoul, the smell overpowered him with memory.

Jeanne, weeping over the bodies of the English soldiers, burned to a crisp in the charred ruins of Les Tourelles. Their skin roasted black, their faces unrecognisable, and the smell...

La Hire looked down at the meat, bile bubbling up in his throat. De Metz, perhaps prompted by the same memory, made a strangled sound. The two knights looked at each other, sick understanding in their eyes.

"Take it away," La Hire said hoarsely. The servants hesitated and exchanged frightened glances.

"Sire – we can't. Henriet said – the Marechal said – you are expressly invited to eat, sires."

"Take. It. Away." La Hire groped for his sword, pulling it out of the tangle of gear by the bed. The servants started back, almost dropping their trays. De Poulengy, in the act of sitting down, goggled at La Hire in confusion. The servants didn't require another hint – they bustled out with their cargo, dropping utensils in their haste.

When they finally were gone, de Metz checked the door again, this time to make sure there were no listeners at the latch. De Poulengy flung himself onto the bed, irritated.

"I don't know about you, La Hire, but it was a long time since I tasted food that good," he began heatedly.

"I hope you never did," de Metz said, his voice bone dry. His face was pale. La Hire shook his head.

"Oh God," he muttered. "Oh God."

De Poulengy looked from one to the other. "Afraid, Jean?" he said. "And you, La Hire, praying? My God, what was it? What was that meat?" Then de Poulengy stared at them as light dawned. "My God," he said. "My God, La Hire, what have you got us into?"

De Metz shook him awake after first watch and La Hire rolled to his feet silently. He settled himself by the door as de Metz took his place on the bed and dropped instantly into sleep.

The room was cold. The fire had died down and only coals glowed on the hearth. La Hire hugged himself to stay warm, bouncing on his toes to get his blood moving and his stiff muscles to loosen up.

A sliver of moonlight through the shutters illuminated de Poulengy's face, mouth open as he drove his pigs to market. De Metz coughed and sputtered and caught his breath. Preoccupied, it took La Hire a few moments to realise he was hearing something besides his companions' deep snores. He held his breath.

A rhythmic grunting came from somewhere below their chamber, ending in two overlapping sounds, a long sigh and a muffled scream. A long metallic scrape, muted by distance, followed, and something heavy rolled. La Hire, a man of war, recognised that sound and his guts froze. He broke out into sweat.

Move, damn you, La Hire! He was numb, and for a desperate moment hoped he was still dreaming. He heard nothing more, though he strained his ears, and he wondered how long the sounds had been going on, or what else he missed before he woke. *Screams?* his mind remarked. *Crying?*

He cursed, but it only helped a little. He thought of de Poulengy and how he would have crossed himself and drawn courage from God. But La Hire had only one prayer, and it was not one that could be used when a man really needed it.

He gathered up his sword as quietly as possibly, buckling the swordbelt around his waist and forgoing the rest of his equipment. Something hard pressed against his chest; running his fingers over it he detected Jeanne's ring, caught in the loose folds of the shirt. He did not remember putting it there, but he held it tightly for a moment.

Better than a prayer, he told himself, though the Maid had no patience for superstitious talismans and would have reprimanded him sharply if she had been there. Still, he felt a little better.

He limped down the long hall, returning the way they had come up from dinner. Many of the torches had burned out, but one or two still flickered, and he snagged one to help him on his way. The stairs at the end of the hall were a descent into utter darkness. La Hire took them slowly, straining to see more than a few steps at a time, but the torch helped little to illuminate the way and only interfered with his night vision. He took a tentative step and stumbled. Grabbing at air, he windmilled desperately through the darkness into an unseen hole below.

The first thing he noticed was the pain – the next thing was the light. La Hire lay on his back on the stone floor, struggling for the breath knocked out of him. He got to his feet with difficulty. Warm candlelight bathed the room, and when he could move enough to look around, he saw it was a circular chamber, draped in velvet and brocade. But instead of a grand hall, here these tapestries hung over a rack and a wheel. Bones littered the floor, and the sick-sweet odour of decay permeated the room. Dried blood streaked the floor and reddened the instruments; a head, quite removed from its torso, stared lifelessly at him. Another body slumped on the rack, and La Hire saw that it was still alive, gasping shallowly every few seconds. He started involuntarily toward the victim when the tapestries swayed and a cold breeze raised the hair on the back of his neck. La Hire turned, his legs stiff and heart pounding, to meet de Rais.

The brave knight who had fought at the side of the Maid, who had argued into the night with La Hire over tactics, who was quick to anger and as quick to charm, was unrecognisable. His hair and beard, always wiry, stood out in tufts from his head. His hose and tunic were as richly embroidered as always, but La Hire noted that de Rais looked like a shrunken stick inside them. Only his eyes were familiar and they burned with madness.

"Welcome, La Hire," he said. "Welcome to my church."

"Sire," said La Hire, his voice rusty. "I am just La Hire but I don't think this is anyone's church unless it's the devil's."

"La Hire!" de Rais said in mock surprise. "It is a miracle! You have regained your faith. Does this mean you will worship with me?"

"What do you want from me?" La Hire asked. De Rais laughed.

"Great La Hire. You are my safe-conduct to God. Or at least past the executioner. If La Hire stands with de Rais, de Rais will not burn."

La Hire shook his head, the old rage filling him.

"By God, if you think I will play this game you are a bigger fool than I thought."

"What, do you think you can stop me? You, La Hire? I traffic with forces greater than you have ever known in your bleak, pathetic life. They have given me strength!" De Rais' voice rose into a shout. "They have given me appetites beyond anything I have thought possible, and they have given me leave to feast in ways that *you* cannot imagine! I burn with desire, La Hire, and I feed at will, and burn, and feed, and it is never-ending –" his voice broke.

In the silence that followed the prisoner moaned. They both looked over at him, and La Hire, his eyes adjusted to the dim light, for the first time saw that it was a boy of perhaps twelve. He felt a muscle jump in his cheek.

"No, de Rais," he said. "I can only help you by killing you, and I will do that in an instant." He moved a few steps toward the boy with the intent of releasing him, but de Rais was faster.

The marechal lunged forward, taking La Hire by surprise. De Rais was wiry and strong, and his fingernails gouged La Hire through his shirt. He threw the captain onto the floor and held him down. La Hire found himself looking up into de Rais's mad eyes. Spittle dripped from the marechal's mouth, and his beard was stiff and pointed, so black it gleamed blue in the light.

"Kill me? I didn't bring you here to kill me. This is a church, after all. God's peace governs here. No. You are here to atone, La Hire."

"Go to hell, de Rais. I have nothing to atone for," La Hire shot back.

"Oh, indeed?" de Rais raised an eyebrow. His mouth opened but it was Jeanne's voice that came out.

"Save me," de Rais/Jeanne said. "Save me from the fire, La Hire." Candlelight flickered in de Rais' eyes, but the pinpoint flames turned into an inferno, and in the midst of them a young girl writhed.

"Jesus!" La Hire gasped, his eyes bulging in terror. He bucked and tried to throw off de Rais' hands.

"In God's name, La Hire, do not abandon de Rais as you abandoned the Maid," de Rais continued, still in Jeanne's voice.

"God damn you to hell!" La Hire roared, wild with fear. "I did not abandon her! I will kill you, de Rais! I will kill you, you child-eating devil! I will kill you!"

Strangling on his rage, La Hire rolled over on top of de Rais, getting one hand free and punching him so hard the marechal's head snapped back against the floor.

It should have knocked him senseless. Instead, de Rais threw his head forward and caught La Hire in the nose with his forehead. Stinging pain exploded in his skull, and blood spurted. La Hire bellowed and shook his head to clear it, flailing to catch de Rais.

The marechal easily captured his hands again and rolled La Hire back onto the floor. With an almost gentle gesture he slid one finger down La Hire's bloody face and placed it on the captain's lips.

Glaring, furious, La Hire stared up at de Rais, his breath coming hoarsely.

"I will kill you," he said again, through clenched teeth. In answer de Rais leaned close to his ear, and in a soft whisper, said, "No. Save me."

This time the voice was his own. La Hire stared. For an instant de Rais looked at him, his eyes pleading. *Stop me*, he mouthed. Then cold air whipped past La Hire, raising the hair on his arms, and the room was plunged into darkness. The weight left his chest. De Rais was gone.

When he could move again, La Hire rolled painfully to his feet and wiped the blood from his broken nose with the back of his hand. Damn you, de Rais, he thought half-heartedly, and searched for a candle.

The darkness gave way reluctantly to the feeble light and La Hire stumbled over to the rack. The boy was still breathing, but blood came from his mouth, and his eyes were staring. Fumbling with the restraints La Hire released him, and the boy fell into his arms, crying out feebly. La Hire lowered himself into a sitting position against the frame, the boy half in his lap. "Shh," he said gruffly, scraping a hand over the boy's hair. "Shh."

He started when he heard familiar voices coming from above. Torchlight winked from the stairs.

"Jean! Bertrand! Down here! Watch your step."

He heard them exclaim as they stopped abruptly at the edge of the trapdoor.

"Name of God, La Hire, what are you doing down there?"

"Not now, Bertrand! Get down here!"

They jumped cautiously into the chamber, staring around them with awe.

"Name of God, La Hire!" de Metz said, taking in the rack, the boy, and La Hire's ruined face.

"Never mind. Did you see de Rais?"

They shook their heads.

"He did this. He's mad. The dinner, now this —" he nodded down at the boy. "Who knows how many victims?"

"Hundreds," croaked the boy. He clutched La Hire's shirt with weak fingers. "Sires, I can see you are men of good blood and have to come to help. Go to Nantes and find Constable L'Abbe. He has suspected the marechal for a long time but lacked proof. My body is the evidence he needs."

"Not your body, boy," de Metz said gruffly, but the youngster shook his head, gulping back the pain.

"No. It's too late. But if you can, sires, find me a priest? And my — my mother? She lives in the village, she must be worried. If you could tell her that I will see her in Heaven —" he stopped, groaning.

La Hire tipped the boy gently into de Metz's arms and stood up. "Let's figure out an escape from here."

It turned out to be a mundane secret; the tapestry behind the rack hid a corridor. They followed the cold breeze coming from the outside and found themselves in the courtyard.

It was cold and pitch dark. Dawn had not yet come, and the torches had gone out. Fog settled over the open space, and they could hear water dripping loudly in the distorted air.

"Go," La Hire told de Metz. "Get L'Abbe and bring him back here —" he glanced down at the boy. He appeared to be unconscious. "And a priest," he finished softly. "We'll find de Rais and hold him for the constable."

De Metz nodded and headed toward the stables with his burden.

They found him in the chapel. De Rais knelt in front of the altar, his body still as stone and as quiet. La Hire and de Poulengy exchanged uneasy glances. They watched from the door as the dim figure bowed his head and crossed himself. De Rais got to his feet, and, still facing the altar, said,

"Have you come to kill me, La Hire?" His voice was quiet, rational.

"If I must," La Hire said. De Rais nodded, as if considering that. He turned at last, his face in shadow.

"I am not a bad man, you know."

De Poulengy's laugh echoed explosively in the chapel. The other two ignored it. De Rais went on with his defence.

"I fought for France beside the Maid, as did you. God will see that. He will weigh it. And I have decided to enter a monastery. I will take a vow of poverty, you see, and I'll be good. Yes. I think it will be a good life. I am tired of this one."

La Hire and de Poulengy exchanged glances.

"I don't think that will be an option, Sire," La Hire said.

"But I am so tired, La Hire. I want to stop, but I can't. Do you think God will understand that?"

If He did, La Hire thought, it will be because there is no God, only a Devil.

"Consider yourself stopped, Sire," de Poulengy put in. He stepped forward, one hand on his sword hilt. "We've summoned L'Abbe."

For the first time de Rais looked directly at de Poulengy.

"You," he sneered. He stepped out of the shadow, and La Hire saw de Poulengy flinch uncertainly. "Who are you to judge me? Go back to France, little man, go back to your sad pinings for a past that never was. You are destined to be nothing but the dung under the heels of great men. First Jeanne, now me –"

De Poulengy lunged, grabbing de Rais by his tunic and throwing him backward. La Hire pulled him off. "De Poulengy, don't!" he said. "He is just trying to taunt you –"

Furiously de Poulengy tried to pull himself from La Hire's grip. "Let me kill him, La Hire! He is evil, he is filth –"

Pressed against the altar where de Poulengy had pushed him, de Rais watched their struggle, laughing. Some intuition made La Hire panic. With a last effort he pushed de Poulengy off and lunged for de Rais, catching a velvet sleeve just as a breeze from the courtyard swept through the chapel, and the candles flickered. But he kept his grip on the marechal, and after a moment, the candlelight came back up. Their faces only inches apart, La Hire caught the look of terror on de Rais's face when the marechal realised he was caught.

"No!" he howled, and twisted one hand free. In the time it took La Hire to register that he held a dagger, de Rais had buried it in La Hire's side.

For a moment La Hire's hearing was preternaturally acute. Above de Rais's thick breathing and de Poulengy's frantic cursing, he could hear the hissing of the candlewax, even the dripping of moisture outside the chapel. He looked past de Rais to the quiet altar, and saw for the first time the stained glass window above the crucifix. At first he thought the armoured figure was St. Michael.

Then he recognised it for who it was. The dawn must have come, because grey light filtered through the leaded glass, shining through the halo behind the armoured head, black hair peeking out around the face, just as it had done in real life. Her banner waved above her, and her armor, plain and unadorned, gleamed with new light. She stood on the walls of Orleans, but her gaze was not fixed on the sight of her most triumphant military victory, but upon La Hire.

"God's blood, girl," he said to her. "What are you doing here?"

"La Hire, how many times have I told you not to take the Lord's name in vain?" she scolded.

He smiled. He never thought how good it would be to see her again. "You never give up, do you? Don't you know my swearing is a hopeless battle?"

"Despair is a sin, La Hire. There are no hopeless battles where there is God."

"Even here, Jeanne?"

"Especially here, La Hire."

"He asked me to save him. To stop him from killing again."

"Then you must do so."

"Will he be brought to justice?"

"If God wills it."

"Damn you, Jeanne! I knew you'd say that."

He expected her to reprimand him again, but she said nothing, just looked at him kindly, and he had to avert his gaze to tell her what he had kept pent-up for ten years.

"I was in a Burgundian prison," he said flatly. "Just to let you know. I would have come, if I could."

"I know."

He plunged on. "I don't know about the others. The King, D'Alencon – I don't know why they abandoned you. I suppose they thought – well, that you were the Maid and you would win."

He dared to look at her then, and her smile was kind, though tears sparkled at the corner of her eyes.

"But I did win, La Hire," she said.

He waited, but she said nothing more, and he noticed that the window was still again. La Hire sank to his knees. Even as de Poulengy hurried to grab him, La Hire looked at de Rais.

"I've come to save you," he said, and pitched face down onto the chapel floor.

He woke up in a different chamber, this one streaming with light from shutters thrown open to the fields outside the castle. The scent of the dead children that clung to the walls of Machecoul had lessened, but La Hire knew it would never be entirely clean.

"He should have died," de Poulengy told de Metz as they stood over the bed. "I've seen wounds like that." He shook his head and went on. "But La Hire just stood there, staring. And then he told de Rais he had come to save him. Then he collapsed."

La Hire grunted. He was still weak and his eyes kept wanting to close. "Did I say anything?"

"No... at least I didn't hear anything. But de Rais said you were talking –" he looked away uncomfortably. "– to Jeanne," he finished. "And he saw behind her a vast army of knights, all stern and sorrowful, and he knelt in surrender to you."

"I didn't see the knights," La Hire said without thinking. De Poulengy looked at him.

"But you saw her?" he said quietly, his voice aching. La Hire exchanged glances with de Metz. It had never been easy for de Poulengy. The rest of them could think of Jeanne as a warrior sent from God or a boy in knight's armour rather than a girl, vibrant and spirited. A son for Dunois, a brother for d'Alencon, a weapon for Charles the King.

De Poulengy had loved all of her in equal parts, the girl, the saint, and the soldier.

"What happened then?" de Metz asked.

"While I was trying to stop La Hire's bleeding," de Poulengy went on, "de Rais tried to kill himself with the dagger, but I took it from him, and then I tied his hands with the altar cloth.

"I didn't want to put La Hire in the hands of the servants, so we holed up in the chapel until afternoon, when I heard you and L'Abbe in the courtyard."

"The boy was all that L'Abbe needed to get the warrant for de Rais' arrest from the Bishop of Nantes," de Metz said. "He told his story to L'Abbe before he died."

La Hire wondered if the boy had seen a priest before dying. He hoped so. Despite himself, his eyes closed. He heard the two knights leave and the door close behind them. With the last of his strength he brought his hands together and began to pray.

~*~

Etienne de Vignolles, called La Hire, and Gilles de Laval, called de Rais, fought by the side of Joan of Arc during her pivotal 1429-30 campaign against the English during the Hundred Years War. De Rais quit the battlefield before Joan's capture and by his own account became involved with witchcraft, cannibalism, and necrophilia. In 1440 he was hanged and burned; his story is the source for the folktale Bluebeard. La Hire's prayer, "God, do for La Hire what he would do for you, if you were La Hire, and he were God," inspired this story.

Theo Ballinchard and the Oranges of Possibility

As with Red Ned Mederos, Theo Ballinchard is an origin story of the Mederos family. It ended up being something more – I find myself quite protective of Theo and I'm very glad to have made his acquaintance. I hope you enjoy meeting him too.

Theo Ballinchard had a fairytale childhood, but as he was neither the eldest son who inherited everything, nor the youngest son whom the cat helped, but only the middle child who always made the wrong choice and then exited the story, it was rather less enjoyable than otherwise.

Down the wet and smoky lanes of Port St. Frey, where the sun never seemed to shine even on the brightest summer days, Theo grew up in the shadow of besmirched brick walls and blackened rafters. His mother and father quarreled and drank and quarreled more, and when they weren't berating each other, they were berating Theo.

Theo knew they couldn't help it. He was hapless, clumsy, and always did the wrong thing. Balto, his older brother, told him so. "How is it, lard-ass," Balto helpfully asked him, "That you always do the wrong thing?"

His younger brother, Corsande, who had fair curls and an angelic face and therefore was beloved of all, always snorted in laughter at Balto's quips.

If Theo fought back, they mocked him for his feeble fists. If he tried any of the retorts that he thought of late at night, they roared with laughter.

So Theo went quiet. When his family noticed, they made fun. "Oh Theo. Giving us the silent treatment, eh?"

Then he learned to make himself unnoticeable. It was a revelation when Theo realised he could cultivate this quality. His mother still saw him sometimes, if she bumped into him in their tiny tenement flat, and she never failed to shriek in alarm. "Theo! You half scared me to death, you dolt! Make some noise, you cursed freak!"

But otherwise, if he ignored himself it would help anyone else ignore him, who might otherwise notice a pudgy lad in dirty clothes with a dirty face and dirty bare feet.

At first he stole food, and at first it was food that he understood. A bun, or a turnip or an onion. He would find a spot under the wharves at low tide and eat his stolen meal, look out at sea, and feel at peace.

Then one day at the market he saw a pile of oranges, fresh off a ship from the southern climes, and there was something about the brightness of the fruit, as if sunshine itself emanated from them, that drew Theo forward. He reached out and touched one, and it unleashed a scent of such glory that Theo forgot he was supposed to be invisible.

"Hey! Street rat! Bugger off!" The vendor shouted, and Theo jerked his hand back in alarm. The pile of fruit trembled and then the whole lot rolled off the table and bounced along the cobblestones. The vendor shrieked and the market exploded in a riot of shouting, and "Stop! Thief!"

The calamity was as good as his talent for invisibility. Theo grabbed three of the oranges and ran, dodging the crowd, getting his toes trod on, and finally escaping down to the harbour. He ducked under the wharf and climbed the cross rafters so he could perch unnoticed on the slimy sea-wracked structure.

He pulled an orange out of his pocket. He smelled it, as if the aroma were food itself. Then he bit into it. It was bitter on the outside and sweet and juicy on the inside. He filled his mouth with the sweetness and bitterness, and crunched the seeds. Then he smelled his hands again, closing his eyes on an ecstasy of taste and smell.

"Had the devil's own time finding you," came a voice from above him. Theo froze, then looked up through the cracks in the boards. He saw hobnail boots, the hem of a duster coat, and muscular legs in leather breeches. "Neat trick, that. Who taught you?"

Theo puzzled over that remark. Taught him to steal? That was the birthright of all of Port St. Frey's less fortunate. Surely the man knew that.

"No one," he said cautiously.

"Well, you've got a knack and we can use it. Get up here."

Theo didn't know what was about to happen, but he knew he couldn't avoid it. It was the fate of the middle brother. He climbed out onto the wharf and faced the man.

From this angle, the man was even more imposing. He was at least six feet tall, brawny, with black hair and snapping brown eyes. He had a dagger at his belt, a walking stick with a knob that looked like it could do a good bit of damage, and dirty lace at his throat. Theo waited for judgment and hoped it wouldn't hurt too badly.

"Go on," the man said. "Do it again."

Oh. That. Theo didn't know if he could do it with someone looking straight at him, but he gave it a go. There was a long silence, and then the man whispered, "Bugger me sideways."

The man's name was Kerrickan and he ran a ring of light fingers all around Port St. Frey. He soon had Theo doing second story work on various jobs. Some were merchants' offices down on the harbor. Theo lifted coin, papers, bits and bobs of this and that. Then came the day that Kerrickan gave him a different assignment. He summoned Theo to his office, which was a nest above an unnamed bar on Tanners Row. There was another man there. Theo figured he knew what was coming next. When Kerrickan was in his cups he'd have Theo show off his talent to his loutish friends. They'd all shout with laughter and make personal remarks ("with a face like that, no wonder he doesn't want anyone to see him!"), and Theo would go invisible in his mind too, just to get through it.

"Theo, my boy," Kerrickan said, "We have a job for you." He looked at the man. This man was far better dressed than Kerrickan, and he had a look about him that said quality. He was fair-haired and he had an expensive watch fob across his waistcoat and a silver ring with a big green stone on his pinkie finger.

"Can you read, boy?" the man asked.

In fact, Theo could, a skill that his brothers often teased him for. But in this case he didn't know if it was better that he could read or couldn't. He looked at Kerrickan for help. Kerrickan nodded at him, so Theo nodded at the man.

The man made a face and produced a piece of paper. He borrowed a pencil stub from Kerrickan's wooden table and wrote on it, then handed it to Theo. "Read that for me."

"Official Merchants Guild of Port St. Frey Trading Charter," Theo read.

"Like a perfesser," Kerrickan said. "Told you."

"It would do no bloody good if he stole the wrong thing," the man said. "Right, boy. Here's what we need you to do."

Three nights later, under a clouded half moon casting diffuse light, Theo stood outside one of the grandest merchant houses on the High Crescent in the shadow of the stone wall surrounding the house. He looked through the gate at the colonnaded portico. There were two lanterns at each side of the front door.

House Jardins had all modern security. There were two men patrolling the house, and the locks had been made special by Tolle & Sons, the finest locksmiths in Port Saint Frey, whose designs were unpatented, the better to keep their inner works secret. He had been briefed on this by the man of quality, and Kerrickan had added his bits of wisdom from his days when he was the boy and he worked for a master. Now Theo waited, and the night air off the harbor was chill, even here high above the city. But it smelled nicer here, and he breathed deep. He smelled sea air and pines, not sea air and sewage or rotting fish, or drink, or urine, or untanned hide.

I'd like to live here, Theo thought. An emotion he could not name ran through him – wistfulness with a side of longing. Somehow this reminded him of the first orange, and the possibilities that it opened up for him. Then the High Crescent night watchman called out, "One of the clock, and may all be well!" And that was his signal.

A man popped out of the front door at the Jardins house and doused the beaming lanterns. Theo's eyes adjusted to the dark, and when the man went inside, and he heard the door closed and locked behind him, he scrambled barefoot over the stone wall and dropped onto the grounds. Theo stole around the side of the house and went up the drainpipe as fast as a rat. On the third floor, he pushed up a window and squirmed inside.

He was in a hallway dimly lit by the moonglow. To his left was the study he was to go to. Theo went down that way, his bare feet padding along rich carpet. At the third door, he turned the knob. The door was locked. Theo's invisibility couldn't help him, but he had been taught the secret to the Tolle & Son mechanism by the man of quality. He soon had it open and darted inside. He closed and locked the door behind him.

The room was small. There was a rolltop desk and a chair. There were large cabinets lining the wall. The helpful moonglow provided enough light to see by.

Working quickly, Theo picked the lock on the desk (another Tolle special), scanned the papers, found the roll of documents the man of quality wanted, and then replaced them with the sheaf of papers in the rolled leather case he'd been given. Easy peasy. Theo put the stolen papers in the case, and went to unlock the study door when he heard voices.

He backed away, and looked around. The room was small and there was nowhere to hide. He could go invisible, but if someone bumped into him, the jig was up.

A key rattled in the lock. Theo made a middle child's decision – i.e., his only choice, doomed to fail – and unlatched the window. He scrambled out as the door was opened.

"Hey! Stop! Thief!"

Theo looked back at the two men. He stood on the tiny stone lip and edged away, his fingers and toes gripping for purchase. It took a moment to gain control over his invisibility but he knew he had done it when he heard someone shout, "Where did he go?"

"Must have fallen. Call the night men – see if they can find his body."

While the alarm was raised and the lanterns and candles were lit all over the house, Theo Ballinchard plastered himself against the stone wall of the grand mansion and shivered in the cold. At length, he forced himself to get moving, inching around the house. The stone of the house was slick with sea air. Theo's fingers slipped and he almost fell, and he realised that he would fall to his death before he reached the drainpipe.

He came to another window with a bit more ledge. He pushed at the glass with hope, and it rattled a bit, but it was latched. He dug for his small knife, and used that to shim between the sash and lift the latch. It took a bit of doing but finally he had the window opened. He slid inside the room.

He looked around. It was a child's bedroom. There were toys and books. A rocking horse, with real horse hair for a mane and tail. A fireplace with a low, cosy fire, emitting warmth and no smoke at all. There was a lump in the bed, a still, sleeping form. Theo felt his heart race, but whoever it was had not been woken by his antics. So he calmed down and had a think.

It was nice and cosy in this room. Theo knew the quality had more things, better things, than the tenement folks, but he hadn't known those nice things included fires that didn't smoke. Or sea air that just smelled of the sea, and not the rest of it. Quality meant they had all the good bits.

Theo didn't mean to, but he set his hand down on a small hairbrush on the dressing table. Before he knew it, the small silver brush was in his pocket, as if it had jumped inside on its own.

He heard footsteps coming down the hall, and the hushed voices of women. They were still whispering as they came into the room. He faded into nothingness. Two ladies, one in a snug wrap and one in a servant's dress, entered the room.

"See, ma'am? She's not been disturbed by all the hullabaloo," whispered the servant.

"Oh, such a relief," said the lady. She scanned the room, passing over Theo without pause. "Even so, let's keep her in bed tomorrow, in case she had nightmares without knowing it. I would love to kiss her on her little cheek, but I would only wake her. Oh dear, did the window come unlatched again?"

She tiptoed over to the window, brushing by Theo, and pulled it shut, latching it firmly. "There. Let's go, before the dear thing wakes."

Although all initiative and curiosity had been beaten out of Theo over the course of his young life, a suspicion wakened in his breast. He waited until the servant and the mother left the room with their candle and closed the door behind them. Then he went over to the bed and pulled down the covers. Sure enough, there were two pillows and a lace night cap, but no daughter.

A giggle from across the room caught his attention and he turned. A girl materialised out of the shadows by the fireplace. She was Theo's age, about twelve, and she had long straight hair in two braids. She was in a night gown, all cosy linen and lace.

"I thought I was the only one who could do that," the girl said, appraising him frankly. "Are you the reason every one's in a fright?"

Theo was well aware that he had a sheaf of stolen papers in his coat and a silver brush in his pocket. Sometimes, there was no choice to be made at all. "Yes," he said.

"Well, you can hide here until it all dies down. I meant to go out, and was preparing to, but then came all the shouting and I knew I wouldn't get far, even with my small talent. I have to focus, you see, and at the slightest distraction, whoosh, there I am again. Then you came along. Would you like the brush? I don't like it very much."

He took the brush from his pocket and laid it back on the table. He knew that she was being kind and it confused him.

"It helps if you forget who you are," Theo said.

She understood immediately. "Oh, is that how you do it? But then how do you come back to yourself?" He was at a loss. He didn't know. "Well, I think it's lovely," she went on at his silence. "I will practice. I'm Felicia Jardins."

"Theo Ballinchard." Was he supposed to bow? Or curtsey? "Why do you go out at night?"

She grew sad, and went and sat down on her bed. She patted the bed next to her and he sat there. The bed was soft and smelled of her and of fresh linens.

"They keep an eye on me at all times during the day. I was very sick as a baby, and mother has always been frightened for my health. So I'm cosseted during the day, and the only time I have is at night. At first I just crept along the hallways. But now I go out into the garden. I'm quite brave. One day, I'll go down to the harbour. I am sure you think I'm not brave at all, though."

To Theo, bravery was overrated. "Why do you want to go to the harbour? It smells." It occurred to him that she wouldn't know that.

She muffled a giggle. "Does it? Well, even a bad smell is better than being stuck in here."

That settled it; she was a lunatic. Theo got up. "I should go."

"Must you? Will you come back?"

Of course not. "I – guess," Theo said.

"Good. Here – I'll show you the best way out."

She took his hand and led him through the halls. First they went up a half flight into the attic, and then down a set of rickety stairs. At each creak she stifled a giggle, until Theo was hard put not to laugh himself. He couldn't remember the last time he'd laughed. At the bottom of the stairs, she opened a small door in the garden wall. It was draped in ivy, barely visible in the dark.

"This is better than the drainpipe," she said. "I discovered these stairs on my jaunts and they are quite unused." In the moonlight her pale face was animated. "You will come back, won't you?"

"I will," Theo said.

After the clean smell of the sea air on the High Crescent, Tanners Row was particularly noxious. Theo covered his mouth and nose with his scarf, which barely helped. He hoped to make his delivery quick, then off he would go to his current hidey, in the crawl space of a spice merchant's warehouse behind Aether's Coffee House. There was a small light shining in the window of Kerrickan's office above the bar. Theo trudged up the stairs and went to his boss.

Kerrickan was sitting still in his big chair, his head cocked at an attitude, as if to say, Well? Theo pulled the rolled case from his coat and held it out.

"Got 'em, boss," he meant to say, but his words failed him. As his eyes adjusted to the dimness, Theo realised that the dark spill down Kerrickan's neckerchief was blood, and Kerrickan's eyes were not staring at him but staring into eternity. Theo felt rather than heard the knife slicing through the air at him, and he went inside himself and rolled, so the knife only nicked his ear. He ran.

He lost his pursuer with ease, and watched from the shadows as the man cursed and ran up and down the alley, trying to find him. Then Theo walked over to his hidey, hunched against the wet cold, the rolled case still in his hand.

For the next couple of days, he laid low and listened as the word on the docks were full of Kerrickan's death, and in Aether's, the gossips were full of the business of House Jardins. They had tried to renew their trading charter with the Guild, but their papers were arrant forgeries, and so House Jardins was drummed out of Port St. Frey. The family had left, the gossips said, gone to Ravenne to live in exile, their trading house and ships now belonging to the Guild. He wondered if Felicia still practiced her invisibility.

Theo kept the papers under the floorboards in his hidey. It made no sense for Theo to think about his future. He was only twelve, or maybe eleven, he never truly knew. There would be no happily ever after for the middle son. But he knew the papers represented something that he wanted, if he could only hold on to them long enough. So he waited and listened and finally knew it was time to take his place in the world again.

Theo got a job emptying slop and washing barrels at Aether's, and he listened to the investors gossiping over their coffee, and learned a thing or two. He learned that a certain man of quality had been nosing about for a boy, a boy like Theo. One investor eyed Theo particularly hard, and Theo thought the jig was up, but then he heard that the man of quality had gone on a long journey, and that investor had invested in the expedition and did not expect the man to return any time soon. Or at all.

Theo kept his head down when he heard that, and his heart eased a bit.

Months passed. And one night, he decided to chance it. Theo went back to the High Crescent, to the Jardins' house. He pushed the ivy aside and ducked inside the garden. The house loomed in the darkness, an empty, silent hulk.

Theo sat down on a stone bench, and looked around. There were statues and huge stone planters with trees in them. Everything was overgrown. He heard creatures peeping but he didn't know what they were. It was cold, but he was protected from the wind. He smelled a familiar scent, and looked around for it. Under glass, illuminated by moonglow, was a small orangery with three spindly trees. Somehow one puny fruit had survived, silver in the moonlight. Theo went over to it, and breathed deep. Saliva flooded his mouth, but he didn't pluck the orange. It didn't seem right.

The story of the middle child never ends in "happily ever after." Theo's life went on as it ought. He worked at Aether's. He met Ned Mederos and became his partner – some say in business, some say in crime, some say both. He kept the trading charter hidden, not even telling Ned. He saw his brothers and parents now and again, but Balto had grown even more of a bully, and Corsande had become crueller than before, and his parents thirstier than he thought possible, so Theo let them go, though it is another kind of fairy tale to think we can ever be free of our beginnings.

Fifteen years passed. Theo was in Ravenne for Ned, and he was walking along Merchants Street when he saw a sign. Jardins Trading and Mercantile Emporium, it said. Theo stopped dead. He forgot his commission for Ned. With a shiver of anticipation, he stepped inside the shop. It was a busy place, like a market under a roof, with goods of all kinds from all over the world at his fingertips. Theo scanned it all and was a kid again.

"Can I help you, sir?" came a voice behind him. He turned. Felicia Jardins smiled before him, an expression that turned quizzical and then aghast with recognition. Theo hadn't changed that much – the round-faced boy had become a round-faced man, fond of his dinner, and he wasn't tall. She had grown, but hadn't become willowy as girls of her station were supposed to, and her face was as thin and pale and pinched as he remembered. She wore an apron over her plain wool dress, and her dark hair was braided in two sombre plaits looped over her ears.

"Do you remember how?" he said.

She flushed, and nodded. "Yes. Your advice worked. And you?"

He hadn't had much use of his talent. He had become invisible in other ways – the chatty, bumbling, stout partner of the more charismatic and dangerous Ned Mederos. No one noticed Theo any more, and he found he liked it that way. But it was like riding a dandy horse. He hadn't forgotten. So he nodded.

Theo and Felicia stepped aside, moving as one. They were alone in a sea of customers, all talking, exclaiming, picking up goods and setting them down, pawing through sales bins, and treading on discarded items. He reached out and took her hand in his. It fit perfectly, and they smiled.

No one saw them go.

About the Author

Patrice Sarath is an author and filmmaker in Austin, Texas, USA. Her short fiction has appeared *in Alfred Hitchcock Mystery Magazine, Weird Tales, ParSec Magazine,* and *Year's Best Fantasy.* Patrice's novels include The Gordath Wood series (*Gordath Wood, Red Gold Bridge,* and *The Crow God's Girl*), The Tales of Port Saint Frey (*The Sisters Mederos* and *Fog Season*), and *The Unexpected Miss Bennet,* a standalone sequel to *Pride & Prejudice.*

Patrice's films include *Do Over,* an award-winning short film about a horse-crazy girl who jumps forward in time to team up with her adult self to get a pony, and *Shakespeare in the Diner: Macbeth,* a retelling of the Scottish play. She has also adapted her short story "Hell: A Rescue Mission" into a short film.

To see her short films and read excerpts of her work, visit her website at www.patricesarath.com.

ALSO FROM NEWCON PRESS
Polestars

Human Resources – Fiona Moore

Fiona Moore's work has been shortlisted for BSFA Awards and a World Fantasy Award. Her stories have appeared in *Clarkesworld*, *Asimov's*, *Interzone* and elsewhere, and have been selected for six editions of *Best of British SF*. "A collection of intelligent, thoughtful, disturbing but ultimately optimistic speculative stories" – *Oghenechovwe Donald Ekpeki*

Back Through the Flaming Door – Liz Williams

A new Fallow Sisters story; a new Inspector Chen story set in Singapore Three; a new tale set on the Matriarchal Mars of *Winterstrike* and *Phosphorus*; a new story from the world of *The Ghost Sister* and *Bloodmind*. All this and more in Liz Williams' stunning new collection. Stories that will enchant, dazzle, and delight, blurring genre boundaries and defying preconception.

Drive or Be Driven – Aliya Whiteley

The much anticipated new collection from a critically acclaimed author who has been shortlisted for multiple awards and is writing at the top of her powers.

"There are no misfires here; readers will think they've hit the standout story of the collection, only to turn the page and find another contender. It's a marvel." – *Publishers Weekly*

Elephants in Bloom – Cécile Cristofari

Debut collection from a French author who has been making a name for herself with regular contributions to *Interzone* and elsewhere. Providing a fresh perspective on things, Cécile's fiction reflects her love of the natural world and concern for its future. Contains her finest previously published stories and a number of brand new tales that appear for the first time.

Our Savage Heart – Justina Robson

The first collection in twelve years from one of the UK's most respected and inventive writers of science fiction and fantasy. A dozen short stories and novelettes, 100,000 words of high quality fiction. A collection that gathers together the author's finest stories from the past decade.

www.newconpress.co.uk